JIGSAW

A Novel by

Craig Simpson

Inchbroom Publishing

Published in 2014 by Inchbroom Publishing

ISBN 978-0-9930336-0-5

A catalogue record for this book is available from the British Library.

Published with the help of Indie Authors Scotland

Cover design by IAS

Dedication

To my wife Marion

Acknowledgements

Thanks to Alison Spencer, and Kim & Sinclair Macleod of Indie Authors Scotland for their help in making this dream a reality.

Chapter 1

"Just you proceed on a need to know basis, Mr Donaldson," the woman said smiling, her green eyes glinting, full of confidence. Steve Donaldson shrugged his shoulders.

"I need to know a lot more lady, if I take the case, like who I am working for, what are the reasons for my help, as I have no wish to flaunt the law just because some well-dressed broad pays me."

The woman allowed herself a wry smile.

"As I said, Mr Donaldson, on a need to know basis is a condition of the job. Money is not an object, but if there is something else bothering you then I'll find somebody else."

"Okay lady, you find somebody else, I don't really care."

"I see! You were recommended to us Mr Donaldson," she replied, as her eyes roved around his poor office with its old desk, beat-up wooden swivel chair and empty chilled water cooler in the corner, which had not been refilled for some time. The blind on the window had been pulled down so that the only lights in the room were from the primitive single centre rose with its yellow-stained shade, and a desk lamp that shone a spotlight ray.

"Us? Who's us?"

The woman smiled. "That doesn't concern you, Mr Donaldson; after all, you are not taking the case."

With that she turned to leave: she was at the door, her gloved hand on the brass handle when Steve reappraised her. She was attractive; she had style.

"You got balls, I'll give you that," he said.

The woman turned around. "I beg your pardon darling, you have obviously been out of circulation longer than I thought, in case you hadn't noticed, I'm a woman, and women, Mr Donaldson, don't have any balls."

"Well, honey, you may not have them physically, but I bet you broke a few in your time."

Again the woman turned to leave.

"Okay! Okay! Sit down, I'll take the goddamn case, but I do need more information than you've given me."

The woman sat down again and crossed her legs, allowing her black designer dress to ride high up her thigh.

Steve averted his eyes. "Let's start again," he said.

"So, where do you want me to start, Mr Donaldson?"

Steve turned away, keeping his mind off those long, long legs.

"First, I need to know who is paying me – you said 'us'? What's the background of the girl you want information on? A photograph would be good, and why you want her found. Little details of her last place of work would also be helpful."

Steve turned back to face his client, just in time to hear the click of his office door.

It was then that he saw the $2,000 in used bills that had been left on his desk. Steve immediately went to this window and, moving the blind, observed the woman entering a black limousine that sped her away into the night. He turned back towards his desk: there was a telephone number, a photograph, and a note:

You're the bloody detective, you find out the information you require.

Steve Donaldson held the money in one hand, and looked again at the photograph. He turned it over and read the name 'Nicky – daughter of Gina'.

He examined the picture again. At least he had $2,000, which was an unexpected bonus, especially at this time of year.

A telephone number was there, so he dialled. The telephone rang out; then a cultured English male voice replied.

"Good evening, the Rosenberg residence."

Steve returned the handset to its cradle and reached for the phonebook. His finger travelled down The Rosenbergs listed, but his number was not there. That would have been too easy. He allowed himself a smile as he pocketed the money and switched off the light.

"Tomorrow is another day," he said out loud, as his eyes made another sweep of his office and he smelled the fragrance of the Dior perfume that hung in the air from his new client with the long legs.

Chapter 2

That had been a week ago and now he found himself on a stakeout on a freezing winter's night, still without much information except that he now had an address to marry with the photograph. He was going numb again and longed for his favourite leather armchair back at his apartment, and his favourite bourbon. He could certainly use a large JD right now to rekindle his circulation.

2:00am and the overspill white light of the diner across the street extinguished and Donaldson wished he had taken advantage of its services. He could see the waitress now. She was of slim build and wore her short, brown hair in a bob style. He watched as she struggled with her keys as she shielded herself from the inclement weather. Donaldson's first instinct was to help her, but experience told him otherwise, and so remained motionless and hidden.

The waitress completed her task, and then pulling the collar of her coat up around her neck, scurried down the sidewalk.

Steve glanced back to the apartment he was observing. There was still no sign of life.

He wondered what the girl's story was. He had so little information and the fact he, a small-time investigator, had been chosen and paid cash in used bills signified discretion. But why?

There had to be reasons.

He checked his leather strapped wristwatch; it was now 4:00am. He decided to call it a night. He pulled his collar up, shrank his head deep down into his coat, and stepped out from the shadows, now feeling the full force of the driving snow as he lost protection and shelter of the alley.

He crossed the street towards the entrance to the apartment.

He did not see the other pair of eyes of the man with a scar on his left cheek watching him.

Chapter 3

Steve scrutinised the entry buzzers of the brownstone's apartments. There was nothing significant and the three nameless ones did not invite any clues. He was about to leave when he heard the swish of tyres and a car engine as it manoeuvred its way through the snow. Its engine grew louder as it approached, then stopped abruptly. The two occupants kissed, then the car doors opened and both rushed towards the entrance, the young woman laughing as she avoided the ponding of the uneven slabs of the sidewalk.

"Terrible weather," Steve exclaimed as he pretended to be fumbling through his pockets and at the same time shielding himself from the winter's night. The young woman stopped in her tracks, flashed her well made-up eyes, smiled, then inserted her pass key into the lock and entered the lobby with her partner.

Steve was quick, he recognised those eyes. They were the same as the ones in the photograph he had in his pocket. He put his foot across the threshold.

"Don't you have a key? Please, identify yourself," she said, staring at him. Steve thought quickly. He remembered George Lubenski, a name he had just read.

"I'm an old friend of George Lubenski's," he said casually. "My car broke down so thought I'd look him up." Steve paused, then added, "Need his help."

"I've never seen you before, you sure you're a friend?"

Steve shrank himself into his overcoat. "Can I wait for him in the lobby?"

"It's a weird time to be visiting, eh!" Nicky said.

Again Steve smiled, paused, then said "Please." Nicky was considering Steve's request when her companion spoke.

"Come on, Nicky, let the guy wait here for George or whoever. We've got the rest of the night with each other. Let's go and enjoy ourselves.

"You a cop?" Nicky said, searching Steve's eyes.

"No! Not me!"

Nicky stepped backwards allowing her coat to fall open. Steve could not avert his eyes from her young, firm figure, her skimpy black chiffon dress, leaving little to the imagination.

Nicky caught his stare.

"Hey! What you starin' at, never seen a pair of tits before?"

Nicky's man friend quickly put his arm around her.

"Hey honey, let's go, don't let this schmuck spoil our evening."

"Okay. Hey, who cares mister, no big deal!" She yelled, then without further hesitation turned to her partner.

"Let's go darlin' we got some partying to do."

Nicky turned to go but not before deliberately letting her coat fall open once again to give Steve a full view. Once she had accomplished his staring eyes, she turned, giggling, and led her partner upstairs, their laughter fading as they ascended out of earshot.

Steve waited in the lobby. He wondered what the girl's story was. How was she connected to The Rosenbergs? Was she connected? What was the link? He knew he would have to find out more about her before reporting back to his client.

Steve re-entered the street, the cold storm reminding him of how long a night it had been. He glanced upwards and watched Nicky passionately kissing her companion. She had no inhibitions as she led him away to another room, which Steve assumed was her bedroom.

Smiling to himself, he pulled his collar up once again and made his way home. He still had not observed the other pair of eyes and as Steve left the scene, the watcher lit up another strong, black

Turkish cigarette, the small flame from the lighter illuminating the scar on his left cheek. Nobody witnessed the small ember after his first drag, as he watched and waited patiently.

Chapter 4

On returning home Steve now appreciated the warmth of his apartment. It was small and simple, but it was comfortable and he felt glad to be off the streets. He hung up his damp coat and walked over to his cabinet, took the dumpy bottle off the tray and poured himself a large Jack Daniels into his wide, straight-sided glass. Sitting lazily in his armchair with his two cushions that moulded to his body, he took a large gulp of the liquor, savouring it as it travelled down his digestive track. Normally he would have sipped the drink, but tonight he was so cold he required the fortification. He poured another large measure as he thought about his evening and his first encounter with Nicky. Sleep overcame him and he fell deeply into his comfortable chair.

A shiver woke him and although he had slept after his long stakeout, the cold had taken its toll and his armchair was no substitute for his bed. He staggered as he stood up, his hair limp, his mouth furred, his bones ached, his tie askew with the collar button of his shirt missing. He grasped his glass of unfinished bourbon, drained the remainder in one gulp and headed for bed. He had no idea of the time, he didn't care, he was exhausted, and collapsed on top of his bedspread, spread-eagled diagonally, falling back into another deep sleep.

Steve Donaldson did not hear the faint click of the lock turn of his apartment door, nor did he hear the soft steps of the intruder as he crossed the living room floor. The shuffle of papers at the magazine rack was not heard either, as the gloved hand flicked through its contents, depositing a letter. The envelope had a smooth edge where it had been opened by a knife or a letter opener. The intruder had taken the empty bourbon glass that Steve had drank from, and placed it on top of the letter after moistening its base with some of the liquor residue, creating a ringed stain on top of the letter, then carefully rested the item into the magazine rack.

The unwanted visitor looked in on Donaldson, still spread-eagled across the bed, smiled, and then with a final sweep of the apartment to make sure he had left no sign of his entry, secured the door lock with its keeper. Somewhere in Steve's mind he heard the quiet click of the tumblers of the door lock, but in his hazy state the sound did not register and therefore it was ten minutes later before he stirred.

He still had a bad taste in his mouth and was still cold. His shirt and trousers wore the wrinkles of his previous evening's exploit. He stood up, his hair sticky and uncombed, the blue growth on his face feeling sharp against his hands as he splashed cold water onto it. He stumbled about his apartment then took a shower, shaved, combed his hair, and instantly felt better, even though his eyes were slightly hooded. It had been a long time since he had been on an all-night stakeout. He remembered young Nicky, how attractive she was and he remembered too how she flaunted herself and teased him before she departed upstairs with her companion.

Steve took his time returning to Nicky's apartment that morning. He was not prepared for the events that started to unfold. A large crowd had gathered, forming a circle. Flashing lights from both ambulance and police patrol vehicles illuminated the air. A policeman was directing the slowing traffic, while his colleague with notebook in hand was questioning bystanders, hoping to gleam information of the incident. A man lay dead on the sidewalk; he had been stabbed.

Steve mulled his way through the crowd. He thought he recognised the dead man, but the throng of people now shuffling together obscured his view. He turned away and looked up at the apartment window where only hours before he had seen his young woman seduce her man friend. She was there!

Nicky, staring right back at him, her frightened expression obvious. Their eyes met, then she disappeared from view, pulling down the window blind. Steve turned back towards the dead man on the sidewalk, but he was already being stretchered towards an ambulance.

He heard the click as the main entrance door of the apartment block opened and Nicky stood there in a long black coat which she held closed by her hand, holding the collar close to her chin, protecting herself. Steve moved quickly, he approached the door and held Nicky's gaze.

"Will you help me, please?" she said, her whole body trembling.

Steve nodded, then turned towards the crowd to see if anybody was watching them. He turned back to Nicky and was about to speak when she grabbed him and pulled him inside with one hand, the other closing the door. Steve stood there, admiring the full view as Nicky wore nothing beneath the coat except for a small pair of black panties and black high-heeled patent shoes. Once again, she pulled the collar of the coat close to her, shielding her body.

"Please help me!" Her frightened eyes watching and waiting for Steve's response.

"You were the man that was here last night, George's friend."

Steve smiled. "Yes I was; did you see what happened?"

"No! No, I didn't. All I know is when Frank left me to go home I heard a shout, a cry. There was the sound of some kinda scuffle in the street, then my buzzer rang." Nicky paused. "It was Frank. He didn't sound the same. I was frightened; I couldn't let him in. I...I should have, I wish I had, maybe...just maybe..." Her voice trailed off. "I heard him, God, oh God, no, he was saying, then another man spoke, I couldn't make it out, sounded foreign. I heard a thud of a heavy weight falling. I shouted his name but there was no answer. Then the intercom line went dead. I panicked at first, and ran to the window, but saw nothing. Then I saw a man standing across the street under the lamplight. He was staring back at me. I screamed, closed my eyes and when I opened them he was gone."

"Did you see his face? Did you recognise him? Had you seen him before? Can you describe him?"

She stared at Steve. "He was of your build, in fact, he looked a lot like ... you."

Nicky stopped speaking and reversed herself back against the door. She was terrified.

"Hey! Hold on, you don't think I had anything to do with it?" Steve shouted, now upset that this girl could even imagine such a thing.

There was an abrupt knock at the entrance door, and a loud voice demanding entry.

The intrusion broke the tension between them, Steve taking his opportunity and quickly grabbing Nicky.

"Let's get outta here," he said, and guided her back upstairs to her apartment.

Nicky struggled. She was shaking, petrified to move.

He held her close. He could smell her perfume. She began to whimper as they made their way upstairs to Nicky's apartment.

The entry buzzer burst into life, its loud intrusion interrupting their closeness. It sounded again then repeated for a third time, with a much louder and persistent tone.

Nicky stared into Steve's eyes and shook her head. Steve held her, the buzzer still ringing with a constant irritation. He strode towards the intercom and was about to answer when the instrument stopped. He paused, waiting for it to resume, but all was quiet. Carefully, Steve peeped out of the window. The crowd had dispersed; there were only the police patrol cars and one unmarked car with an emergency flashing light fixed to its roof. He watched as the officer took a look at the deceased body before it was placed into the ambulance, then signalled his permission for the medics to proceed. The ambulance sped off, siren wailing, lights flashing.

The detective in charge was conversing with one of the police officers when he casually glanced upwards to the apartment window. Steve jumped back, not sure he had been seen. A few moments lapsed then the door entry buzzer once again burst into life, it's annoying, penetrating sound piercing the air.

Nicky, now whimpering held herself close and started to cry.

"I'll need to answer this, I think the guy down there saw me."

"I don't want to talk to anyone," Nicky replied, her eyes wide and frightened.

Steve stared at her, and thought for a moment.

"Get back into bed, come on, quickly!"

Nicky just stood there, motionless. Steve repeated his order and started removing his own clothes.

"What! What are you doing?" Nicky exclaimed, now uncontrollable and not understanding Steve's actions.

"Get back into bed!" The buzzer continued to sound. Steve picked up the intercom.

"Yeah?" He attempted to sound sleepy.

"This is detective Chandler of NYCP, can I come in, please? There's been an incident and I need to ask some questions."

Steve paused before answering.

"Didn't see anything, but you're welcome to come up," and with that he pressed the release switch for the main door. Steve knew that the police would have gained entry anyway, so there was little point in refusing them. He also knew it was only a matter of time before they came asking questions, and he wanted to make sure that Nicky would not compromise herself before he could derive more information from her for his own purposes.

"Nicky, for the last time, get back into bed!"

Steve was now fully undressed and deposited his clothes over a chair.

"Where do you work? Come on, where?" He had no time for hesitation.

Nicky's eyes closed momentarily, her long eyelashes accentuating her obvious beauty.

"The Blue Parrot, I'm a dancer," she replied softly.

"Okay, listen, I picked you up, we had a few drinks and I spent last night here with you. We didn't answer the intercom the first time because we were otherwise engaged … understand?"

Nicky nodded, still shaking and not understanding why the man in her bedroom was about to lie to the police.

"Where's your bathroom?"

Nicky pointed to the full panelled mirrored door that was ajar. Steve quickly grabbed a large, white bath towel and wrapped it around himself. There was a knock on the apartment door.

"By the way, I'm Steve," he said, giving Nicky a reassuring smile.

"Nicky Martin," she replied, allowing a small smile to soften the expression on her face.

Steve ruffled his hair with his fingers and opened the apartment door. He expected the usual format;

after all he had been through the same procedure when he was on the Force.

"Lieutenant Chandler, NYCP," the man said, displaying his identification shield in its leather wallet. "And this is Detective Sergeant Johnston," who also held his shield high for Steve to see.

"We'd like to ask some questions regarding the attack outside."

"Attack? What attack?"

"May we come in?"

Steve held the door open for the two officers.

"Look, I don't live here," he blurted out. "I'm with the young lady, we met last night at her club, we made out here all last night. We don't know anything about any attack."

Chandler surveyed the room, then fixed his eyes on the young woman approaching from the bedroom.

"And you are?" Chandler asked, staring at her.

"Nicky Martin, Officer," she replied, almost releasing a smile.

"Did you see or hear anything of the attack outside? A man was stabbed at the entrance door of these apartments."

Nicky started to tremble, Steve, nervous of Nicky breaking down and exposing his cover, came to her rescue.

"How can I put this, Lieutenant, Miss Martin and I didn't hear or see anything, we returned late and were totally absorbed in each other's company, if you get my drift," Steve smiled, making his statement more believable.

Chandler observed Nicky who had not yet spoken. He waited for her confirmation, but nothing came.

"Where do you work?"

"The Blue Parrot, I'm a dancer. We met at the club, we were making out and came back here, and I don't think the rest is any of your business."

Chandler smiled. "There's been a murder, everything is my business," he said dryly. "Can we have your name, Sir, just for the record, you understand?"

"Donaldson, Steve Donaldson."

Steve gave his true name, full in the knowledge that it would be checked out and a false name at this stage would do more harm than good. He also gave his true address. Steve motioned to Chandler with his head to speak privately with him and both men moved to the other side of the room.

"Listen, Lieutenant, I don't really know this girl. We met last night like I told you. Our emotions were high, things progressed, and we enjoyed each other's company and Miss Martin certainly knows how to keep a man interested. In fact, Lieutenant, I don't think I would have been aware of anything, even if a bomb had gone off."

Chandler grinned. "She's that good, eh?"

Steve smiled, his eyes glinting, agreeing with Chandler's assumption without saying anything.

"You married, Mr Donaldson?"

"No, divorced, which is why I never refuse good company, especially when it is packaged like Miss Martin." Steve glanced over at Nicky and smiled.

"Okay, so neither of you saw or heard anything. Here's my card just in case you do remember something, even some small detail you may think is unimportant may just be crucial to this case."

The detectives departed and once out of earshot Nicky started sobbing, then collapsed into Steve's arms. He held her. He had to find out everything that happened between her and the dead man. The police would be back when he wasn't there and Steve still needed her story, and hopefully any connection to The Rosenbergs.

He spent time with Nicky, gently coercing information about her current life and her relationships before attempting to prise her history.

It was slow, Nicky being reluctant to divulge any of her past. The name Joe Marshall surfaced and Steve attempted to press her for more information.

"Hey! There's nothing to tell. I'm a dancer in a club. I dance and they pay me. The club takes their share. Anything more I get to keep."

Steve listened as Nicky carried on. "Sometimes you meet someone like Frank, and for a while it's okay – you both know it ain't going to last so you have fun while you can. Then Joe Marshall came along. He was different." Nicky sighed, and shrugged her shoulders.

"He was too serious, wanted to take me away from my dancin'. Wanted to change my life, give up my guys ... It wouldn't have worked, I love dancin', besides, I'm good at it."

Steve wondered how he could contact Joe Marshall, who could possibly provide more information on Nicky's past. It was obvious. Nicky still cared for him but their relationship could never have been sustained.

"What about your family, Nicky, your mom and dad?" Steve asked.

"Hey, you a cop? You ask a lot of questions!" Her voice was brutal. Nicky's mood had changed.

"Get outta here. Get out now!" she shouted.

Somebody had killed Frank Coulson. Steve knew Nicky was implicated, but the question was, how? Did Frank's death relate to his own enquiry? He hoped not. He stared at Nicky, and headed for the door.

"No! Wait! Stop! I don't want you to go, stay! Please stay! I can't be on my own." Nicky was shaking, quivering like a little girl. Steve held her. He felt her relax, just a little.

"You're not a friend of George's, are you?" She whispered, her soft voice sobbing between breaths.

Steve didn't reply. He just held the vulnerable young woman in his arms and stared into her wonderful big, brown eyes.

Nicky shrugged and pulled herself away. " I think you should go now," she whispered.

"I'll leave you my number, maybe we could meet again?"

"Jesus, first it's that cop, Chandler, now you. Joe Marshall was the same, all wanting to protect poor little Nicky. All of you leavin' your friggin' numbers for me to call! Well, I don't think so Mister, I don't need you or your help, understand? I'm Nicky Martin, the best dancer on the street! Get it?"

Steve let Nicky have her outburst. "You wanted my help earlier this morning when Frank's body was discovered outside. Did you see who murdered him, Nicky? I'd like to help you."

"Get out! I don't need you or anyone else, now just get out!"

Steve realised Nicky as a volatile personality. Up one minute, down the next. Great when it's good, tragic when it's not. A walking time bomb.

He attempted to retrieve the situation, after all, if he was to learn more about her background, they would need to part for the moment on good terms.

"Listen, I do want to help you, Nicky. If I hadn't been here earlier, that cop Chandler would have taken you downtown, and then what kind of state would you be in? Maybe Joe Marshall could help too, between us we ..."

"For fuck's sake, Joe Marshall and I were over a long time ago, so don't go there. And besides, it's none of your business, now for the last time, Mister, whoever you are get out! Get out!"

Nicky's mood had changed once more. So had her wonderful, gorgeous eyes.

Chapter 5

Steve returned to his apartment, his mind on the case. Joe Marshall couldn't be that hard to track down. Maybe Marshall could fill in some blanks on Nicky's background, maybe even her mother, Gina. Steve would contact his ex-army buddy, George Hunter, who now worked in the Records Department at Social Security.

Steve unlocked his apartment door. Something felt different, but everything appeared to be in place. He checked each room quickly, and then his door lock. There were two small parallel lines down its side; someone had gained entry while he was out. Again, Steve scrutinised his apartment. He checked the handset of his telephone; maybe it was even bugged.

There was nothing. Everything seemed normal, and yet it wasn't. He'd had an intruder.

It was growing dark outside now, the winter weather making everything cold and grey. Steve positioned himself at the side of his window. He had extinguished the living room light and allowed his eyes to adjust to the darkness as he searched the street outside. Was his intruder watching? He didn't know. Steve stood silently for a long time before he gave up. He had checked all sockets and picture frames, but found nothing.

With one final glance of the street below, and satisfied no one was observing him, he sat in his leather chair and poured a large Jack Daniels. Steve sipped the Tennessee bourbon and let his mind reflect. Everything to do with this case was bizarre. The $2,000 he'd been paid was a lot for such a simple job. He'd also been recommended, but by who?

The telephone number he had been given was The Rosenbergs. Where did they fit into all of this? Nicky's photograph with her mother's name, Gina. Was Gina a Rosenberg?

Steve dialled the telephone number again. The same well-spoken English accent answered, "The Rosenberg residence." Steve held his breath for a moment.

"Hi! Can I speak to Gina, please?"

There was a silence at the other end of the line.

"Who's calling?" The English voice enquired.

"Is Gina available?" Steve continued. "This is a personal call."

There was a longer lapse of time, and then a woman's voice came on the line.

"May I ask who's calling?"

Steve wasn't completely sure if it was the same voice of the woman who had hired him.

"My name is Steve Donaldson. If you're the person who hired me, I have the information you want."

The line went dead. Steve stared into his handset. He had been cut off. Slowly he returned the instrument to its cradle and mused over this latest reaction.

He was tempted to return the call, but changed his mind.

Next day Steve decided to visit his friend George in the Records Department at Social Security, maybe get a lead on Joe Marshall and hopefully more information on Nicky.

George had served with Steve in the army. He had an introverted personality, but was meticulous and exact, being in administration. His challenge was that he could not bend from any rules or regulations, and therefore remained a corporal with limited expectations. Steve had always befriended George when others made fun of him, and the two men, although having completely different natures, were good friends.

Steve rechecked his apartment, and then closed the door before finally placing a small strand of hair across the lock. If the hair barrier was broken or missing then he would know that he had an intruder again.

Steve met George and gave him his brief, then

after their usual catch-up, departed, Steve continued with his day, but for all his experience was not aware of the man following him. The man with the scar on his left cheek kept a discreet distance, and followed his quarry all day, noting who he spoke to and where he visited.

It had been a full day and Steve returned to his apartment. The taped hair was still in place, so no one had entered. He re-examined the score marks on his lock, their new shine contrasting with the aged keeper indicated that they had been made very recently.

Steve closed his apartment door and walked swiftly to his window. He searched the street below, watching daily life taking place as the festive season approached.

The traffic was busy as usual, and snow had begun to fall, causing pedestrians to rush like ants towards shelter.

Steve almost missed the solitary figure in the black trench coat wearing a soft hat pulled down shielding his eyes. In fact, he had begun to turn away from his window when he noticed the motionless figure. Everybody else was scurrying except for the man in the long black coat, and, although their eyes didn't meet, each knew that observation had taken place.

Steve bounded out of his apartment, leaving his door wide. He was still fit and it didn't take him long to reach the street, and across the busy road to where the man had stood. He was gone. Steve rotated his body, his trained eyes registering every detail and every person in the vicinity. He was wet again with the prevailing weather. A car passed, causing surface water to splash over his shoes. He looked down to assess the ingress of water at his ankles, and saw the end of an extinguished cigarette. He bent down and examined it, it was plain ended and he could smell the residue of the strong tar. Turkish, he thought to himself. His observer had obviously dropped it before vanishing, after Steve had spotted him. Steve knew his watcher would not be far away, and probably observing him as he stood from a new vantage point.

Wet through, Steve returned to the warmth of his apartment. He discarded his wet clothes onto the bathroom floor, took another shower and wondered why he was being observed so closely. His recent connection with Nicky Martin and The Rosenbergs left him pondering his thoughts. He did not hear the intruder enter, and place the gold bracelet watch in his jacket pocket. There was a click as his apartment door lock was returned to its keeper, and this time Steve heard it. He darted from the shower and out into the hallway, wrapped only in a white cotton towel. He checked the corridor, then the stairs downwards. There was no movement. He glanced upwards; again nothing, then he observed the damp patches on the treads of the stairs. He quickly leapt up the stairs and bounded out to the corridor of the next landing. There was a young woman unlocking the door of her apartment, and Steve's sudden appearance in his towel caused her to turn around.

"Hey, honey, that's a bit brief for this time of year," the woman said smiling, her eyes admiring the view.

"Did you see anybody come along here?" Steve questioned, his voice urgent.

"There ain't been anybody else but you honey, you sure you don't want some company? I could keep your warm … real warm."

The young woman was staring at Steve, eyes wide, her lips smiling, and Steve was then aware that his towel had slipped to his ankles, exposing his full body, especially his manhood. An elderly woman appeared further down in the corridor, and realising she had been seen, promptly disappeared back into the safety of her own apartment. She did not want to get involved in the shenanigans of younger people. Steve, now aware of his nakedness, forced an embarrassed smile, picked up his towel, and returned to the stairwell. The young woman's voice called out again.

"Hey, it's apartment 12B honey, if you change your mind."

Steve heard the invitation, but ignored her. He returned to his apartment on the first floor. Whoever it was that was watching him was good, very good.

Steve suspected the possibility of a person with a military background, as nobody just comes and goes without a trace. Nobody just disappears. Whoever his watcher was, Steve knew he would be close. He once again observed the street below, hoping to catch a view of his intruder. He was unaware of the situation on the floor above.

Chapter 6

Louise Volosso was Italian. She was attractive; striking looking with dark hair and lovely brown eyes. She had grown up an American, but still held her roots close to her heart. Both her parents had passed away many years before, her father dying of a broken heart at the loss of his wife. Louise had never married, she had always wanted to settle down, have kids, make spaghetti, have friends to share her life, but it hadn't panned out that way.

Her life was like so many other New Yorkers; she worked hard, played hard and somehow got through life without depending on others. The family she once craved never seemed to be in the offering, so she accepted her life as it was, and made the best of it. She was, however, always on the lookout for Mr Right, a handsome guy who would sweep her off her feet, and take her away from her routine life, but that was just in storybooks, it never happened to real people.

Louise had many affairs, especially as she frequented many bars and jazz clubs in the city; with her bubbly personality and attractive figure it was not hard to find a companion for an evening.

She was also a friend to her workmate Sylvia, and both women often shared each other's company with a pizza and wine.

Louise Volosso in apartment 12B was in the middle of changing her clothes when the knock came to her door. She was only wearing her black stockings, lace bra and panties when she heard the sound. Quickly covering herself with her robe, she walked to answer her caller, whom she assumed was her naked man with the towel.

"That was quick, honey, come to take up my offer?" She said, smiling confidently, opening the door. The black-gloved hands grabbed her throat, as she was forced back into her flat; she tried to scream, but no sound came. The power of her assailant was too much for her. She lashed out with her hands and feet but they had no effect, as she was forcibly pinned to the floor, the weight of the man on top immobilising her. She heard the zip of his trousers and attempted another resistant defence. Her eyes, now fully wide open, were filled with terror. Tears welled up as with one hand her attacker removed her underwear, whilst still keeping her pinned, unable to move. The strength of the man was unbelievable, and she wasn't ready for the skull-shattering blow, as he hit her about the face and head, before violently raping her. The rape over, she lay confused and whimpering, and certainly didn't expect or feel the super sharp blade of the stiletto as he quickly and efficiently cut her throat. Her blood poured freely onto the carpet, and her black satin robe. Her head turned to one side. Louise Volosso was dead. Her attacker pocketed her underwear, checked the corridor was empty, then returned to the street, disappearing into the crowded pavement, mixing with the throng and vanishing from view.

Steve was still observing the street from his window, but had not seen the man in black leaving the building. He sat down in his chair and listed the facts on a sheet of paper:

1. *Good lookin' lady hires him to locate a young girl by the name of Nicky. The telephone number of the reverse side of her photograph was the Rosenberg residence.*
2. *Nicky Martin located and is entertaining a male companion she met at her place of work – The Blue Parrot.*
3. *Her male companion is found dead outside her apartment, stabbed to death – Frank Coulson?*
4. *The young woman – Nicky Martin requests his help after the stabbing of her companion.*
5. *Flat broken into without apparent signs of entry – nothing taken.*

6. Joe Marshall – close friend of Nicky Martin. No whereabouts known – waiting on information from George.
7. Another forced entry to apartment – nothing taken – why?
8. Chased suspect in stairwell, but the man vanished – where to – possibly resides in the apartment block.
9. Possible witness to the intruder – woman in flat 12B, second floor – attractive – should speak to her again.
10. The man observing him wears a long black coat, soft hat and smokes strong tar cigarettes, possibly Turkish – who is he – what is his mission, who is he working for – The Rosenbergs?

Steve appraised his list. The common factor was Nicky Martin and The Rosenbergs. He knew now more than ever that he had to find the connection. He couldn't understand the murder of her punter, Frank; also he could not understand an intruder entering his apartment when no theft had occurred. He thought long and hard about the man in the black trench coat who smoked the Turkish cigarettes. Why was that man observing him?

It then occurred to him. If nothing had been stolen from his apartment and certainly no bugs had been placed, then maybe something had been added. Steve now methodically and slowly searched each section of each room of his apartment. He didn't know what he was looking for, but in any event found nothing.

He thought about the attractive woman who had hired him. She had mentioned 'us'. Maybe the man in black was her partner. Steve realised there was more to this case than just locating young Nicky Martin. He therefore planned to visit The Blue Parrot that evening.

First of all he would rest. It would be a long night ahead.

Louise Volosso was not missed from work the first day, but after three days her workload was piling up and her absenteeism drew the attention of her boss.

"Where's Louise," he asked Sylvia. "Is she sick?"

"Don't know, I've tried to contact her but there's no reply."

Her boss frowned. "I need this stuff done," he said, pointing to the backlog on Louise's desk.

"Maybe she's too ill to call or answer her telephone?" Sylvia suggested.

"Whatever, just go and find out what's wrong. I need this work done."

Sylvia nodded, then headed for her friend's apartment.

She knocked and knocked without success on Louise's apartment door and was about to leave when she spotted an elderly woman peeping out from along the corridor.

"Excuse me! Excuse me!" Sylvia shouted as she ran in the direction of the onlooker's apartment.

The elderly woman closed her door and stood inside, waiting. She saw things, but never got involved. Life was too precious to become involved. Sylvia knocked frantically on her door, she knew the woman had seen her at Louise's apartment.

"Please, please, open your door. I'm concerned about my friend, Louise Volosso who lives down the hall. She's not reported for work for at least three days now, I just wondered if you knew anything." Sylvia talked to the apartment door, the tone of her voice anxious and sincere.

"Please, open the door … please."

There was a brief pause, then Sylvia heard the tumblers in the lock operating. The door opened ajar, the strong chain lock visible, and the lady's firm grip told Sylvia she was not being admitted.

"I wonder if you could help me, I'm concerned about my friend Louise. You may know her, Louise Volosso, she lives along the hallway, number 12B, you must know her, very attractive, striking looking, dark hair, lovely eyes, always well dressed."

Sylvia moved her eyes in the direction of her friend's apartment as she spoke.

"I don't know her," the quiet, small voice of the lady replied.

"Are you sure?" Sylvia pressed.

"I keep myself to myself, you can't trust anybody these days."

Sylvia scribbled her name and telephone number and handed it to the elderly lady.

"If you see her, please tell her to contact me."

"I don't see anybody, I've already told you, I keep myself to myself, it's safer that way."

Sylvia smiled. "Well, if you do see her, please give her this."

With that, she passed the note to the woman who promptly responded by closing her door, the click of the latch securing the lock.

Sylvia returned to her friend's apartment. It was all quiet, she knocked on the door once more, again without response, so she wrote a note.

Hi Louise
Worried about you
Boss concerned too
Urgent you call me
Love Sylvia xx

Sylvia was back on the street and glanced up at her friend's apartment shrouded in darkness. She felt a chill run through her bones. Something was very wrong.

Sylvia's boss listened to her report. He shook his head. "Did you check the hospitals?"

"No, anyway that would take all day."

Her boss considered Sylvia's comments. "Okay, use our telephone, see if you can track her down. He then resumed his duties, leaving Sylvia alone at her desk, thumbing the Yellow Pages.

Old Mrs Winston sat in her chair. She would normally be watching television with the volume turned up, her hearing wasn't so good these days, but there was nothing wrong with her mind. She read, and re-read Sylvia's note. It had Sylvia's telephone number. Mrs Winston remembered the last time she saw Louise Volosso. She seemed a lovely girl, very attractive. Then there was that naked man with the towel.

Nervously, she dialled 911.

Chapter 7

Lieutenant Chandler's workload was immense as usual. The crime statistics in the city never let up. It was mainly youths running riot, high on drugs; committing crimes of robbery, muggings, and, worse of all, rapes and murders.

His department would arrest the offenders and the smart lawyers in suits and judges would set them free. The politics of it all, absurd. Chandler had been promoted several times in his career, each time bringing more responsibility, which meant more time spent at his job, causing his family life to suffer.

His wife, Christine, and their only daughter Lucy never saw much of him as he was always working. Stuart Chandler's social and family life was a mess; he lived for his job, working tirelessly, keeping the streets predominantly safe, but his workload always increased and as the years rolled by arguments between him and his wife was more frequent and bitter.

"You're married to that goddamn department," his wife would shout. "What about me and Lucy? Why can't we be like normal families, do family things? Why, why, why! Why can't you just say no for once! Let them find someone else. Please Stuart, stay home just for today."

It was always the same old rant as far as Stuart Chandler was concerned, and somewhere deep down he wanted to spend time with his wife and child, but he knew the ever cascading crime that landed on his desk would not disappear. He was a public servant, fighting the garbage on the streets; attempting to keep law and order for most of the city's inhabitants.

Organised crime was the biggest enemy as their infiltration and connections within the establishment allowed the criminals to walk free.

Chandler's divorce was amicable, and although Stuart missed his family desperately, he could not compromise his career and its long hours.

Officer Johnston handed the small piece of paper to his boss.

"We got a call, maybe something or nothing. An elderly woman, a Patricia Winston called, concerned about a neighbour she hasn't seen or heard from for the last few days."

"What!" Chandler exclaimed. "That's not our department," then rethinking and sighing, "Get a patrol car to drop by and check it out."

Chandler turned his back to resume his telephone conversation with the district attorney concerning another case. It was not going well. He slammed the handset down so hard it jumped back off its base onto the desk.

Always not enough proof.

"We need more proof," he yelled. "The guy's got a list as long as your arm and he's as guilty as hell, but no, the goddamn DA wants more proof!"

Johnston put the white slip of paper in a tray, and instructed a policewoman to follow it up as a general enquiry, who put the slip into a different file marked 'pending'.

Two days lapsed and Detectives Chandler and Johnston found themselves sat in their unmarked car sipping a takeout coffee and hamburger. They talked casually with each other.

"You still married, Johnston?" Chandler asked, his mouth full of burger and relish.

"Oh yeah, wouldn't have it any other way, Lieutenant." Chandler nodded.

"I used to think the same, in fact I used to be a lot like you, loved my wife, family, home; loved my job, but with promotion came more responsibility and it all just seemed to slip away over the years. Don't let that happen to you, Johnston. You have any kids?" Chandler asked, now taking a gulp of hot coffee.

"No, but we're working on that," Johnston replied, smiling inwardly, reminiscing of the good time he had enjoyed with his wife a few nights before.

"Well, take my advice. Work on your marriage. Don't let this crap job swallow you up. Keep something back for you and your wife." Chandler's voice trailed off to a whisper as he added, "I wish I had."

Johnston listened to his boss quietly; then the call came over the radio.

Chapter 8

The blue neon light flashed intermittently between the name of the club and the blue outline of a parrot. Located on 45th Street between Eleventh Avenue and West Side Highway, the club exuded certain opulence. Steve entered through the heavy wooden door, and found himself in a large, marbled foyer with fine antiques and a large reception desk. He approached the two attractive young women, dressed in long, black satin gowns, high heels, evening gloves and diamante jewellery.

"Good evening, sir, may I take your coat? Are you a member?" the dark haired young woman asked, giving Steve a sexy smile.

"Yes, you can take my coat, and no, I'm not a member."

"Well, you'll need to complete a registration form, pay a joining fee and a small subscription for this evening."

Steve's eyes locked with the hostess. There was an instant chemistry between them.

"Membership lasts for one year, and we will send you a reminder nearer the time. We also host adult theme evenings throughout the year; the girls love them, and our prizes are fabulous."

A blond receptionist took Steve's money, and handed him his membership card with The Blue Parrot logo on the cover.

"Maria will escort you into the club; have a lovely evening, Mr Donaldson."

Steve's eyes locked once again with Maria's. She took Steve's arm and led him up the marbled staircase, held the velvet curtain back while he entered the dimly lit bar. His eyes were still adjusting from the bright chandelier lights of the reception to the almost dark glow of the inner club as Maria introduced him to Francoise.

"This is our new member, Mr Donaldson, take good care of him."

Steve turned to Maria. "Will I see you again?"

"Quite possibly, we shall see, we are very busy tonight".

With that, she smiled, and then returned to her duties at reception. Francoise took Steve's arm. "Are you dining tonight, Mr Donaldson? Would you like me to find you a companion? What type of girl appeals to you?"

"No, I'm not … is there a floor show this evening?"

"Yes, there's always a cabaret and it's a good one, but it does not commence until later. You see, that gives our guests time to relax, have a meal, and enjoy the company of one of our hostesses, unless of course they are in the Dancing Parrot Bar."

"The Dancing Parrot Bar," Steve echoed. "What's that?"

Francoise came closer to Steve; he could smell her perfume, her heavy makeup concealing her true age.

"That's were the main bar is, and of course, our dancing parrots. Shall I escort you?"

Steve's eyes, now fully accustomed to the light, observed the tables of the red dralon booths, housing wealthy businessmen with their hostesses; drinking champagne, escaping from the reality of their lives. He watched for a moment, thinking how insincere it all was, but then maybe the men who frequented this kind of establishment didn't want commitment. They craved the company of a younger attractive woman who would release them from their boring lives. He returned his eyes to Francoise; she was attractive, blonde and obviously older than some of the other young hostesses, but she had a certain warmth to her personality.

"I'd like to see that, maybe I can return later, Francoise, and you could accompany me?"

"Oh monsieur, impossible, I don't sit, monsieur."

Francoise smiled, she would have very much liked to have accompanied Steve, but she had played that role many times in her career, and preferred her present position of manageress; always ensuring that every client was happy and each girl was accommodating their guest, and extracting as much money from them for the club as possible.

"What type of girl do you like ... blonde? Brunette? I can organise it. Obviously, it would be better to sit now, get to know your hostess, enjoy her company, and relax before the cabaret commences. The club is busy tonight, later it may not be possible to find you a hostess, or even a table."

"Does Maria accompany guests?"

Francoise held his expression. "Maria is at reception and rarely sits with customers."

"But ... she does sit?"

"Oui, but very, very rarely, and only if a special request is made for her company."

Steve understood the club's main function, give their customers lovely hostesses who would never refuse a meal, champagne, or cigarettes. Get them to spend their money in the club; give them a reason to return on a regular basis. Every girl was warned; no boyfriends, no relationships; what they did outside the club was their own affair, so long as it did not interfere with the club's policies. The management would not tolerate customers sitting with their girlfriends. A jealous partner or pregnant hostess would not be good for business, and always ended up the same way; with the girl's employment being terminated. Steve scanned the club again. There was no sign of Nicky Martin.

Francoise guided Steve upstairs to the Dancing Parrot Bar. He admired her attractive figure, in her scantily clad, sparkling basque with seamed stockings and silver high-heeled shoes.

The Parrot Bar was full of men drinking and shouting at the lap dancers on stage; their fists full of dollars, enticing the provocative dancers to perform close to them. There were three golden parrot cages on stage, each at different heights, and beside each cage, a long, slender pole.

Flashing coloured lights that were recessed into the floor illuminated the catwalk from the stage, and the dancers' provocative moves delighted their male audience. Francoise had not categorised her latest member as being the type to watch and pay a lap dancer. Maybe she was wrong. She had been wrong many times before in her life when it came to her judgement of men.

"There is only one condition, Mr Donaldson, a very strict one. You must not touch the dancers, or attempt to touch them during, or after, their performance. No matter how close they come to you. Do you understand, monsieur?"

Francoise then diverted Steve's gaze to a group of bouncers at the bar.

"You don't want to mess with them."

Steve thanked Francoise, and then searched the stage in front of him. He saw Nicky; she was in one of the parrot cages, dancing. He moved closer to the stage where the lights were brighter. He was progressing quietly when the interruption came.

"Hey bud, you won't see or get much with no dollars in your hand," the man with the bald head said, then laughing, turned his attention to a tall, black dancer in front of him, beckoning her close, holding up his money. She moved her body, enticing her victim, then smiled and blew the man a kiss as he stuck $50 in her G String. She danced seductively and exclusively for him for a while. Steve watched the young dancer; her punter was suitably satisfied.

He turned his attention to Nicky.

Nicky's cage door opened and she started to descend. Steve was jostled with the surge of other spectators to obtain a position in the front row next to the dancers.

Nicky's pale blue sequined costume was very brief; her blue headdress and plumage feather matched her heavy blue stage eye makeup. She arrived at the bottom of her pole, using it as a prop. She held it with outstretched arms, her knees bent, her shoes balancing on the floor, her body moving up and down seductively. She arched her back, tossed her head backwards; then her eyes met Steve's. She almost lost her balance, but managed to regain her control and continued dancing. She did not, however, dance so freely, as her mind was on Steve and did not hear the chants and applause of the other customers.

Steve moved away from the side of the dance floor and stood at the bar beside the muscular bouncers.

"Jack Daniels on the rocks," he shouted, and the barman suitably obliged. Steve was still observing the floor show when he overhead the conversation between the two henchmen. They were talking about Nicky.

Nicky, thinking Steve had departed, regained her confidence, and danced more enthusiastically. Her antics on stage were leaving little to the imagination, and the crowd loved her.

"She's fantastic, just a pity anyone who becomes involved with her ends up hurt, or even dead, as in the case of that guy Frank Coulson."

"Yeah, there's no proof she had anything to do with that, but there's no smoke without fire."

"Hey, remember that boyfriend of hers, what was his name, Joe something? I heard she really fell for him."

"Yeah, he was going to take her away from all of this."

Nicky was commanding the stage now, and the crowd egged her on.

"Can you imagine taking her away from all of this? No chance."

Both men laughed at the very thought; they agreed that whilst Nicky was a star, no one would want her for a girlfriend. She was trouble. So volatile.

Steve listened carefully to their comments without making it obvious. He took a final look at Nicky on stage, and decided to leave. Francoise spotted Steve as he entered the cabaret section of the club.

"Oh, monsieur, I hope you haven't come back for a table, all booths are occupied," she said softly.

"That's alright Francoise, I won't be staying; maybe some other time."

He drew a $20 bill from his pocket, and discreetly slipped it to her. She hadn't provided any service to warrant the tip, but Steve hoped it would stand him in good stead if he required information in the future. Francoise smiled as Steve descended the marble staircase to the reception foyer. There were two different staff on duty, but as he approached, Maria appeared.

"Did you enjoy your evening, Mr Donaldson?"

Steve turned around, please to see her.

"Yes, very much, didn't get to watch the cabaret unfortunately."

Maria smiled. "Maybe next time," then added, "I hope there'll be a next time, Mr Donaldson." As Steve adorned his coat, he did not feel the card with her name and number being slipped into his pocket.

Chapter 9

Lieutenant Chandler and Detective Sergeant Johnston arrived at the scene to find police and ambulance in attendance, and a crowd all waiting to catch a glimpse of the dead body. Chandler entered the apartment block, passing the two patrolmen on duty.

"It's on the second floor," one of them said to Johnston.

They entered the apartment which was now an official crime scene, the photographic boys busily flashing their cameras from different angles as the dead body of the young woman lay half-naked, the brown colour of dried blood from her neck staining the carpet.

"There's no sign of breaking and entering," an officer told Chandler. "In fact, the chain was off the latch, which means she may have known her attacker."

"Did anyone hear or see anything?"

"We're checking that now. We're interviewing all residents as we speak, well the ones we can get a hold of at the moment. It was reported by a Mrs Winston, she lives down the hall."

Stuart Chandler walked around the rest of Louise Volosso's apartment.

"Nothing else disturbed?"

The policeman shrugged his shoulders. Chandler returned to where the body lay. She was attractive.

"Why in god's name when these violent attacks and murders take place, no one ever sees anything?" he said, shaking his head. Forensics were now in attendance and examining the body before allowing it to be taken to the morgue for further analysis.

"Johnston, make a list of everybody who lives in the block; find out where Ms Volosso worked and contact any friends or family, you know the drill. Oh, and Johnston, I want everything you can find on this woman; if she's got a parking ticket, I want to know. There's a beast out there and I want him. Let's hope this is a one-off case and there's no more repeats. You said earlier that this address sounded familiar."

Johnston nodded. "It was the same address that was called at two days ago regarding the missing neighbour; remember sir, we passed it for a routine follow-up."

Chandler shook his head. "Who called it in?"

The patrolman on duty came forward. "A Mrs Winston, Patricia Winston. She lives down the hall. She's in shock and won't say too much."

Chandler nodded, acknowledging the policeman's comments.

"Did she know the victim?"

"I don't think so Lieutenant, as I said she keeps her own company."

"Thank you, officer, you've done a good job. I'll speak to her before I leave."

He turned towards the medical officer. "How long before you can give me a more accurate time of death?"

"We're in the process of bagging everything, making sure Charlie will have all the information from the crime scene at his disposal."

Charlie O'Brien was the chief coroner and worked closely with Stuart Chandler. He was a New Yorker but being descendant from an Irish family, had a fiery temper, especially when overworked, and the very nature of his job brought its own stress, as time was never on his side.

The medical officer knew what Detective Stuart Chandler was about to say. He raised his hand. "Don't even ask for it tonight, they are stacking bodies downtown like an epidemic, and you know Charlie, he won't be pushed."

"But I've a strange feeling about this one."

"Chandler, you always have a strange feeling about all your cases, you know Charlie O'Brien as well as I do; he'll give you his opinion once he has the body and has completed his diagnosis.

Chandler shook his head. He knelt close to the dead woman's body. "Why? The attack was so violent, it was not just a lover's tiff, and yet Louise Volosso had admitted her murderer to her apartment, or that was how it appeared.

Patricia Winston was in a terrible state, and had a woman police officer attending her until she calmed down.

"Hello, Mrs Winston, I'm Lieutenant Chandler, and this is Sergeant Johnston. I understand you called this in."

Patricia nodded while holding her small linen handkerchief with its floral motif close to her eyes and sobbing.

"I never knew much about Miss Volosso. I keep myself to myself. It's not safe out there, you know."

Chandler wanted to smile, but didn't. He knew what she meant; after all, he dealt with it every day.

"Did you see anyone?"

"No, I don't go out; it's my legs, you see."

Chandler stared at her legs; they were both swollen with elephantiasis. He paused.

"Then what made you make that call, Mrs Winston?"

Patricia Winston stared back at Chandler; her eyes filled with fear and now wishing she had not got involved. She took her time, then softly mumbled.

"The young woman who knocked on my door two days ago.

"What! What did you say?" Chandler pressed.

Patricia repeated her statement and added, "A lovely young woman, who was very concerned for her friend, Miss Volosso. She missed her as she had not been in touch."

Again Patricia burst into floods of tears at the very thought of the horrific murder that had taken place along the corridor from her apartment.

"What young woman was that?" Chandler asked, eager to obtain the necessary information, but knowing from experience he would need to be gentle and patient if he were to secure more co-operation from Patricia Winston.

"Oh, I don't know, never seen her before, she left me a note."

"May I see that, please?"

"Oh, now, what did I do with it?" Patricia was again upsetting herself.

Chandler consoled her, he needed that information.

"Oh, yes, I know," then she abruptly stood up, steadying herself. She crossed the room, opened the lid of a tin, and fished out Sylvia's note with her details.

"Here you are, Lieutenant," she said, stretching out her arm and handing Chandler the slip of paper with the name and telephone number.

"Is there anything else you can tell us, anything at all, anything unusual recently?"

Chandler's question hung in the air. Mrs Winston negatively shook her head.

Chandler turned to leave when Mrs Winston shouted. "There … was … the naked man with the towel!"

"A naked man in a towel?"

"Yes, he was handsome in a rugged kind of way. I keep myself to myself as I've told you, but let me see; it was few days ago; Miss Volosso was arriving home. I heard some noise just before that and peeped out. Miss Volosso was standing, unlocking her door, when a man who came out of the stairwell distracted her. He was wearing nothing except for a white bath towel. The last I saw of him was when his towel dropped to the floor, and he was in full view of Miss Volosso – naked. They said something to each other, but I was too embarrassed to stay, so I returned to the safety and privacy of my apartment. Anyway, I didn't want to get involved."

This was the kind of information Chandler had been seeking. Maybe this case was moving forward after all.

"Did anyone else see this man?"

"Not to my knowledge. Well, not on this floor, maybe someone else saw him, after all, he was only wearing a towel, but then again he did come from the stairwell."

"Did it appear as if Miss Volosso knew this man?"

"I'm not sure of that. He saw me and disappeared."

"So he didn't approach Miss Volosso at all?"

"Certainly not when I was in the corridor, maybe after I closed the door, I can't say."

"Mrs Winston; Patricia; is there anything else you remember?"

Patricia shook her head. "No."

Chandler nodded. "Look, if anything pops into your mind, no matter how little, or how unimportant, please call me on this number. It's my direct line."

"You've been very helpful, I may need to talk to you again, but don't worry, this young policewoman will stay and look after you for a while."

Chandler paused, and faced his witness.

"Oh, by the way, did you recognise the man in the towel?"

Patricia Winston closed her eyes for a moment, then answered in a sure-full voice. "No, Lieutenant, I didn't, but to be honest I wasn't exactly looking at his face." She afforded herself a small laugh. Lieutenant Chandler also allowed himself a smile, and returned to the crime scene for one last look. He gave Johnston Sylvia's note.

"Check this out, maybe we'll turn up something, and Johnston, I want a list of all occupants in this building; owners as well as tenants."

"I've already put all that in motion, sir."

Chandler and Johnston returned to the station house. The day had started badly, and had got steadily worse.

"Did you see the state of that girl? What kind of animal does that, sir?"

"I don't know, Johnston; I just hope it's an isolated incident. The puzzle is, there's no sign of breaking and entering, so she either expected someone, or knew who was at the door, and judging by her lack of clothes, there's been no argument, 'cos there's no sign of a struggle anywhere in the apartment. Whoever killed this woman knew he'd have no difficulty gaining entry, and as I have already said, the way she was undressed possibly expected her caller."

"She obviously did struggle when she was held down with force; if the bruises on her thighs are anything to go by, and the attack was violent, but the way her throat was cut looks like a professional job to me. I believe, Johnston, we're searching for someone with specialised skills, someone who's close, but someone with a motive. There's something puzzling me. If you were going to attack your lover, you wouldn't allow yourself to be seen, especially if you were only wearing a towel. Patricia Winston never mentioned any knife, albeit she wasn't looking at the man's face, or indeed his hands, but bet you ten to one that the cut made across her throat is from a special blade, and not the sort of knife you'd find in a lady's apartment. You know, our man is very strong, he did after all hold that poor bitch down while he assaulted her."

Just then, Johnston was handed the list with the names of the owners and tenants who resided in Louise Volosso's apartment block. He scanned it quickly, not knowing what or who he was looking for, and handed it to his superior.

Chandler appraised the list. "Johnston, break this down. I want to know where each person works, what they do, how long they've lived here. I want to know what they had for breakfast, what they have in their fuckin' tea. Okay!" he shouted.

Chandler grabbed a coffee from the vending machine, took one sip, and choked.

"Goddamn it! Can't we get a decent cup of coffee around here no more?" he shouted, as he threw the plastic cup and its contents into the bin. He returned to his own office, slamming the door.

Johnston knew his superior. His boss was under immense pressure, and certainly didn't need the publicity of a rapist and murderer on the loose.

The rest of the station left Chandler to his own devices; they had seen it all before and felt sorry for Johnston, who, being Chandler's closest colleague, always took the brunt of these moods and outbursts when they occurred.

It was only a matter of time before normality would regain itself, but until then, life in the station would be hell.

Chapter 10

It was 3:00am when Steve left The Blue Parrot; a light snow fell, indicating that the freezing temperature had risen. He was about to make his way home when out of the corner of his eye he observed the tiny red glow of a cigarette. Steve decided to walk in the direction of the smoker, but kept his head down and collar up, shielding himself from the inclement weather. He looked up as he passed by the stranger in the black coat and hat, although he couldn't see his face; instinct told him that it was the same man who had been surveying him. He walked on, then quickly ducked into a doorway, stood for a moment, then cautiously retraced his steps. The man had gone. Steve strained his eyes in all directions, but the man had simply vanished. Something made him glance down at his feet, and there it was, a plain cigarette butt, floating in a puddle on the sidewalk. Steve slowly bent down, keeping his eyes on the street, his fingers fumbling in the dark, grey water, before tracing the cigarette end. He smelled the same strong, Turkish tar; however there was still no trace of the smoker.

His gaze returned to the club's entrance. Some of the girls were leaving, so he waited patiently for Nicky, hoping she would be alone. She appeared, and was about to enter a cab that was waiting. Without any hesitation, Steve jumped in beside her, and gave the driver Nicky's address.

"What you doin' here? Thought you'd gone home. You seen enough tonight!"

"Yeah, I saw enough; saw your whole act. I was at the bar."

"Listen, mister, I do a good job. I get paid well. I make these sad guys happy. Take them out of their reality for a while. They enjoy themselves."

"What about you, Nicky? Where do you go in your mind?"

The taxi made steady progress, the driver complaining about the snow.

"What are you afraid of, Nicky? Who are you running from? What's your story? Your reality, Nicky?"

"It's not Joe Marshall!" Nicky snapped. "If that's what you're thinking. I like Joe, but it would never have worked."

"I know that," Steve replied, his voice steady but quiet.

"You know nothin'. Nothin', you hear? I had to protect him."

"Protect him from what?"

Nicky fell silent. They were almost at her apartment.

"Is it alright if I come up?"

The cab driver watched both of them in his rear view mirror. Steve couldn't see his face, just his eyes staring back at him.

"Come on, let's have some fun." Her mood had changed as she turned her charm onto Steve.

The cab driver grinned, his eyes glistening, betraying his thoughts. Steve also smiled as he paid the fare.

Nicky poured some drinks and danced to the music she selected. She was becoming lost in its rhythm, and Steve joined in, hopeful that he may derive more information on her background and story. It was not to be, as Nicky slowly began to discard her clothes as well as Steve's. Overcome with emotion, they headed for the bedroom.

It was mid-morning when Steve woke. Nicky was still sound asleep. He quietly slipped out of bed, didn't shower; just dressed, and left, hailing a cab to return home. He did not see the watchful eyes of the man in black. Another Turkish cigarette butt fell to the ground as the man buzzed Nicky's apartment. It took a long time for Nicky to respond. She was hung over and still sleepy.

"Parcel for Miss Martin," the caller said.

Without thinking, Nicky clicked the entry door open.

"I'm on the second floor, number six."

She returned to the bedroom to find her wrap to cover her nudity. There was a knock at the door.

"Come in, I'll be out in a minute," she shouted, searching for her other black mule slipper. She was still searching when she heard the footsteps behind her. She turned around, but the blow was too much for her, and she fell to the ground, her wrap falling open, revealing her young, fit body. Her assailant dragged her by her hair, yanked her head backwards, and held the silver-polished deadly blade to her throat while he raped her. She lay helpless on the bed. He tied her hands and feet, then sat astride her, smiling as he beat her senseless.

Nicky almost died that day; in fact her attacker left her for dead. He searched the bedroom, found what he was looking for; a lovely little white thong, which he pocketed. His gloves protecting his fingerprints, he smiled again at Nicky, who lay unconscious on the bed, satisfied with his work.

Johnston sat at his desk, reminiscing of the conversation he had with his boss about how the job had affected and changed his life. His chief's words echoed in Johnston's mind. *"Don't let this job turn you into me; don't let it take over your life."*

Johnston was still completing his paperwork when the call came in.

"Goddamn it, not another one!" This was what he had feared after they discovered Louise Volosso's body.

"Johnston? Johnston?" Chandler shouted again. "We've got work to do."

Both detectives responded to the emergency call. They recognised the address. It was where their man had been stabbed only days before. Now there was another incident; a violent rape and beating. The girl involved was still alive, but only just. The medics were on the scene when the detectives arrived.

"Fuck me, what son of a bitch did this?"

Johnston just shook his head, not believing his eyes. It was only a few days ago, maybe a week at the most, when they had questioned this very woman in connection with the stabbing on the sidewalk outside her apartment. Chandler scanned the apartment with his eyes; whatever monster did this, did not come here to steal, he came to teach a lesson, and meant to kill her.

"She must know something, or someone for this attack to have taken place. Once again, there's no sign of forced entry."

"Maybe she saw the stabbing?" Johnston volunteered.

Chandler considered this comment. "Where did you say she worked?"

Johnston brought out his notebook. "The Blue Parrot Club, she told us she was a dancer."

"Okay, we'll start there, 'cos there's one thing for sure, this young thing won't be dancin' for quite some time."

"Excuse me, Lieutenant, but there's something bothering me." Johnston thumbed through his notebook. "Remember when we interviewed this young woman a week ago, well her boyfriend, or punter, was here, a Steve Donaldson."

"So what?" Chandler replied, his eyes still on the physical wreck of Nicky.

Johnston continued. "It's maybe nothing ... but ..."

"But what?"

"He was wearing nothing but a white towel."

"And? ..." Chandler pursed his lips.

Again, Johnston continued. "So was the man that Patricia Winston observed in the corridor before Louise Volosso was murdered. He had nothing else on but a white towel. I'm also checking the list of names of all the occupants in Miss Volosso's block of apartments, and there's a Steve Donaldson residing there."

Johnston now had his chief's full attention.

"Could we be so lucky?" Chandler said, his eyes full of anticipation.

"Let's pay our Mr Donaldson a visit."

Chapter 11

Steve had heard about the attack and death of Louise Volosso, and assumed it was his man who wore the black trench coat but the question was, why? Why had this innocent woman been the subject of such a vicious crime? What was her connection? Was there a connection? She was attractive, and he recalled her expression and smile as his towel fell to his feet.

Steve thought again about Nicky and on all the incidents that had occurred since he had taken the case.

1. *The stabbing and death of Frank Coulson.*
2. *The ever-watching man in black, who smokes Turkish cigarettes.*
3. *Someone had entered his apartment, although strangely nothing seemed out of place.*
4. *What was the connection to The Rosenbergs?*
5. *Who had recommended him – that question was still unanswered.*

6. Nicky Martin is a dancer. The Rosenbergs, the man in black. His client – what was the common factor?

Steve didn't understand, and poured himself another large Jack Daniels as he once again turned these events over in his mind.

"You got the warrant?" Chandler asked.

Johnston nodded, holding up the document.

"Okay you guys, everybody ready – lets go," he shouted, as he and his fellow officers burst into Steve's apartment, their guns held high in outstretched arms, all pointing at Steve's head.

"What the hell?" Steve yelled, jumping out of his armchair.

"Steve Donaldson, I'm arresting you for the murders of Frank Coulson and Louise Volosso, and the rape and assault of dancer Nicky Martin. You do not have to say anything…" Chandler started, as he read Steve his rights, while another officer brutally cuffed Steve's wrists, snapping the bracelets onto his skin.

"Hey, man, what the fuck are you talking about?"

"Fuck off, asshole," Chandler replied, kneeing Steve from behind. "We have a warrant to search these premises. Take him away," he shouted to his colleagues.

"Hold it, hey, you can't just … now hold on … you can't … what the hell are you doing?"

Chandler stood close to Steve now, and whispered in his ear.

"It's all over, big boy. You've screwed your last pussy. I'm taking you down, and by the time I'm finished with you, they'll throw away the key."

"Listen man, I don't know what information you have, but I'm innocent – you've got the wrong man."

"Hey baby, half the inmates in the penitentiaries are innocent, or so they claim. Isn't that correct, Johnston? Now get this son of a bitch outta my sight."

Chandler surveyed the apartment with a scrutinising sweep of his eyes.

"Okay, boys," he shouted. "Search this place, pull it apart.

"What are you looking for?" Steve yelled, his wrists now bleeding and beginning to hurt. "What do you expect to find?"

Chandler smirked. "Oh we don't know yet, but we're sure it's here and it's also what's not here."

"Not here?" Steve echoed, looking puzzled.

"Yeah, not here," replied Chandler.

"Like what?!"

"Like your letter opener."

"What?"

"Your letter opener, Mr Donaldson, the weapon you used to kill Frank Coulson. The same letter opener we have with your fingerprints all over it. You left it behind at the scene, remember? That was careless, or did someone witness the murder?"

"Witness what? No one witnessed anything, 'cos I wasn't there, and I certainly did not kill Frank Coulson. I don't even know a Frank Coulson."

"Is that right, you filthy son of a bitch. I don't think that's correct, Mr Donaldson," Chandler said, then inflicted another blow to Steve's lower abdomen, which saw Steve shrink to his knees.

"Nicky Martin saw you. Didn't she? Didn't she?!" Chandler shouted into his ear, nearly blowing him deaf. "Look, you fuck, you're ex-job. We've got your prints on file. We have the weapon that you used on poor Frank. We interviewed you at Nicky Martin's; we probably interrupted you. Do you turn them on first, the act with the towel, then enjoy raping before beating them? We probably saved Miss Martin's life that morning we questioned you in her apartment. I mean she was very frightened. Had you threatened her? You probably scared her out of her wits, and then you returned to finish the job, didn't you? But you made one mistake, Donaldson. No, correction, two mistakes."

"One, Nicky Martin's alive. Only just, but she'll identify you. It's only a matter of time and two, the only other person to see you in your towel was Louise Volosso, and you couldn't let it go: you'd had to have her, you bastard; you fucked her violently then slit her throat. A very tidy job. A specialist with a particular style of knife. Where is it, Donaldson? Tell us, or have we to beat it out of you? Because let me tell you, you're going down for a very long time."

"Listen, Lieutenant," Steve's mind was racing. "You've got this all wrong. I had nothing to do with any of those events. I'm innocent."

"We have a witness, Mr Donaldson. One you forgot about, but she remembered you.

"She? Who, what's going on here?"

Chandler laughed. "Where's the knife you slit Louise Volosso's throat with, after you raped her?"

"Hey man, this is all some sick job, right? I mean, I've no idea what you're talking about."

"Were you at The Blue Parrot club last night?"

Steve hesitated, then answered slowly. "Yeah, but what has that to do with this?"

"Did you go back to Nicky Martin's apartment?"

Again Steve hesitated. "Yeah, so what? You interviewed me at her apartment last week."

"Did you have sex with her?" Chandler asked menacingly.

"That, Lieutenant, is none of your goddamn business."

"Oh, none of my goddamn business?" Chandler repeated. "Well, let's see," he snarled as he administered a blow to Steve's kidneys. "You bet it's my business, you motherfucker son of a bitch."

Steve stared at Chandler in disbelief.

"What do you mean?"

"Did you have sex with Nicky Martin last night?" Chandler shouted.

"Yes, we did. We fell asleep and I left before she woke." Steve realised that there was no point in denying the question, as Chandler must have a reason for asking.

"What kicks do you get, Donaldson, raping these girls? And in Nicky Martin's case, tying her up after you've taken your pleasure and beaten her within an inch of her life?"

Steve's face was a picture. He was appalled and frightened. "What! What the hell are you talking about?"

"Take him away," Chandler shouted, gritting his teeth and then kicking over a chair with sheer anger.

Chandler looked at his men. He scanned Donaldson's apartment once more.

"Take it apart, leave nothing unturned," he said again, raising his voice.

He then went to join his prisoner in the waiting patrol car. Steve was handcuffed, seated in the locked rear section of the car, the steel cage separating him from the driver and Chandler.

"Listen, Lieutenant, I'm innocent. I've told you, I haven't done any of those things you accused me of. Sure, Nicky – Miss Martin – and I got it together, but she was sleeping soundly when I left. She was not assaulted and certainly not beaten. She was sleeping like a baby.

"Save it, Donaldson. I hope you have a good councillor, because you're sure gonna need one."

"Listen, someone's setting me up. I'm innocent. I'm working on a case. I'm not about to beat up a possible witness."

Chandler listened to Steve's ramblings, but chose to ignore him. As far as he was concerned, he had his man.

The ordeal at the station house was terrible. Some of Steve's former colleagues still worked there, and the whole department went quiet when he was led in. He was put in an open cage for all to observe along with the other low life.

Steve knew the procedure well enough, but had never experienced the humiliation first-hand. How had all this happened? He couldn't quite put it all together. What seemed a simple contract had turned into a nightmare. There was a large bald headed bruiser watching him as he entered the cage.

"Hey, shit face. You're a cop. I remember you."

Steve glanced at the inmate addressing him, then turned away, choosing to ignore the man.

"Hey, motherfucker, I'm talking to you. Don't you turn your friggin' ass away from me."

Steve didn't respond, but the blow to the back of his neck was significant and he collapsed, unconscious. The inmate's boot crashed into Steve's abdomen, as he lay helpless on the floor. It was sometime before Steve woke to find himself in a solitary cell on a stone bed with no mattress, only a pillow at this head. His vision was blurred and his head pounded like a drum. He felt sick and disorientated. Slowly the sequence of events of that day returned to his mind. He rose, finding it difficult to stand, staggered to the heavy steel door and banged as loud as he could for assistance. Eternity lapsed, then the peephole slot opened, and a pair of eyes met his from the other side.

"I want to see Lieutenant Chandler," he yelled at his captor.

The peephole slammed closed with no words spoken, no acknowledgement of his request, all there was were the heavy footsteps of his guard disappearing down the corridor. Again Steve banged on his cell door. This time he drew no attention.

Chapter 12

Steve Donaldson once had a very different lifestyle, and he let his mind wander back through the years before he joined the Marines and Special Forces. He was born Steven Arthur Donaldson. Steven, taken from his mother's father and Arthur, from his own father. Arthur had worked in the steel industry all his life and therefore was a tough individual, who expected his wife to keep the house perfectly and always food on the table, no matter whether the union was on strike or not. The steel workers had their share of industrial action, and as with all progress, there were casualties. Steve's father, Arthur, was one of many who lost employment, and on that sad day when his father stayed home because he was out of work changed their lives forever. He started drinking more with fellow workmates in the same predicament, the union hand-out being spent irresponsibly. Arguments followed between his mom and dad, and Steve couldn't wait until he was old enough to leave the so-called family home.

He felt sorry for his mother who, bless her soul, had given her all and supported both him and her husband through all adversity. She could not, of course, maintain the house, care for Steve and give justice to her job, to say nothing of attempting to satisfy her husband's demands, and soon became ill with exhaustion as she realised everything she held dear was going downhill.

Steve remembered the day his mother was taken into hospital because the cancer had spread. The family's lack of funds had prevented treatment that would have eased her pain, and so Steve's mom died a tired, broken woman of an incurable illness.

In life she had always sought the best in people, always gave more time, smiled at everybody, never complained about her own problems, and always had an ear for others in trouble. Steve's mother always defended her husband when Steve or anyone else criticised him and point out his shortcomings. But with the struggle over the years all taking its toll, she died holding her son's hand, while her husband, who had slipped into a self-pity condition was drinking with his so-called pals in a local bar. Steve cried for days after her death, and decided he would need to make a life of his own. His mother had made him promise on her death bed to care for his father, but Steve knew in his heart that it would never work.

He left the note addressed to his father on the large dresser in their living room, took one long, last look around at the house in which he was born, and with a tear in his eye pulled his rucksack over one shoulder, and closed the door on his childhood.

Although only 16, he had saved enough money to travel south on the Greyhound, hoping to find a new start. A job, a roof over his head, and who knows, maybe a future. The bus had been travelling for two hours, and although other passengers were conversing with each other, Steve had slept; not just with the trauma of leaving home, but with the fear of being totally alone in the world, with nowhere to go.

He awoke with the silver bus pulling to a halt, and the bustle of fellow passengers alighting. A holdall suddenly landed on top of him, with a young man trying desperately to retrieve the offending bag, and apologising for his clumsiness. He offered to buy Steve a beer, who declined at first, then accepted his kind offer.

Andre Gomez was Mexican, and although smaller than Steve, was strong. He had a good physique and his eyes had a certain alertness about them. Their conversation was hesitant at first, each waiting for the other to take the lead. Moments passed and then Steve enquired of Andre's destination. His reply changed Steve's life.

"I'm joining the Marines," Andre proudly replied, a smile breaking across his face.

"The Marines?" Steve echoed in surprise.

Andre laughed as he sat upright, with shoulders back and chest out, determined to create an impression. "There's a war comin', you know, I want to be part of it."

"Do your parents know? I mean, do they really know, Andre? Or have you left home like me?"

Steve could have bit his tongue out there and then, as he did not mean to divulge the fact that he had left home under difficult circumstances. Andre paused, and stared into the eyes of his new companion.

"Amigo, don't be shy, we all have a cross to bear. Hey, look at me, I'm Mexican and going to be a US marine. Plenty of people say I won't make it, but I've got news for them. It took guts to get this far and I can't afford to mess this opportunity up."

Steve appraised Andre again. He was so positive; he had ambition, a goal, a future. Steve instinctively knew Andre Gomez would make it as a US marine, and probably a damn good one at that.

Andre talked about his family, his eyes motionless as he recalled old memories. He stared at his beer glass. "Where were you planning to stay tonight, Steve?" he asked, without changing the direction of his vision.

Steve took a deep breath, his tongue forming a bulge in his cheek. Then he let out a sigh. "No plans, really, I have a little money, suppose I was just gonna ride the Greyhound until that runs out, find a job, and somewhere to live."

"Doin' what?" Andre pressed.

"I don't know!" he snapped. Maybe leaving home wasn't such a good idea after all, he thought. Maybe I should take the next bus back, take that row; that would surely be waiting, then wait until I have a proper idea, some more money, and a definite plan for my life.

Andrez Gomez appraised Steve, wiped the beer froth from his chin with the back of his hand, and rubbed his hands together.

"Why don't you come with me, join the Marines? It'll be a great life. Something to belong to; something to be proud off. Unless of course you do really just want to stay on this bus until your money runs out and take potluck. But Steve, I think you're better than that. You only have to believe in yourself."

Andre glanced out of the diner's window. Other passengers were reboarding the coach.

"You comin' or not?" Andre said, standing up. Then he grabbed Steve's arm, not waiting for an answer.

"Let's go," he said.

"But I don't ..." Steve stammered.

"Shut up, asshole, get your butt out there and come with me. Hey man, you've nothin' to lose."

Steve heard Andre Gomez's words. This could not be happening.

Both men reboarded the Greyhound, sitting together this time. They were silent for a while, then started to speak simultaneously.

Both men laughed, talked more about their families and their different upbringings until both fell asleep, while the silver Greyhound ploughed onwards to its destination, eating the miles surely and steadfastly, the drone of its engine becoming just a distant hum.

Steve joined the US Marines along with Andre Gomez. They were good friends, and throughout their training always stood up for each other. Andre, being Mexican, suffered taunting from other trainees, but nobody metered out punishment like Sergeant Joe Brewsbaker. He hated Gomez and took great pleasure in abusing his authority with beatings and imposing extra duties on the man.

Andre Gomez of course always bounced back, no matter how unjust or horrible Brewsbaker's torture was. Joe Brewsbaker was a big man, with a large face and bulging cheekbones. His crew-cut hair and broad shoulders, together with his obnoxious, tough attitude, sent out the appropriate signals to all, and therefore was used to getting his own way.

Andre Gomez was the exact opposite. He was good looking, with jet-black hair and of a slim build, but very strong, both physically and mentally. He therefore knew how to survive and could, for the most part, handle Brewsbaker's punishments.

Steve was also strong. His body was well-toned; his dark hair, lean face with its prominent cheekbones and jaw line suited his full six-foot-four height, and the fact that he and Gomez were close also reflected his share of punishment from Brewsbaker and his lackeys.

Time passed as Steve lay on his bed in his cell, and once again allowed his mind to wander back through his years, when he met his first wife, Gill. He loved Gill and still did. It was just his career in the Marines and the special overseas opps that eventually took their toll, to say nothing of his own change in personality.

Steve resigned from the Forces and joined the New York City Police as a detective. His specialist skills stood him well, but his non-conformity brought some resentment and he found himself working more as a loner rather than a team player.

His marriage eventually broke down when Gill could no longer suffer the long hours his job demanded. After separating from Gill, Steve never really settled, so left the Force and set himself up as a private investigator.

Steve thought once more of all the events that had occurred since he took this case. It all centred around Nicky Martin; he didn't know why, and he believed Nicky didn't know either.

Chapter 13

It was some time before the police squad finished searching Steve Donaldson's apartment. They had as instructed been meticulous, and had bagged various items which they catalogued with a brief description of where they were found. The apartment looked like a bombsite. It had been ransacked, but ransacked methodically. A patrolman was left to guard the area as this was now a crucial part of evidence, and had become a crime scene.

All items found in Steve's apartment were forwarded to Forensics with a copy of their description to Detective Chandler.

Chandler held the paper with his left hand and scrutinised the list.

"You found all these in that apartment?" a surprised tone in his voice.

"Yeah, Lieutenant, most unusual to find all these at the same time in the same location."

"Did anybody check the trash can?"

"Yeah; that's where we found the white thong, obviously from one of the girls. We think probably Nicky Martin as Miss Volosso was dressed in black."

Chandler checked the list again. What motivated a man to commit such crimes, he thought.

Steve Donaldson, by all accounts, did not fit the profile of a serial rapist and murderer, but Chandler had long since given up being surprised at situations and people he came across in his job.

"Donaldson's been calling for you, Lieutenant." Chandler looked up from the list.

"Has he now?" Let's make him sweat a while longer. Anyway, I want the lab reports before I talk to him again." Chandler sat at this desk and re-read the items found at Donaldson's apartment.

Item1 – gent's gold wristwatch; bracelet strap – found in jacket pocket left hand side.

Item 2 – card from Maria/telephone number on Blue Parrot Club business card.

Item 3 – black lace panties – possibly from Louise Volosso.

Item 4 – white lace thong – found in trash can – possibly from Nicky Martin – the thong matches other underwear found at Miss Martin's address.

Item 5 – photograph receiving Medal of Honour and Purple Heart for service to his country.

Item 6 – photograph with other servicemen – note special forces emblem on shoulder.

Item 7 – letter to Steve Donaldson – found in newspaper magazine rack.

Item 8 – membership card for The Blue Parrot night club. Found in top pocket of jacket and telephone number of Maria.

Item 9 – photograph of ex-wife, Gill and daughter Beckie.

Item 10 – large cotton white towel – bathroom – no bloodstains.

Item 11 – half bottle of Jack Daniels and glass – taken for fingerprinting.

Item 12 - $1,500 cash – used bills.

Chandler shook his head. "All this found in one location. Either our Mr Donaldson is very stupid, or he has a fetish for collecting woman's underwear. It's astonishing. There's something from each victim; the watch, a letter, two pairs of panties. Then there's the letter opener he used to kill Frank Coulson. He's obviously picked up Nicky Martin at the Blue Parrot. Maybe got jealous when she was fooling around with Frank Coulson? In a rage, he's waited for him to leave his precious Nicky's apartment, then killed him with the letter opener. Stole his watch to make it look like a mugging. Gets back with Nicky Martin on the pretence of protecting her, and all the time his rage was building inside of him, building until it erupted.

"Don't know what he was doin' at Miss Volosso's dressed in a towel, and allowing himself to be seen, that was careless. I believe he saw Louise Volosso and took his revenge out on her in an attempt to quell the rage within himself, but found that he still wasn't satisfied or fulfilled. No, it had to be Nicky Martin and so he returned to have sex but this time he was going to teach her a lesson. He'd already thrown Miss Martin's panties in the trash when we burst in.

"I think we're dealing with a sick old vet whose career as a PI has taken a nosedive. He's not the hero anymore. He's lost his wife, his family. He's been married to the job too long. I can understand all that; I walked in the same trap myself, but he's lost it completely and resents his lifestyle.

He's taken out his frustration on these women. Nicky Martin possibly rejected him after a while. God knows, she doesn't fit with him, does she?"

"And Frank Coulson," Johnston interrupted.

"Oh, Frank? Frank was just her next punter who took Nicky away. His Nicky, and given his experience in the Forces, and coupled with jealously, raging within, he just did the natural thing and took him out. I don't believe he would have left his letter opener at the scene. He's been disturbed or seen by someone. Possibly even Miss Martin.

"What do you want me to do now," Johnston asked.

Chandler hesitated. I want his service record pulled. I want to know everything about this son of a bitch."

"His record may be classified, sir, given that he was in Special Forces."

"Special Forces my ass. I don't give a damn. I want that record. This is a murder enquiry. Hey, Johnston, contact his ex-wife; pull her in. I want to talk to her."

"Is that all, Lieutenant?"

Again, Chandler paused. He sifted through the items that had now been brought to him. He stopped at the Blue Parrot card with Maria's telephone number on it.

"That's all, Johnston. I'll take this one. We may just have prevented this Maria becoming the next victim."

With that, Chandler sat down at his desk to again read the letter found in Donaldson's magazine rack.

Hi Honey,

I'm sorry we couldn't be together last night. It was just one of these things. You weren't there and Frank was. I was told I had to entertain him, you know what I mean. He's got connections, I guess. Anyway, I didn't expect you to turn up at my apartment that night. He was only a one-night stand. Please believe me.

Will make it up to you. I promise.

Love Nicky xx

Chandler read the letter over and over. He noted the ring stain where Donaldson's glass had rested. The poor son of a bitch must have been getting drunk as he poured over this letter, his imagination running wild. Of all the things his Nicky would be doing with Frank Coulson.

However, that was no excuse to commit these crimes. Chandler wondered about Steve Donaldson. After all those years of service as a marine in the Special Forces, his time as a cop and his career as a Private Eye; the price he'd paid losing his wife and family. Was it all just a case of Donaldson snapping, or was he a predetermined rapist and murderer as the facts suggested, using his specialist knowledge to commit those crimes?

Chandler held his own thoughts of the man he held in custody and knew whatever the reason, Steve Donaldson would find it very difficult to get out of the evidence surmounted against him.

There was no post date but the faded ring stain of Donaldson's glass did indicate that his suspect had had the letter in his possession for some time. Enough time to dwell on. Enough time for jealously to mount. Enough time for his emotions to take over and enough drink probably to drive him insane and out of control, but then although out of control when beating Nicky Martin, definitely very much in control when murdering Louise Volosso. What was her connection?

Chandler wished he could interview Nicky Martin but she was still in a coma. Her mind and body had closed down with the trauma of her attack.

No matter what her lifestyle, no one deserved a beating like she had sustained, but two other facts frustrated Chandler; both Louise Volosso and Frank Coulson would not be making any statements. He would need to interview Donaldson, he knew that, but he would let him stew a while longer.

The DA surely couldn't dismiss the evidence against his suspect on this occasion, so Chandler felt confident that he could make his case stick. He had all the evidence, the motive, the weapon for at least one murder. He wanted of course more than anything to tie all three cases together, and prove Donaldson was guilty which would send him down forever. One of the challenges was that Forensics had not matched any sample of blood from Louise Volosso to Donaldson. It was only the black panties found in Donaldson's apartment that cross-matched as those of Louise Volosso's underwear. That should have been enough but Chandler wanted to be absolutely certain. He knew he had to find that vital missing link, otherwise Louise Volosso's murder would be treated as an isolated case.

Johnston appeared at that moment.

"Any luck tracking down Donaldson's ex-wife?" he asked his sergeant.

"Yes, we've located her but haven't made contact yet, thought I'd better speak to you first."

"Why, what for?" Chandler asked, a puzzled expression on his face.

"Well, Donaldson's service record is a no-no. Can't get any co-operation."

"This is a bloody murder investigation!"

"I know, Lieutenant, but no matter what I tried or who I spoke to I got so far, then nothing; a brick wall. Apparently his file is coded and access is prohibited.

Stuart Chandler stared at Johnston in disbelief. As police, there were no barriers in obtaining information so what was so special about Steve Donaldson and his file protected by a code?

"Did you find who could access his file?" Stuart Chandler asked in a sarcastic tone.

"That information is also classified."

"What! So we have a murderer and rapist on the loose, walking about committing all sorts of crimes, and because of some stupid code nobody can gain access to the guy's records? Is that what you're telling me?"

"Well, Lieutenant, that appears to be the case but he ain't walking about, sir. We've got him downstairs and the evidence we brought in from the search of his apartment; surely that'll be enough to convict him?"

Johnston paused before concluding his statement. "Maybe we don't need his goddamn file."

Stuart Chandler listened to his officer. Maybe his sergeant was right, but he had been denied access to information on a man held in custody and the prime suspect on multiple murder and rape charges, and Chandler did not want to go to the DA half-cocked just to have the rug pulled from under him by faceless people who, for whatever reason, wanted and protected Steve Donaldson's history. There was something nagging at the back of Chandler's mind but he couldn't bring it to the surface.

"Get his ex-wife in here. Don't tell her what it's about. Make up an excuse, anything, but don't release any information on the murders and rapes until I've spoken to her. By the way, were you given any name that could access the file.

"Well, not so much as a name, but as I understand it, authority has to come from the President.

"The President?" Chandler echoed. "Who the hell have we got downstairs? Who has that kind of protection?"

Johnston pointed out the obvious. "Steve Donaldson, sir."

Chapter 14

The metal slide on the peephole of the heavy cell steel door opened and a pair of eyes scanned the cell. Steve lay on his concrete bed and, although hearing the movement, made no attempt to stand. The guard, happy that his prisoner could be seen, unlocked the door; the loud noise of keys turning in the lock brought Steve to his feet.

"Okay, okay, stay back," the guard said, his baton at the ready as he approached Donaldson to cuff him. Another officer stood in the doorway in case there was any attempt to escape or attack.

"Where are you taking me?" Steve asked, his voice rough and his eyebrows lowered.

"They want to see you upstairs."

Donaldson was shuffled along the corridor and prodded in the back a couple of times by his guard. He was escorted to the interview room where one of his hands was cuffed to the chair. That meant one hand was free.

Stuart Chandler realised he would need to be courteous with his prisoner. He could place Steve Donaldson with place, time and motive where Nicky Martin and Frank Coulson were concerned, but it was Louise Volosso's rape and murder that Chandler wanted to prove. He needed Patricia Winston to identify Donaldson.

Chandler sat across from Steve and stared at the man in front of him. Another officer joined them and the two policemen checked their wristwatches and recorded the time the interview commenced. They pressed the tape recorder button.

"Interview commencing at 3:30pm, Wednesday, 18 December. Let's start with Nicky Martin? How long have you known her?"

Steve paused, his memory counting the days and the incident when he first met Nicky when she had arrived home with Frank Coulson.

"It was approximately 15 days ago," he replied.

"Are you sure? Absolutely sure? That was the first time you met Nicky Martin? Now, I urge you to take your time, and think carefully."

Steve realised that if the question was being repeated, then the police had a reason, which obviously had contradicted his first answer.

"Yes, I'm sure," then thinking out loud "unless you mean when I first saw her, which would be in a photograph that my client gave me, but as far as meeting her, yes, 15 days ago would be about correct; she was with her man friend.

"Hold on! You refer to a photograph. What photograph would that be, and may we ask the name of your client and who was Miss Martin's man friend?"

"Well, my client name remains confidential, Lieutenant." Steve then thought to himself he wished he actually knew who his clients were. After all, that was one of the reasons he stuck with the case, to find out more.

"Her man friend was just another punter, I expect. I didn't know him. He had certainly never seen him before. And may I add, Lieutenant, at that point I knew absolutely nothing about Nicky Martin."

"So you're telling us that you had no prior relationship with Miss Martin, and you had no knowledge of the fact that she was a pole dancer at The Blue Parrot nightclub?"

Steve nodded his head. "That's correct."

Stuart Chandler went quiet for a moment, then continued his interrogation.

"Can you then explain, Mr Donaldson, why, when I personally interviewed yourself and Miss Martin the following day, after Frank Coulson was found murdered outside her apartment block, how you told me you had met Miss Martin at The Blue Parrot club the evening before, and you both had returned home together and you spent the night with her?"

Steve remained silent.

"That was all a lie," Chandler said, slamming his palm on the table, which made everybody jump. Everybody that was, except Steve.

Steve knew he couldn't now tell the truth of how he met Nicky and Frank the night before, and how it was Frank who'd spent the night with Nicky, and not him. So he said nothing.

"Explain yourself, Donaldson," Chandler pressed. Steve looked at the other officer.

"Believe me. The first time I met Nicky Martin was ..."

Was when Chandler, interrupting Donaldson, now standing up and shouting, "Was it when she was with her man friend? Was it when I interviewed you in her apartment when you were wearing nothing but a towel, the same as you were when you visited Louise Volosso?"

"What! Louise Volosso has nothing to do with me!" Steve exclaimed.

"Not what our witness says, Mr Donaldson. In fact, she could give a very full and accurate description of you, especially with your towel at your ankles," Chandler said smugly. "In fact, you seem to like flashing yourself Donaldson, where young women are concerned."

"Look, I've already told you! I was on a case for a client to track the whereabouts of Miss Martin. I was even paid upfront in cash but I wanted to know more about Nicky Martin's story. So I did go and meet her, at her apartment, which was the first time I met her, just before you came along. If I hadn't protected her with an alibi you'd have had her downtown, accusing her of all sorts, and I would never have been able ..."

Again, Chandler interrupted, and again shouted "never been able to screw her and then beat her to a pulp. What did she have on you, Donaldson, or was it just your rage taking over because she was having an affair with poor Frank Coulson? Was that it? Frank was just the poor unlucky son of a bitch as you would have reacted no matter who she took home?

"I put it to you, that's why you took your same rage out on Miss Volosso. Again, in your towel, you forced yourself on her, raped her at knifepoint, then in accordance with your specialist training, you cut her throat. Where is the weapon? What did you do with it?"

Steve shook his head. I've already told you. I had nothing to do with Louise Volosso's murder. I didn't even know the goddamn woman. "

"Handy, her living in the same apartment block, wasn't it? You nursing your feelings, your rage rising. You must have noticed her coming and going, I mean who wouldn't notice a lovely young attractive woman like her? Full of style. Warm and inviting. A friendly personality. Maybe too friendly, eh, Donaldson?"

"I didn't know Miss Volosso. I never saw her before ..."

"Oh, so you do now admit you did see her. You have denied that previously. Go on, refresh all of us. Tell us the goddamn truth. You're going down, Donaldson. You won't escape this time, so do you want to make it easy on yourself, or shall we do it the hard way?"

Steve reflected for a moment. It was those long, long, legs that had swayed him to take this case. Those legs and $2,000 he had been paid up front.

Chandler stared irritably at his prisoner. "Okay, shall I make it easy for you, Donaldson? You met Nicky Martin at The Blue Parrot club where she was employed as a dancer. You and she became involved, you both saw a lot of each other, if you pardon the expression, until one night she went out with Frank Coulson. You became insanely jealous Steve, and I must say, after meeting Miss Martin myself, I can fully understand your feelings.

"Yet Nicky began to see Frank on a regular basis, didn't she? Again and again she went with him – you couldn't stand it, Steve, could you? So you were going to put a stop to him, and then teach poor Nicky a lesson." Chandler was fishing.

"Louise Volosso may have been unintentional but you still took your rage out on her. She just happened to invite you in, probably on impulse after seeing you in your towel. You just couldn't resist her, Steve, could you? But things got out of hand, and I believe the beast inside of you took over, and the rest we know."

Chandler stopped, hoping Steve Donaldson would now confess to his summary of events.

Steve negatively shook his head. "You've got this all wrong, Lieutenant. All wrong."

"Well, how do you explain the letter she wrote to you."

"What letter?"

"The one we found in your apartment. The one with your stained glass ring on it. The one you read over and over again while getting drunk with liquor and jealousy."

Chandler then dropped the said letter on the table in front of Steve. He watched his suspect as he eyed the evidence in front of him.

"As I was saying, Steve, you couldn't handle the fact that Nicky had moved on. So you waited for poor Frank to leave Nicky's apartment then you went for him with your letter opener. The handiest weapon you had after digesting her letter.

"You killed him, Steve, stabbing him repeatedly until he was dead. You then stole his watch to make it look like a mugging and robbery. Didn't you! Didn't you?" Chandler repeated, the emotion and rage rising in his voice.

Steve composed himself. "I've never seen that letter and I don't know how you found it. I don't have any idea of its contents and I can't explain how it was in my apartment when it was planted there. Also, you say the murder weapon was a letter opener. Well, that doesn't mean it's mine. You're fabricating evidence, Lieutenant."

Chandler's eyes widened. He produced a sealed plastic bag, its contents secured the bone handle letter opener.

"Recognise this? I believe it's yours?" he said, before Steve could respond.

"Steve's mouth fell open as he viewed his own knife.

"Is that the murder weapon?" he asked.

"You know it is. It's got your prints all over it. Who saw you, Steve? Who, or what, encouraged you to leave this behind, stuck in Frank Coulson's body?"

Steve again shook his head.

Chandler then threw another package on the table. It contained a gold bracelet wristwatch.

"You took this off Coulson, Donaldson, didn't you, as you left him to die on the sidewalk? You made your assault appear as a mugging gone wrong. This piece of evidence was also found in your apartment in your overcoat pocket. What were you going to do with it? Taunt young Nicky with it, teach her a lesson? Teach her that she could dance and play at the club, but outside she was yours and only yours, Steve? Is that it? Is that what this is all about?"

Steve now realised why his apartment had been broken into, and on more than one occasion. The man in black who smoked strong, Turkish cigarettes was setting him up as the fall guy, probably; but what Steve couldn't understand was why? And on whose instructions?

"I'm being set up, Lieutenant. You've got to let me go so I can prove my innocence."

Chandler started laughing. "Hey, bud, Mr Special Bloody Forces, I can promise you one thing for sure. You ain't goin' anywhere for a long, long time.

"Interview concluded, time 4:45pm. Take him back to his cell," Chandler instructed, as he left the room to find Sergeant Johnston, whom he hoped would have more new evidence.

Chapter 15

Karen was the daughter of wealthy banker Henry Laithwaite, whose bank held the vast Rosenberg Diamond Company Account in its portfolio, so it was only a matter of time before she was introduced to Ralph Rosenberg. Karen was beautiful; her charisma attracted all when she entered a room, and was therefore never short of admirers or suitors. Karen, however, was attracted to Ralph; his family fortune being the main factor, but also Ralph's strength of character and his appetite for power and ambition certainly suited her needs. So, after a short courtship, they married.

The wedding was an elaborate affair, the guest list reading like a who's who. They honeymooned in Europe, taking in the sights of London, Paris, Venice and Rome and attending many social events as invited guests of honour.

Karen loved all the attention fraternising with the international jet-set, and certainly felt at home in their company.

A visit to one of their diamond mines in South Africa had been arranged which didn't really excite Karen, until she was presented with a huge diamond of some fourteen carats. The uncut stone and the celebration of the find was published worldwide.

Their marriage, wealth, and the diamonds, especially the uncut stones, all added to the fantasy. It all seemed like a fairy tale. Photographs of the uncut stone appeared in all the broadsheets and the usual bidding for exclusive articles from wealthy international magazines were unparalleled.

Karen loved and enjoyed the limelight; her beauty and extrovert personality invited many interviews. Ralph by comparison preferred the company of his business associates, and therefore did not attend many social events.

The publicity offered from the media machine often caused Ralph and Karen to clash. She needed and wanted their adulation, and being wealthy herself as the daughter of Henry Laithwaite, meant she thrived in the spotlight. The more the media wanted, the more she gave, and the more beautiful she became.

Once back in residence in New York, the couple settled down together and any time Ralph travelled he took his new bride with him. Unfortunately, Karen did not share Ralph's enthusiasm for the business side of things, and as time passed Ralph would make these trips on his own, leaving Karen at home with her social calendar.

When they reunited Ralph's homecoming was a joyous occasion, and they both enjoyed an active sex life; their passion for each other all-consuming. Karen especially had a high sex drive, and her appetite for Ralph's body was very demanding. She was not afraid to experiment in their lovemaking; in fact the more bizarre the better. She was outrageous and Ralph loved her for it. That was until their first child was born.

Karen announced she was pregnant, and Ralph was deliriously happy. Their son arrived and Ralph was so proud of himself that he allowed the media back into their lives. Karen, in her usual prowess, posed for photographs and interviews, enjoying all the adulation that the new birth of her son had brought. Ralph too shared some of the attention, until he grew tired of the cameras, the notepads and the microphones shoved in his face everywhere he went, and so he made other arrangements to allow his movements to be more private. His wife Karen was the one the Press loved. She always embraced them, her appetite for attention never dwindling, her beauty never failing to impress.

Four years passed when Karen found herself pregnant again. Once more the family was the subject of the media attraction, but Ralph on this occasion did not want a repeat of their intrusion into their private lives. Karen's eagerness for the media was the exact opposite and arguments started between them.

Karen gave birth to Gillian two months' premature and the baby girl being so small was kept in hospital. Ralph and Karen visited their daughter every day, and were relieved when Gillian was strong enough to be allowed home. Ralph organised a large party for the occasion, but although the rich and famous were in attendance, there were no media.

Chapter 16

The man with the scar on his cheek stood patiently, observing the social security office entrance from across the street. It was 5:15pm and the heavy rush hour traffic was in full swing, horns blaring as impatient drivers weaved their way in the wintry conditions.

George Hunter appeared, ready to join the mayhem of pedestrians making their way home, or the bars for their regular happy hour. He didn't have many friends, and being a creature of habit made his usual journey home. He always stopped at the same newsstand to purchase an evening paper, which he enjoyed in the privacy of his own apartment.

The man in black crossed the street, his head low, his face hidden by his fedora that was pulled down, now in pursuit of his target.

"Murder! Murder! Violent rape!" the newspaper boy shouted, hoping to attract more sales as George purchased his copy. From nowhere, George felt a hand on his shoulder.

"No, don't turn around. Keep walking," the voice instructed.

"What do you want? I don't have much money," George answered, attempting to turn his head towards the voice.

"I said, keep walking and don't turn around. Trust me."

George felt the blade of an object in his kidneys.

"I've come on behalf of Steve Donaldson. He can't make it. Got another meeting with Nicky. I'm helping him with the case. Have you got the information yet?"

George wondered why Steve had not contacted him about his assistant. This was most unusual and not like Steve at all. He always worked on his own. So George decided to withhold any information from this stranger. He would simply state that there was no trace regarding Steve's enquiry and therefore nothing to report. That decision made, George walked more freely and eventually arrived at his apartment block. He entered the foyer and headed for the elevator.

"Stop right there," the voice said in a broken English accent. What floor are you on/"

"The third," George replied, wondering now why, if this man did work with Steve, that he didn't know that already.

"Okay, we'll take the stairs."

George's panic returned as the man pushed him towards the stairwell. They entered the dimly lit apartment with its plain décor and furniture. There were many books and magazines, together with old newspapers stacked everywhere. George Hunter obviously was a hoarder, who didn't have many visitors.

He turned to face his adversary. The man's dark eyes stared back at him.

"So, what's the case you and Steve are working on," George stammered.

"I can't tell you that George, but we, Steve I mean, requires the information. Time is running out.

"Well, I haven't got …" George stammered again, "… anything to report."

"What! For Christ's sake, Steve is depending on you."

"Why, why didn't Steve contact me himself, then?" George stammered, attempting to be brave. He did not like the appearance or attitude of the man before him.

"Steve's a bit preoccupied right now," the man said, affording a smile.

George stepped back. "Look, I haven't been able to trace any information on Joe Marshall." The name was out before he knew it. He could have bit his tongue. George put his folded newspaper down on the chair.

"So, you don't have any address or information on Joe Marshall? Steve will be disappointed," the man in black said drily.

"No, I don't, Joe Marshall may have moved to another state, who knows where, my enquiries are discreet, I have to be careful." George was shaking uncontrollably now.

The dark eyes stared at George as the interrogator's brows frowned. "You sure about that George?"

"Yes, yes, I'm sure. I would have contacted Steve to meet me at the usual place and give him the information."

"So! Was Joe Marshall's connection with Nicky ever explained to you?"

"No, no, I don't get involved. I only provide info for Steve if I can, and only when he asks. That's why I don't know about you. Steve and I have an arrangement and if I had any information, it would be for his ears only. George was recovering his posture and attempting to be cool and confident.

"Well, Steve can't make it."

"Why should Steve make it?" George replied. "I didn't contact him to meet me."

The man in black moved towards George so swiftly, and held George close, their faces almost touching. He could now see the deep scar on the man's cheek and detect the stale smell of the Turkish cigarettes.

George started to tremble again. He thought quickly, his heart pounding. Maybe if he gave the man the information he would go and then Steve could sort it out.

The grip on George's throat tightened.

"Okay, the information is in my briefcase on the couch," George's eyes moved in the direction of where his briefcase lay.

"And are you going to give me that report?"

"Yes, yes, of course. I just had to be sure you knew Steve."

The man's grip lessened, and allowed George to move. He took out the small piece of paper and handed it to the man holding him. The dark, piercing eyes held George tight again as he read the note, then dropping the report, fished into his coat pocket and produced the deadly stiletto.

It was so quick that George hardly felt a thing, as he stumbled to the floor, overturning his chair where he'd left his newspaper, which still fell open at the front page with the headline of murder and rape in the city.

The blood from George's throat spilled, staining the remainder of the article.

His assailant pocketed the report with Joe Marshall's details, switched off the light, and vacated the apartment.

Chapter 17

Gina Gordino was Italian, stunningly attractive. Her long dark hair with its natural sheen complemented her taught, young tanned skin. Her wide green cat-shaped eyes and full smiling lips exuded a friendly nature and her willingness to help others made her very popular.

Gina came from a proud family and although her father had passed away, her mother kept the family's high standards, and generated much love on her daughter.

Another handsome, young Italian who lived in the same neighbourhood was Peter Berio. Peter was always finding an angle on how to get things done, and it was inevitable that Gina fell for him. Peter was always one step ahead of his friends; one-step further up the ladder. He was engaging, ambitious and most importantly, had the desire to become successful. He could be charming, impetuous, but he could also be cruel, direct and uncompromising, but who wasn't who was brought up in the world of hard knocks?

Gina was busying herself with housework when Peter arrived at her mother's house early one evening.

"I've a date with Gina," he informed Mrs Gordino.

"A date with Gina?"

"Oh yeah, I'm taking her dancing tonight," he replied, a broad smile beaming across his face.

He was smartly dressed in a new suit and felt good and very confident.

"Gina. There's someone here for you," her mother shouted.

"Who's that, mamma?"

"I think you better come and see for yourself."

Gina appeared, her face slightly embarrassed when she saw Peter.

There was a moment's silence, then Peter spoke, his hand fidgeting with the brim of his hat.

"I've come to take you dancin'. Remember, we discussed it last week."

"Dancing! Tonight! You mean, tonight? Dancing?"

Peter laughed. "Yes, dancing, you know the kinda thing, the guy gets to hold the girl and swing her about a bit." Peter smiled. Everybody else just laughed at him.

"What is it?" he said, still smiling. Don't tell me you've forgotten? I mean, how could you forget a date with me?"

Gina and her mother laughed again. Peter was trying to win Gina over as well as her mother, and he was winning with his irresistible smile and charm.

Gina blushed and was about to offer an excuse when her mother suddenly spoke. "Actually, Peter, Gina was about to go and take a bath. You were not expected for another hour."

"Of course, I'm an hour early. How stupid of me, but I just couldn't help myself. Got this new suit," he raised his lapel with his hand, "and I just had to see you."

Again, everybody laughed. They all knew the whole situation was nonsense but Peter got full marks for initiative.

"Peter, you come, sit by me, you, Gina, go and get ready for your young man.

There were many nights like that when Peter would simply turn up and spin some yarn to request Gina's company. They were seen together everywhere and it wasn't long before they were accepted as a couple.

Peter's connections with the family and organised crime in New York increased and as time passed his duties and responsibilities multiplied, and the more successful he carried out his errands for his friends, the more his recognition with them flourished. This brought Peter Berio new wealth and he was able to lavish more expensive gifts on Gina and her family.

Gina never understood what Peter did for a living. He had always just told her it was business.

Sometimes it worried her but Peter seemed to float about from place to place but he always seemed to be doing well and therefore she learned not to question him.

Sometimes he was away for days at a time. Other times he would be working nights with little or no explanation.

It was a lovely, sunny day when Peter arrived at Gina's. He had been away on business and she had missed him.

"Hey babe, how you doin?"

"I've missed you, Peter," Gina replied, her voice high with excitement.

"Missed you too, honey."

Gina was kissing and hugging her man. How she loved him, she thought, feeling so good to be in his arms.

Peter disentangled himself from Gina. "Hey honey, look what I've bought."

Gina stared at the beautiful red, shiny new convertible with its cream seats, white walled tyres and chrome wheels. She gasped.

"Is this really yours? It must have cost a fortune! Can you afford it?"

"Hey, no problem honey. Business is good, you know."

Peter held Gina close again, and then speaking softly, "I've something to ask you."

Gina pulled back. "What is it? What have you been up to? How can I help?"

Peter smiled, as he produced a small blue box from his pocket.

"Gina Gordino, you know I love you. Will you do me the honour of marrying me?"

Peter was down on one knee as he snapped open the blue box, revealing a small, beautiful diamond ring. The diamond had been cleverly set on its claws and crown which gave it an illusion of being much larger and more expensive than it actually was.

Every passer-by stopped and stared at the couple as Peter waited patiently for Gina's reply.

"Get up, Gina whispered. People are watching us." She was smiling but didn't want an audience.

"What's your answer?" Peter said, gazing into her eyes, his handsome smile full of expectation. Gina and Peter's eyes were trapped; locked together. Then her reply came in a loud outburst.

"Yes, yes, yes! Now stand up, kiss me."

Peter, delighted, jumped up, kissed his fiancée, while swinging her round and round.

It was a day of celebration. Gina was on a cloud. The happiest girl in the world.

Peter and Gina married and were blissfully happy, even although Peter's business sometimes took him away for days at a time. Gina never complained. She had already experienced her husband's temper after an awful argument when she enquired as to his whereabouts. When pushed, Peter became so unreasonable he lost control; Gina therefore learned not to question her husband and never met any of his business associates; sometimes they would collect him by car. A horn would peep twice and Peter would kiss her and go. Mostly those occasions were at night and many times he never returned until the small hours of the morning.

Gina actually enjoyed her life. There was no shortage of money and when Peter returned from any long trips she was always showered with gifts. She never really knew whether these presents were genuine or given as an apology for something he had done in her absence.

Four years passed and the day Gina fell pregnant marked a turning point in their lives. The celebration of Lisa's birth was fantastic. Parties were thrown and many friends, including some of Peter's business associates, attended to congratulate the happy couple.

It was on one of these occasions when the day over spilled into a party at night. Everybody had departed and Gina questioned Peter about some of his friends. She was sure she had read about them in the newspapers and what she had read wasn't good.

"Leave it. I've told you, Gina, business is business and doesn't concern you," he yelled. "Do you want for anything?" he shouted, waving his hands at their possessions.

Gina didn't listen; she kept talking over him, asking questions that didn't concern her. She did not see the blow coming. Peter had had a lot to drink and the last thing he needed was a wife ranting on and on, doing his head in. His temper overflowed and he lashed out, hitting Gina square on the cheek. The blow caught her eye and she fell, stunned by the fact and shock of the attack, hitting the floor. Not understanding what had just happened she hurried away and locked herself in the bedroom. Gina held her baby daughter close while Peter banged on the door, shouting obscenities. Gina was terrified of what he would do to both of them. Her left eye was closing rapidly as the swelling from Peter's punch took effect. She fully expected her husband to break down the door but everything was quiet. Too quiet, the stillness and the sound of silence deafening.

Had Peter gone out, or had he fallen asleep in a drunken state? Gina waited, listening; straining her ears for any sound. She heard nothing.

Cautiously, she returned Lisa to her bed and quietly unlocked the bedroom door. She opened it ajar and peered out. She couldn't see Peter; there was no sign of him. Gina fully opened the door and stepped into the hallway. She was not prepared for the assault that came.

He was there, waiting patiently, stalking his prey. He yanked her head back by pulling her long, black hair so hard that Gina thought it was coming away from its roots. She screamed. He dragged her to the bedroom and forced her to the floor. Lisa was crying.

Gina was struggling to break free. Peter ripped off her dress, exposing her femininity. He kissed her forcefully and she retaliated by biting him. He laughed.

"You bitch whore!" he shouted, wiping the blood from his lip. "You'll like this, whore. You want it rough," he yelled, then forced himself inside her panties and brutally entered her. Gina screamed again. The roughness of the sex was hurting her and her anguish grew as she heard her baby crying louder and louder. Gina panicked and attempted to struggle but the more she did so, the rougher and more violent Peter became.

Peter withdrew from her and in that split second Gina lashed out with her long nails, ripping at his cheek. Peter lost no time and his ghoulish laugh echoed around the room as he once again took control and dragged Gina along the hallway and into the lounge. There he held her down, calling her names and beating her. He had lost control, Gina was almost unconscious as he violated her again, thrusting and thrusting his manhood into her violently and bruising her thighs, riding her hard until he was fully spent. Then, exhausted, he rolled off her and lay on the floor. Gina couldn't move. She was paralysed, emotionally distressed, her lip and nose bleeding, her face black and blue from the swelling from the punches.

Gina slipped into unconsciousness. Peter lay on the floor, beads of perspiration forming on his forehead; his back soaked from the fight and the rape.

Outside a car peeped its horn. Peter ignored it, so the driver repeated his signal, but when no response was received Marco entered the house to investigate. He found Peter and Gina.

"What the fuck have you done, you stupid motherfucker son of a bitch? You crazy, Peter. Did you do this?"

Peter smiled at Marco. "She's a bitch, just like that bitch crying."

Marco now became aware of Lisa screaming from the bedroom.

"What happened, Peter?"

"She was asking questions; too many goddamn questions," Peter replied, rubbing his hands through his hair. "She wouldn't stop, nag, nag, nag. I've had a few drinks, Marco, but I've had it with her. It's over, we've gone way beyond the limit this time."

Marco knelt beside Gina. He was feeling her pulse, it was there, but only just.

"So what do you want me to do, Peter?" Marco asked as his eyes surveyed the room, still disbelieving what his comrade had done.

"Do?! Marco, do?! Get me the fuck outta here."

"And what about the kid," Marco pressed, his eyes moving in the direction of Lisa's screams.

Peter stared back. "I don't care about that brat. As I said, Gina was pumping me for information on the organisation; she recognised some of our people. She threatened to go to the authorities," Peter lied. "I, I had no choice, Marco, no choice." Peter let his words fade, he needed Marco to support him.

Marco fell silent for a moment.

"Do you want me to call an ambulance?" he said, fearing the outcome if he didn't.

"Hell, no, let her be. If she dies, she dies," Peter replied dryly.

"And the baby?" Marco pressed, "what about the baby?"

"What baby, Marco?" Peter replied as he brushed himself down and fixed his tie.

Marco stared at his colleague in disbelief. He had heard of Peter's reputation and temper. He could, it was said, detach himself from any situation with no emotional hang-ups.

"Peter, we'd better go."

Both men looked round at the devastation in the house, at Gina lying unconscious on the floor, hearing her daughter Lisa screaming from the bedroom.

Peter started blankly into Marco's eyes. "Let's go," he said.

The screech of the tyres from Marco's car alerted neighbours and it wasn't long before they investigated the Berio household, with its front door open and all lights blazing. The discovery of Gina and Lisa horrified the district and a full description of Peter was released through the media network. The general public, shocked at the brutality of the crime, demanded justice.

Peter's bosses were not amused. The incident had focused attention on Peter and therefore on the organisation. This kind of behaviour was unwelcome and could only bring problems to their door. They had spent enough time and money buying insider help, infiltrating most positions in the system. They did not need one of their soldiers creating such a mess, undoing all their work. They therefore had no choice. Peter Berio had to be dealt with. Anyway, Peter knew too much. Too much knowledge of contracts they had. Too much information and, more importantly, too much about the people involved.

Under close supervision at a meeting with Michele Salvadori, Peter swore that Gina actually knew nothing. He had not divulged any of the organisation business to her or anyone.

"What does she really know?" he was asked.

"She knows nothin', Godfather, nothin', I swear."

"So you unleashed your temper, raped and beat her nearly to death because she knew nothing?" The Godfather spoke quietly but sharply.

"Godfather, please, I had too much to drink that day. She was nagging me; I lost control," Peter paused, then added "A husband and wife domestic, Godfather, that's all."

Michele Salvadori sat back in his high-backed leather chair. He studied his solider before him.

"Godfather, I wouldn't tell her, besides I have my oath to uphold." Peter was attempting to placate his position. He had to regain the trust of his Godfather.

Michele Salvadori waved his arm, signifying for Peter to leave. "Stay within the confines of this house Peter, I will give you my decision after consulting with your other superiors." The Don now lowered his head as if reading other paperwork on his desk. Peter bowed and vacated the large book-lined study.

Michele Salvadori summoned Joseph Cambrio, the family's Councillary. He related the Berio situation.

"What could be our exposure legally, Joseph?"

"Well, if Peter is apprehended he will be found guilty of his hideous crime, that's a certainty. If we defend him, maybe get him a lesser sentence, it will, no matter how you look at it, bring unwelcome attention to the organisation. Once Peter's in custody the Feds will undoubtly press him. He'll be offered a deal and although we know Berio is strong-willed his connection to ourselves is obviously a threat."

Michele Salvadori nodded his head, taking in all his councillary's opinion.

Joseph Cambrio continued. "Gina and her daughter, that's another factor."

"Explain," Michele Salvadori replied.

"Well, if she brought a divorce action against her husband that would start legal proceedings which would expose all his assets and liabilities. We know Peter's led a lavish lifestyle but inevitable enquiries and evidence would require to be produced to substantiate his income.

At that Michele Salvadori interrupted. "Could bring the authorities to our door."

Joseph Cambrio nodded at his Godfather.

"Thank you, Joseph. As usual you have been forthright in your grasp of this situation. You can go now."

Joseph Cambrio hesitated. "Godfather, before I take my leave, may I request a favor?"

Michele Salvadori again gestured with his arm, signifying his agreement for Joseph to speak.

"Let me speak to Gina Berio off the record. She may know nothing and it can't do any harm to know in advance her thoughts and her plan of action."

"You think that is wise, Joseph?"

Cambrio nodded. "I do. Besides, she has a daughter to think of and I don't imagine a mother would want to jeopardise her future."

Michele Salvadori again sat back in his chair.

"Okay Joseph, go speak to the Berio woman. Find out what she knows if you can without alerting her too much and also what her plans are."

"Thank you Godfather," Joseph Cambrio replied. "I think you've made a wise decision.

"I want a divorce, Mr Cambrio. Peter Berio and I are finished. I don't want him to have visitation rights either. He's never to be anywhere near me or my daughter Lisa."

Joseph Cambrio realised that Gina Berio was still hurting and bitter.

"Look, your husband will have legal entitlement to have contact with Lisa. That's the law, so maybe you should reconsider divorce actions. Maybe you'll feel differently given time. I can understand you're upset but given time possibly a reconciliation should be considered."

Gina, astonished at Cambrio's suggestion of reconciliation with Peter, replied.

"No, Mr Cambrio, that wouldn't work. In fact, it'd be worse, me wondering when a repeat performance was going to occur. Peter would just think he could do this and get away with it, so that's not a solution.

He's in a lot of debt, Gina. He owns nothing. You have to think about Lisa. She can grow up here in this house with you; your life can continue as normal."

"Is this normal to you, Mr Cambrio?" Gina then turned her head and swept back her hair to reveal the rest of her injuries. "I … Mr Cambrio, will maybe not survive a next time and I've no wish for that monster to be anywhere near my daughter. Now, maybe your people could rethink this situation and come up with a suitable alternative. I'm not greedy, Mr Cambrio. Provide enough money to put a roof over my head and something for Lisa's education. I'll make my own way after that.

Also, I want you to understand I don't know anything about any of the people you represent, except what I read in the newspapers and believe me, I want it to stay that way, which is why a divorce from Peter without contact to Lisa is the only way it would work.

"Mr Cambrio, let me state my position more clearly for you. As far as I'm concerned, Peter Berio may as well be dead. He's your problem. Your friends created him, so deal with the matter in whatever way you want, but keep him away from me and my daughter. No access, no rights, no contact … ever. Do you understand? A fresh start, Mr Cambrio, for me and Lisa."

Joseph Cambrio understood only too well and he paused before replying.

"What if such an agreement was made and sometime in the future your circumstances change, and you require more assistance from ourselves? How can we guarantee against that?"

"There'll be a letter, Mr Cambrio, to ensure my and Lisa's protection, provided I accept help now and cannot approach or threaten you in the future. Also on the understanding that all protection would be nullified to prevent me going to the authorities, or indeed me helping them with their enquiries."

Joseph Cambrio admired the woman before him. She was negotiating for her life and that of her daughter. He sat back. This was the information he had come for. He could now report back to his Godfather although he knew the families he represented did not like loose ends.

Joseph discussed his findings with his Godfather, who listened patiently.

"Summon the heads of the other families Joseph, make them aware of Peter Berio's conduct. We will have a meeting to decide Gina Berio and her daughter's future."

"So, what does the broad know?" a member asked after listening carefully to Joseph's plea for clemency.

Joseph did not reply for a moment. "Don't actually know. Maybe not much! Maybe nothing! Maybe something! I don't, or can't, answer that honestly."

"So why risk anything? Why don't we just take her and her baby out? A tragic accident! A five-minute report in the local rag. No big deal," the family member said. "And then Peter, her husband, he just gets what he deserves – matter finished. Chapter closed."

Joseph Cambrio turned these statements over in his mind. He knew what was being suggested was normal practice and in most instances an absolute and final matter of dealing with any situation.

Joseph thought hard. Gina Berio had impressed him. She was more intelligent than most of the other wives or bimbos that their soldiers took up with.

Joseph started his reply, his words slow but deliberate for effect.

"I ... I think we'd all be making a mistake if a hit was organised on this woman and her child. Obviously the Authorities are aware of Peter Berio's connection to us, but Peter Berio is the only connection and we all know he can be a hothead, although he has an impeccable record for getting things done. This incident is different.

"If Peter is no longer part of our organisation we prove to everybody that we didn't condone that type of behaviour. The Authorities have therefore no lead to follow. Gina Berio and her daughter have no love lost. They don't want any contact with him; or us for that matter, except to have enough for a new start. The slate is to be wiped clean and she be allowed to restart a new life without interference. She does not want to be looking over her shoulder for the rest of her life. In fact, she'll retake her maiden name, Gordino. I believe, gentlemen, that if we do the honourable thing on this occasion then we have nothing to fear from Gina Gordino.

"Peter Berio, on the other hand, has been stupid; we all know that, but more importantly he flipped; lashed out without any thought of the exposure to the organisation. I therefore put it to you. It's not Gina Gordino we should be discussing here but the fate of Peter Berio."

Joseph clasped his hands and bowed his head, letting the full impact of his proposal and advice to take full consideration.

"We say nothing. Do nothing. A small payment from some insurance bond, but no big cash deal that can be traced back to us. Let her go with her life. Consider this gentlemen. Take her out; the public sympathy would be intolerable. The Authorities would have to act and bring justification."

All eyes stared at their councillary, Joseph Cambrio.

"The decision, gentlemen, is yours."

All the members were still staring at Joseph when Michele Salvadori's voice from the head of the table spoke clearly and calmly.

"Joseph, you have acted as councillary to all the families over many years and we have all come to admire your work and advice as you have always acted most properly on each count and brief you have been given, but please, on this occasion would you leave the room so that we may consider your proposal between us? There is no prejudice against you Joseph; I believe this is a matter for all the families to be in agreement before we come to a final decision."

Joseph stared back at his Godfather. In all his years acting for the organisation he'd never been requested to leave. He was used to answering questions from each member on their own merits and eventually coming to a conclusion.

The Godfather nodded at Joseph and gestured with his hand for him to leave.

Joseph didn't speak. He just moved the heavy leather chair away from the table, excused himself, vacated the wood-panelled boardroom and took a seat outside.

It was a fully 20 minutes before Luigi opened the door and requested his presence.

The Godfather spoke. "We have considered your proposal and reasoning of your councillary. We all agree that your advice and request in this matter is most unusual and not in keeping with our conditions and upkeep of discipline within the organisation."

Joseph felt dismayed. They were going to solve problems in the usual manner; dispose of the Berio's and take whatever consequences came.

"But ..." The Godfather continued, "We have today made an exception."

Joseph was still in his mind deliberating on the consequences that the Authorities would undoubtedly unleash on them when he realised the families were going to heed his advice. He now sat eager and alert, listening to every word.

"As I was saying, Joseph. This woman and her child are to be allowed their freedom, but on a condition that should she speak to anyone about her husband's connections, and if any repercussions come of it, she and her daughter will die."

"Thank you, Godfather, and thank you all," he said, as he nodded his head at all the family heads seated at the table. "I believe you have all decided wisely," he said in a more relaxed tone.

"Joseph, I have not completed my statement," the voice from the head of the table interrupted.

Silence reigned around the room. Some faces stared at Joseph, others bent forward looking down at their hands.

"As I said, should this Berio woman, her daughter, or a member of her family, friends or others divulge any information at any time, not only will they die but you – yes, *you,* Joseph, shall be held fully responsible for their actions and suffer the same fate."

So this was it. They always had to have a get-out clause, a backup plan, with strings attached. The stillness reverberated around the room. Here he was, Joseph Cambrio, Councillary for the largest and wealthiest family in New York, and now he had to put his own life on the line as part of his judgment. Joseph thought now, hell, he could just change his mind, which would certainly seal the fate of Gina Gordino and her daughter Lisa.

He stared at each of the faces that he knew so well.

"Great!" he exclaimed loudly and confidently. "I believe you are all very wise and have come to the correct and proper decision. I will stand by the condition you have set."

All the faces stared back at him, almost in disbelief. It was obvious, they all thought he would have had a change of heart.

Joseph stood first, and then everyone followed. Their Godfather had the final say.

"Before we depart, gentlemen," he paused. "Joseph, do you have a personal interest with this Gina Berio or her daughter?"

All eyes rested on Joseph.

"No," he replied, emphatically. "Absolutely not." Joseph spoke the truth and his voice carried it.

"Then I admire you, Councillary. Gentlemen, regarding Peter Berio. You all know what must be done. A tragic accident as we discussed. Keep in touch with our Councillary here. Whatever debts Peter Berio incurred, see to it that an amicable settlement is made on each of them. As far as the woman and her daughter, they have their lives and nobody is to take any further action against them. "Is that understood by everybody?"

Michele Salvadori paused, waiting for any objections from the heads of the other families. There were none. The faces in the good suits departed, leaving Joseph and his Godfather alone.

Michele Salvadori slowly paced round the boardroom and came to rest beside the marble Michelangelo-styled fireplace.

"Joseph, a payment of $20,000 is to be made to the Berio woman. Make it an insurance bond that has matured. But that's all. I trust that will be sufficient to ensure her silence."

"Agreed," replied Joseph.

His Godfather had been generous, especially when he thought what the alternative decision could have been.

Chapter 18

Time passed and of the two Rosenberg children, Mark grew closer and closer to his father, an intimacy that Karen could not compete with. Mark was then sent away to private school, his education thorough and, with his own hard work and application, achieved high accolades from his tutors. His achievements, both academically and on the sports field, caught the imagination of the Press who frequently attempted to set their own profile of the young man.

There were many attractive women from prominent wealthy families and Mark played the field as and when it suited, but his heart and true vocation was like his father's, close to the family business, and slowly he immersed himself into the world of diamonds and commerce.

Gillian was completely different from her brother. She was like her mother; attractive, vibrant, full of energy and being a young woman from a wealthy family didn't care about business, and therefore tended to live life on the social calendar. Sometimes her photograph would appear in newspapers and magazines; most often showing her in uncompromising situations: either drunk or scantily clad while attending some unorthodox nightclubs. Gillian's activities did not please her father and the fights between them caused upset throughout the household. Karen would inevitably take Gillian's part and attempt to placate Ralph, which never worked. The family arguments went on for days and Ralph was relieved to be away on business.

Mark, now eager to learn all aspects of the business, would accompany his father, and in turn they grew closer and closer. Karen, on the other hand, resumed her social calendar and didn't care whether the Press photographed her on the arm of some wealthy suitor in Ralph's absence. Karen and Ralph's marriage was now really in name only as each led separate lives.

When they met up with each other at their opulent mansion in The Hamptons, both attempted to have a truce even if only for their children's sake, but each time an argument always ensued.

Conversation was always the same, pleasant to each other until the topic of Karen's latest suitor surfaced and then accusations would fly, the end result inevitable. Gillian's escapades were always mentioned; her wild and wayward lifestyle and carefree attitude did not please Ralph and the press releases on her behaviour did nothing to help the family's reputation.

"What the fuck do you care?" Karen screamed at Ralph. You're never here. So what does it matter whom I'm with?"

"It matters, Karen, because you are my wife; you are a Rosenberg," Ralph replied, shouting.

"Oh yeah, the great bloody Rosenberg's; let's protect the great family name," Karen retaliated, a sarcastic tone in her voice.

"Can't you just behave a bit more maturely?" Ralph said quietly, trying to placate the situation. "You have a lovely lifestyle; there's no shortage of money, you entertain your friends. I have no problem with that, but all this dating other men: I don't like it."

"Well, ha ha ha, Mr Ralph Rosenberg doesn't like it. It's bad for the family name, I mean, let's not forget the precious family name and reputation. What do you want me to do, Ralph? Stay at home night after night, lock myself away? Become a good little housewife; attend to all your needs? Be your exclusive whore in the bedroom; ready whenever the mood takes you? Anyway, you're not home often are you? Who's in your bed, Ralph, when you're in Europe, or South Africa? You don't think about the family then, do you?"

Ralph denied the accusations.

"Oh deny it if you dare, it's still hush hush, isn't it?"

It was all flooding out now, and Ralph just stood and listened. "I need to be out of here. I enjoy and need the social events; the company of people. Is that so wrong?"

Ralph paused before replying. "Look Karen, maybe we've allowed our marriage to slip, but surely we can salvage some of this; sure I admit I'm away a lot, the business needs that attention, and then of course there's Mark. It's good for him to see, learn, become involved with every aspect of the industry, because the more I teach him, the more he learns and the more prepared he'll be to take my place when the time comes.

"Oh, its precious Mark now, is it?"

"He's your son too, Karen," Ralph shouted.

"Oh, and is Gillian not your daughter?"

Ralph fell silent again. He never forgot about Gillian but with all her frolicking and drug habit, the arrests by the police and the costs of bailing her out on numerous occasions, to say nothing of the cost of Ralph's pride and attempting to keep as much out of the Press as possible, was always too much for him to bear.

"No you won't reply to that, will you Ralph? You've never really loved her, unlike your precious son," Karen continued, raising the tone of her voice, her eyes flashing, wide-open with rage.

"Let's leave the kids out of this Karen, this is between you and me," Ralph kept his tone and voice level, in an attempt to appease the situation.

"Oh! How convenient. I never really see Mark, he's always with you, and as for Gillian she's in her own relationship, so don't you dare blame me because I socialise and have friends."

Ralph's mind was racing.

"Gillian in a relationship?" he said, out loud, the astonishment in his voice showing his surprise.

Ralph repeated the statement again whilst staring at Karen and waiting for his wife to respond. Karen was silent. She just glared at her husband. Words could not express what she was feeling.

"Do I know the boy, his family?" Ralph asked, desperate for information. Just maybe, maybe at last his daughter had found someone meaningful to settle down with.

Karen started back at her husband, her green eyes searching his face. She had always dreaded this moment between them but he has to know and right now the question hung in the air. She might as well be honest with Ralph and hoped that the news she was about to impart would not have too many consequences.

"Okay, Gillian is in a relationship. That's got to be good, hasn't it? Maybe she's changed, maybe I've been wrong," Ralph waited for his wife's response.

"Has the relationship been going on for long? Has it calmed her down? I mean, where is she, is she here in the house? Can I speak to her?" Ralph let his questions sing across the room. Karen listened, then slowly replied.

"No," she said, turning her back. "No, you don't know the family and for that matter, neither do I. And yes, her relationship has been going on for some considerable time."

"Have you met him, then?" Ralph interrupted, now anxious to hear more, a smile beginning to spread across his face, lightening the tone of his voice and softening the words between them.

Karen paused. It was a long pause. She turned to face her husband, picked a cigarette from its packet, fired up the Gold Dunhill lighter, inhaled and blew out blue smoke high into the air.

"Yes, I've met her," Karen replied, letting the full weight of her reply sink in.

Ralph took the comment but didn't comprehend, then shaking his head, "you said her, you do mean him, don't you?" His voice was quiet, but his words were trembling.

Karen's green eyes with their scared expression looked back at her husband.

"You heard what I said, then, taking another drag, "they've known each other for quite a while and they're very happy together."

"They?" Ralph interrupted. "What are you telling me?"

Karen shook her head, rubbing the palms of her hands together, her forefingers of her right hand still holding her cigarette.

"Our daughter is very happy, Ralph. Her partner, Philippa, is a lovely girl. She's well mannered, considerate, and they are very much in love.

"What! What the fuck are you saying?" Ralph's voice and mind were out of sync, both working overtime; it had gone passed the screaming to a high-pitch gasp of disbelief.

"Yes, Ralph, your daughter – our daughter – is a lesbian, and has been for some time. She's found herself. Philippa is good for her. They're good for each other. Wait till you meet her. Keep an open mind, you'll like her if you give her a chance."

Ralph was pacing up and down, his face burgundy red with shock and anger.

"Meet her?" he yelled, "What's her name? Philippa? I don't think so. Where is Gillian now?" Ralph demanded, his tone fierce and his temper rising. Is she at this thing's house? When can I speak to her? When? When?!" he yelled.

Karen could see the temper and the tension in her husband and somehow was enjoying seeing him stressed. She paused momentarily. "She's upstairs, they live here. They've just never been here when you or Mark are at home, but they feel right with each other and they have decided to come out and make it public, but not before telling you first. Giving you your place, so to speak."

Ralph had not heard all of his wife's statement. "Here! Now! In my house? Living here! Under my roof! Here! Now! Public! Living here! Upstairs! Now! Upstairs! Upstairs! Fuckin' son of a bitch, I'll kill her."

The rage was more than Karen expected, Ralph was uncontrollable. He was so exasperated he couldn't get any more words out. He paced the room.

"They're actually here?! How could you allow such behaviour, you're outta control, Karen. Fuck, fuckin' useless!"

"She's happy, Ralph," Karen replied calmly. "They're both happy, please try and understand."

"Oh you! Don't start! Try and understand! Well, I'll show you understanding!"

With that, Ralph stormed out of the room and sprinted upstairs. Karen was running at his heels, trying to catch him. She had never seen her husband in such a rage; she was begging him to stop.

Ralph violently opened the bedroom door and strode to the bedside where Gillian and Philippa lay sleeping.

Ralph flipped. He lost control. He spread back the sheets in temper to expose the two naked bodies huddled together and then yanked his daughter's head, pulling her by her hair from the bed onto the floor.

Both girls, now awake and stunned by Ralph's actions, had Philippa staring at him in disbelief.

Gillian started yelling at her father for which she received a heavy-handed blow across her face, its mark starting to swell.

"You get out of my house! And don't ever come back! You hear?! You're no daughter of mine!" he yelled. "Get out! Get out! Do you hear?!"

Gillian attempted to compose herself, still holding her face where her father had struck her.

"But, but father..."

But Ralph interrupted her. "Is this true? Is this thing what you're into?" he said, pointing a shaking finger at Philippa.

Gillian was trying to regain control. "Philippa is not a thing, she's a person, and I love her."

"Love her!" Ralph echoed, "You don't know the meaning of the word."

Philippa attempted to speak. "Mr Rosenberg, she began. She did not expect the blow from Ralph as she too was struck with the same forcefulness that he had inflicted upon his daughter.

Philippa fell off the bed to the floor and Gillian, seeing her partner hurt, attacked her father from behind, punching him in the kidneys and at the back of his neck.

Ralph shrugged her off and Gillian fell to the floor.

"What's your goddamn name?" he screamed at Philippa. "What's your name?" he repeated. "Answer me, bitch!"

Philippa was in shock and could not believe the temper and violence that Mr Rosenberg had unleashed, and so answered the question. "Philippa Jesson," she replied, still holding her jaw.

"And do you have parents, Philippa bitch Jesson? Where do they live? Do they know about the kinda thing they have for a daughter?"

"My parents are dead," Philippa shouted. "I'm originally from San Francisco."

"Oh, San Francisco. Well, you can fuckin' return to San Francisco because you're not welcome here. Do you hear?!"

"Ralph!" Karen shouted. She was still standing in the doorway, a witness to the whole event.

"Let it be, calm down, you've had your say, let everybody get back to sleep. We'll discuss all this in the morning."

Ralph turned to face his wife. "In the morning? That'll be fuckin' right you bitch. They're out tonight. Right now. Do you hear? Out of my house, out of my life. Cut off."

Then he turned towards Gillian. "Did you understand that, lezzie, whore, slut! You disgust me, you fuckin' bitch." Then, once again, turning to Philippa, "you, you corrupted my daughter, you thing. You deceitful pervert. Get outta my house.

"Father, father, you don't understand!"

Ralph turned to face Gillian.

"I love her," she said as she glanced at Philippa and repeated her undying love. "I love her so much."

Another violent blow struck her as her father's hand connected with her face once more.

"You deceitful pervert. Get outta my house."

"Father, father, you don't understand."

Ralph turned to face Gillian.

"I love her so much."

Another violent blow struck her as her father's hand connected with her face once more.

"Get out – whore – and take your lezzie friend with you."

Karen now attempted to intervene and approached her husband to calm him down and hopefully appease the situation and protect the two girls.

"Get to fuck, you slut. You condone this?" Ralph shouted at Karen, not fully aware of his actions as he hit her with the same ferocity that he had administered on Gillian, causing her to reel and fall to the floor.

Karen stared back at her husband in disbelief but remained on the floor as she did not want another assault if she attempted to stand.

"Gillian, Philippa, you both better go, get dressed and let me know where you're staying and I'll bring the rest of your belongings. When your father realises how stupid and wrong he is…"

"Stupid and wrong, am I?" Ralph yelled. "Well, for your information I know all about you too, Karen."

"Me, you're way off the mark, I'm no lesbian!"

"No! No, you're not, but you're a whore, a slut and a two-timing one at that."

"I don't know what you mean," Karen replied, attempting to regain her composure. She had a worried expression on her face; Ralph had been behaving differently towards her this time.

"You and Hugh Sullivan."

"Who? Hugh and me? For goodness sake, Ralph, we're just good friends."

"Oh, good friends are we Karen, well, I have a file on both of you and the photographs are more than enough proof for any court that you are more than good friends.

I bet he enjoyed all those sexy poses you cock-sucking whore. Karen, I've seen the photographs – you disgust me.

Karen's mouth fell open. Her eyes met the floor. "How? When did you? We were always discreet. I've never wanted to hurt you Ralph but you were never here. Please, I'm sorry." Karen stood up and stared at her husband, hoping that her admission may just soften his temper.

Hugh Sullivan was a property tycoon, very wealthy and loved the social world and limelight. He'd had many beautiful women on his arm, but once he had met Karen Rosenberg they were seldom apart.

The gossip columns attempted innuendos but were never confirmed and even before Ralph had indeed employed a detective, arguments would surface regarding their relationship. The Rosenberg marriage was not a happy one.

"I'm divorcing you Karen, and you won't get a dollar." Ralph started laughing. "And I wouldn't bet on Hugh Sullivan either, 'cos he's running for senator and can't afford any scandal. He'll drop you like a hot potato, because that job is more important to him than you, Karen. Of course, once he's sighted in our divorce action he'll lose his candidacy and will be out of the running and you, Karen; you'll be out of my life like these two here, but I'll have the satisfaction of knowing you'll be out of Sullivan's life too."

"I'm sorry Ralph, please let's talk about this."

"You're sorry? I bet you are. Sorry you've been found out." Ralph paused, then continued in a quiet, calm voice. "I suggest you leave tonight. Go with these disgusting creatures but get out now. Our marriage is over Karen, you and I are finished. Do you understand?

"No more expense accounts, Karen. No more socialising on my credit cards. You're out of my life and my will and you know what, I'm so glad. Glad to be rid of you and this thing here at last. Now all of you, get out before I do something I may regret."

"Ralph!" Karen shouted, her green eyes wide, her mascara running down her cheeks. "Can we discuss this tomorrow morning?"

"Tomorrow, Karen? Don't you understand I don't want you in my home one minute longer than it takes you to walk through that door. Now get the fuck out you screwing tart bitch and you, Gillian, take your whatever it is Philippa and do the same.

"I don't want any of you to darken my door ever again. Understand!" Ralph was shouting again. "You're all out of my will, you're all cut off from any allowances, expenses, credit cards; everything revoked. Go and make your own money and let's see how you spend it."

"You can't do that Ralph," Karen replied calmly.

"Just you watch me you bitch." Ralph strode from the bedroom and ventured downstairs to his study. He poured himself a large malt whiskey, downed it in one gulp, and poured another. The liquor hit him hard. He felt the sudden pain in his chest, his arms heavy. He was struggling for breath. He dropped his crystal glass and began gasping, inhaling deeply, struggling for air. He staggered towards his study door and opened it in time to hear the click of the heavy front door close as Karen, Gillian and Philippa departed. Ralph slumped to his knees. He did not remember his own study door closing as he hit the floor and fell into an unconscious state.

Clive Richards, aged 70, was tall and thin, with sharp features and bright blue eyes. His grey, left-parted straight hair, combed backwards, completed his distinguished appearance and gave the image of confidence and responsibility. His immaculate attire was always in keeping with his honoured profession and Clive exuded a certain discretion when attending his duties.

He had served the Winchester family for many years at their country pile in Surrey before Ralph made him an offer, which, after much consideration, he accepted, and emigrated to the United States.

Clive had become close to his master and a mutual understanding and respect grew between the two men, Ralph relying on Clive to run the family home and attend to the daily routine while he attended to his business of diamonds.

Clive became Ralph's confidante, his discretion exemplary, and even Karen Rosenberg was, for most of the time, impressed by Clive Richards.

Clive resided in his own cottage within the grounds of the Rosenberg mansion and therefore it was not unusual for him to arrive early for his daily duties.

It was another cold start; a heavy winter's day. Clive arrived and approached Emma, the household cook, as she busied herself in the kitchen.

"Is the master up yet?" Clive asked, after checking his coat.

"I ain't seen nobody, Mr Richards," Emma replied. "In fact, its unusually quiet today." Clive nodded.

"Maybe Mr Rosenberg is still in bed?" Emma continued.

Clive nodded again, but made no comment. "I'll go and light the fire in the study, make everything ready for him when he appears. You want some breakfast, Mr Richards?"

Clive smiled. "That would be appreciated; give me half an hour."

Clive then made his way upstairs to the main entrance hallway with its black and white chequered floor and approached the study.

The heavy oak wooden door was closed but not locked, and yet it would not yield at Clive's attempt to open it. Clive, curious, now shouldered the door and slowly pushed it ajar. There was still a heavy resistance. He kept pushing, then he saw the arm of his master, Ralph Rosenberg.

Clive, now aware that his master was unconscious behind the study door, mastered all his strength to gain entry. He quickly attempted to revive Ralph, putting him into the recovery position. Ralph's lips were purple blue, his face ashen white and Clive realised he'd been there for some time. There was a pulse but only just. Clive lifted Ralph's eyelids but there was no response. He began to panic, so ran back to the kitchen to Emma and get her help.

"Go find Mrs Rosenberg. The master has had some form of stroke, or heart attack and is unconscious. I'll call an ambulance."

"Oh lordy, no!" Emma cried, stopping everything and following Clive to the study.

While Clive called 911 Emma went in search of Mrs Rosenberg. There was no sign of a struggle in the study, only the broken glass on the floor and the bottle of malt resting on the large Louis XIV desk.

Emma returned, panting and out of breath. "There's no one else in the house, Mr Richards, sir."

"What do you mean; no one? Have you tried Mrs Rosenberg's room?"

"I knocked sir, but nobody replied."

"Did you go in, Emma?"

"No, no Mr Richardson, it's not my place and …"

"Oh for Christ's sake, wake her up; oh, never mind, I'll do it."

"Mr Richards," Emma replied, attempting to defend her actions. "It's not for me to go into private quarters, but I saw Miss Gillian's room. It's empty, but a bit of a mess. Something obviously has happened in there.

Ralph turned towards Emma. "What do you mean?"

"Well, the bed sheets are all over the floor. There was broken glass on the carpet. I didn't go in, but the door was open and there certainly isn't anybody about."

"Emma, keep holding Mr Rosenberg's wrist; I'll be back in a few minutes."

Emma was crying now, her emotions consuming her body at the sight of her master lying helpless on the floor.

Clive bounded up the broad stairway towards Karen Rosenberg's bedroom. He knocked sharply, but didn't wait for a reply. Instead, he turned the ornamental brass handle and entered.

There was no evidence of Karen Rosenberg having spent the night, so where was she? Clive then checked Gillian's bedroom. It was as Emma had said, all in disarray. Something had obviously occurred. He didn't have time to work it all out.

He ran back downstairs to the study. "Where's that goddamn ambulance?" he shouted.

Sirens were heard and Clive opened the large, electric black and gold gates to allow the ambulance's entry to the driveway of the Rosenberg mansion.

"What happened?" one paramedic asked, looking up at Clive whilst administering an oxygen mask over Ralph's face.

"Don't know. It was my evening off last night and I only discovered Mr Rosenberg this morning. Also, there appears to be no one else in the house, which is unusual because Mrs Rosenberg is normally always here when her husband returns from a business trip; but there's no sign of her or her daughter. I checked upstairs, but..." Clive let his words trail off as he watched his master being trolleyed to the ambulance. The other paramedic was on his radio.

"May I come with him?" Clive asked and after a nod from the paramedic. Clive boarded the ambulance.

"Find Mrs Rosenberg. Tell her what happened," Clive shouted to Emma, as the rear doors of the ambulance closed. The vehicle sped off, its sirens wailing and lights flashing.

Chapter 19

Steve sat in his prison cell; his hands clasped over his head, his elbows digging into his knees, and stared at the cold, grey concrete floor. Gina was Nicky's mother according to the information he had been given by his client, but who was Gina? Was Gina his client? He didn't really know. How stupid that sounded. His only lead was the fact that when he had telephoned the Rosenberg residence and asked for Gina he was connected to a woman, who listened but then hung up. The fact that there had been no response from that quarter worried him.

Steve knew he'd been set up and with the evidence Lieutenant Chandler had he was certainly going down for crimes he did not commit.

There was obviously a connection to The Rosenbergs but what was it? If the man in black was working for them to trace Nicky, why involve himself? Why frame him? And who beat Nicky within inches of her life?

These questions rotated round and round in his head and he realised he could not solve anything from a prison cell.

The metal viewfinder of the cell door slid open, breaking Steve's concentration.

"Okay bud, you're wanted upstairs, get your ass back against the wall," the guard shouted as he unlocked the door with one hand, whilst his other held his baton.

"When will I get out of here?" Steve asked, his eyes watching every move of his captor.

"The way I heard it, you're going down for a long, long time," the guard said, smiling.

"Oh, yeah, you think so?" Steve replied matter-of-factly.

"Oh yeah," came the reply as his guard hit Steve squarely on his lower back with his baton.

Steve stiffened, ready to react.

"Don't even think about it," his guard grimaced. "Although it would give me great pleasure in teaching you a lesson."

Steve glanced at his guard. He didn't reply, just shook his head.

"You're askin' for it," the guard taunted. "So, please try 'cos I'm the one who's gonna give it."

Steve stood still, appraising the officer and, although ready to take him on, paused and held up his hands in acknowledgement, and strode from his cell.

Steve was once again delivered to Chandler's office.

"If he's gonna give you any trouble Lieutenant, just holler and I'll soon teach the son of a bitch a lesson," the guard said, hitting his baton off the palm of his hand.

Chandler smiled. "Thank you, Dennis. I don't think that will be necessary; besides, by all accounts Mr Donaldson here is probably more than a match for any of us.

Police Officer Davis just smiled, unaware of Steve's background or his superiors reference to it.

Chandler raised his arm, dismissing the officer, and once the door was closed motioned Steve to sit down.

Silence reigned between the two men. Then Chandler spoke.

"I don't like you, Donaldson. Your type, your methods, your history, and I was of the opinion that this was an open and shut case which would give me great pleasure in putting you away for a long, long time. Let me explain.

"I like to know the background of any potential suspect. It helps me to hopefully understand the person, and helps me solve the crime. I'm thorough, Donaldson, and as I've already stated, don't like loose ends. I also think I'm good at my job and need to satisfy myself that I've left no stone unturned before indicting an arrest to be brought before the courts. It's all evidence you see; I put away the bad guys. The good suits very often set them free so I always do my best to ensure all the evidence and motive are all there and can be substantiated, so the bloody smart-arse DA will put the case forward of convict.

"So, you now realise I, for my own reasons, need your history, and your service record, Donaldson, is part of your history - part of your makeup - possibly even the cause of you inflicting those brutal attacks on these young women and Frank Coulson."

Steve shrugged his shoulders. "I thought you said you had all the evidence you require to send me down."

Chandler, staring at his suspect, nodded in agreement.

"Yes I do, Donaldson, believe me, but as I said, I'm thorough and there's something bothering me which doesn't tie-up. Someone's telling lies. Someone's trying to cover something up. Attempting to hide information that's probably relative to this case. I don't want to put an innocent man down just because I chose to let some small detail go, but I will Donaldson, so help me I will; if I don't get cooperation. I do believe I have the right man – that's you – and these hideous crimes will stop when you're convicted, but there's something nagging at the back of my mind. You've say you've been set up?! Who hates you enough, Donaldson to see you go down, quite probably for the rest of your life? Who – Donaldson – who?"

Steve sat there, now full in the knowledge that Lieutenant Chandler was privy to some small detail that, if investigated, may just save him.

"There's no one that I k now of," Steve replied, as he searched his memory.

"You obviously have a loose end, Lieutenant, let me go and I'll promise to keep you informed while I prove my innocence."

"Let you go?" Chandler said, laughing. "I believe you mean that, Donaldson."

Chandler paused, bent forward, staring into his suspect's eyes.

"You're not going anywhere Mister. You'll do time for a long stretch and if I had my way you'd burn in hell. I'm only having this conversation, as I need to satisfy my own conscience. Anyway, when Nicky recovers she'll identify you, and if my hunch is correct she witnessed the murder of Frank Coulson and you committing it. We also have our eyewitness regarding Louise Volosso. Donaldson … I want you to explain why you raped and killed her. Was she just there when your appetite for sex and violence took over, or did you manifest her demise too?

"You see, Donaldson, the plain fact of the matter is, if you can't think of anyone who'd want to frame you, it's probably because you did actively commit these crimes. You could be suffering from schizophrenia, but I believe that if examined by doctors they would confirm that you're as sane as I am.

"Yes, Donaldson, you'll be convicted. I just need more on your background for my personal satisfaction."

"I've got to get out of here Inspector, to prove my case. I'm happy to work with you on this. Anyway, I've no choice. Please believe me when I say I didn't commit these crimes. My life was normal until I accepted my last case to trace Nicky Martin and since then it's been a nightmare."

"Who's your client, Donaldson?"

Steve shrugged his shoulders. "That's confidential, Lieutenant, but the real truth is, I don't know."

Stuart Chandler stood up and let out a loud belly laugh. "You don't know? You don't know! Well, I've heard some in my time but that! That …"

Chandler banged his hand loudly on his desk, the sudden movement and sound would have made most people jump, but Steve just sat there, motionless.

Chandler bent forward, his eyes inches from Steve's; he could smell Donaldson's stale breath. "Now you listen to me, you son of a bitch. I'm not playing games here. If you don't start cooperating, I'll say to hell with my conscience and put the case to the DA. After all, the evidence is airtight, the witnesses. That is, the case is otherwise foolproof. Fuck you, Donaldson. Fuck you."

Silence reigned again between the two men.

"You do know your friends in authority won't lift a finger to help you, they'll just put you down as another statistic, an old vet that has flipped. They'll cover their asses and disown you, so why keep silent?"

Steve understood as he listened to Chandler, who by all accounts was probably correct. No one would give a shit and if his file was protected now it would be near impossible to effect any information once he was convicted. How could he help himself? There would be no point in discussing any missions. Any information on that front would be irrelevant. No, the only way to save himself was to somehow be released and put the Nicky Martin case together and unlock her true story, therefore proving his innocence.

Chandler's telephone rang, its piercing sound interrupting his interview with Steve Donaldson.

"Another one?" Chandler responded, his eyes staring at his prisoner. "Any idea of time?" he asked.

"Maybe a few days ago; we'll know more when we get the body to the morgue. It's the same MO sir, except this time, it's male so there's no sexual attack, but we believe the same weapon was used to cut his throat.

"I'll be with you in a few minutes," Chandler replied.

Johnston returned the handset of his telephone to its cradle and waited patiently for his boss.

Chandler shouted and a uniformed officer appeared. "Take this man back to his cell."

"Hey, hold on, I thought we were..."

Chandler put his forefinger across Steve's lips. "Not today, sonny," he said, and then repeated his order to the officer, who led Steve away.

Steve heard George Hunter's name, and the comment; 'his throat was cut, same method'.

Lieutenant Chandler and Detective Sergeant Johnston attended the murder scene. Once again, there was no evidence of forced entry and no signs of struggle. Either George Hunter knew his killer, or the killer was already waiting, but one thing was for sure, the weapon, inflicting the cause of death was the same, as that used on poor Louise Volosso.

"Maybe there's a link, Sir?" Johnston offered.

Chandler shrugged. "Anything's possible."

"Do you think it's Donaldson, Lieutenant?"

"If it was, we have him in custody; we just have to prove a link between George Hunter and him, and of course a motive and time of death, and just possibly a link to Louise Volosso. That would suit the book," Chandler said, nodding his head, his eyes set on the now blooded headlines of the newspaper.

Chandler checked its date. His suspect was in custody, but the date on the newspaper clearly indicated that the murder had been committed before Steve had been arrested. Chandler just required the time of death, which hopefully forensics would establish.

"Both detective examined George's apartment, did Donaldson confess anything, Lieutenant?"

"No, says he's been set up, what an asshole."

"Pity, I heard he was a good cop when he was on the Force, even although his methods were, shall we say, unorthodox."

"Yeah! Well he ain't so good now," Chandler replied. "Listen, Johnston, I need the actual time of death here. It's imperative we have urgent cooperation from forensics. Seal and search everything. If we can tie Donaldson to this, then that's another piece of the jigsaw coming together. I do believe there's a connection between Hunter and Donaldson, we just have to find it. I want his background, Johnston, and don't come telling me he's some hero with a military coded file," Chandler said sarcastically.

"Find out if this guy has any family or friends, even although it looks to me that he's been a bit of a loner." Lieutenant Chandler's eyes observed the gloomy apartment with its basic furniture and old stacked newspapers and magazines.

"Oh! By the way, did you ever locate Steve Donaldson's wife and arrange to bring her in?"

"We did, Lieutenant. In fact, I'll just get an update on that."

Chapter 20

Detective Sergeant Johnston was on the telephone, arranging details to bring Gill Donaldson to New York to assist them in their enquiries.

Meanwhile, Stuart Chandler visited the Downtown Hospital on William Street, in the hope of obtaining a statement from Nicky. There was no change in her condition and the doctors were not too hopeful.

"There is nothing we can do, Lieutenant, until she comes out of her coma, and even when that occurs it would be some time before we can assess any damage sustained, and quite a while before she can make any statement. She has, after all, taken quite a beating. She's lucky; she has youth and is also very fit, otherwise she wouldn't have made it. Let me warn you, Lieutenant, the mind is a funny thing and even with Miss Martin being strong; her nerves have been damaged. In short, Lieutenant, Miss Martin's responses have shut down."

"What chances, realistically, does she have, doc?"

The doctor shook his head. "There could be permanent damage. The brain can sustain a lot, but everyone's different. Remember Lieutenant, it's not just the rape or the awful attack, it's the shock. Therefore, we cannot predict the outcome of whether Miss Martin will recover unscathed. You say you have the man who inflicted this on this poor young woman?"

Chandler nodded. "Yeah, doc. But I need solid evidence and a testimony from Miss Martin could be crucial."

"Have you any other evidence?"

"Yeah! But just as you tell me that you cannot make a judgment on Miss Martin's condition until she regains consciousness, then it's the same with us. We don't have all the pieces of the jigsaw and we do need them if we are to convict our man. We have got to investigate every avenue. We have to be sure. Besides, there are many loose ends to tie up, which is why Miss Martin's testimony is vital."

With that, Chandler left the hospital. He checked the time on his wristwatch; he'd better radio in. Maybe there would be a new lead or development, that would move the case forward, and if not he would go home and rest before going to The Blue Parrot nightclub later that evening. He contacted his sergeant. There were no further leads and Gill Donaldson was being brought in the following day.

Chandler rested. There was something nagging at the back of his mind. Something just not quite right.

It was midnight when he entered The Blue Parrot. He approached the reception desk and asked for Maria.

"Are you a member, sir?" the young blonde hostess asked.

"No, I just need to speak to Maria. Personal matter.

"I'm sorry, sir, we don't allow personal relationships in the club."

"Is Maria available?" Chandler pressed, ignoring the young hostess's comments.

"Excuse me sir, while I attend to this other gentleman. I'll be back with you in one moment." The other arrival puffed a big cigar, his eyes glinted and he showed off his large teeth with his broad smile.

"You look fantastic tonight, Tracy."

"Thank you, Mr Burrell, let me sign you in."

Stuart Chandler hadn't waited any longer. He had already disappeared upstairs. He was standing inside the red velvet curtain, observing the cabaret act when Tracy appeared at his side.

"You can't just walk in here. You will have to come back downstairs to reception."

Just then Francoise appeared. "May I help you, sir?"

But before Chandler could reply, Tracy interrupted. "This gentleman has not registered and as far as I know is not a member. He was enquiring about Maria."

Francoise turned to face Stuart Chandler. But before she could speak, Chandler flashed his badge and held it up for both ladies to see. Francoise gestured to Tracy to return to reception.

"I'll take care of this gentleman," Francoise said coolly. "It's …?"

"Lieutenant Stuart Chandler."

"Please follow me, Lieutenant, we'll go somewhere more private.

Chandler smiled. He was admiring the view of Francoise as he followed her to a private room at the back of the club.

"We're legitimate," she said emphatically.

"Listen, Miss …"

"Francoise. Please call me Francoise."

"Okay, Francoise, this is not an official visit. Well, not yet anyway. We believe there's a girl working here called Maria."

"Maria," Francoise echoed an astonished tone in her voice. "Yes, do you know her?"

"Yes, of course, Maria's been here nearly as long as me. What is this all about?"

"I'm not in a position to divulge that information at the moment. We're investigating the attack on one of your girls."

"One of our girls, Lieutenant?"

"Yes, Nicky Martin. She's been beaten within inches of her life. She's in a coma.

"Nicky," Francoise repeated. "I ... we ... we're all just thinking she's been assaulted by one of her punters. You know, Nicky has many men friends, I mean, we've all told her not to be so careless. Protect yourself. But she never listens. So what has Maria to do with all this?"

Chandler raised his right forefinger and tapped it next to his nose. "Probably nothing, Francoise, but she just may know the man who committed the crime."

Francoise paused for a moment, allowing the lieutenant's last words to sink in. "I shall go and find her, monsieur. Please wait here."

Fifteen minutes passed before both ladies returned. Francoise didn't want to leave.

"I'll be alright, Francoise. I've nothing to hide from the lieutenant." Silence filled the air for a few moments.

"So, how can I help you, Lieutenant?"

Chandler observed his witness. She was very attractive with beautiful green eyes and dark hair that complemented her skin tone.

Chandler fished into his pocket and withdrew the club's card with her name and telephone number on it. He offered it for inspection.

"Do you remember who you gave this to?"

Maria stared at the card. "Yes, Lieutenant, it was a Mr Steve Donaldson. He was here last week, and I was very attracted to him, so I slipped my number into his overcoat pocket." Maria then added, "I'm not in the habit of that kind of behaviour, Lieutenant. In fact, Steve Donaldson is the first man I've given my number to. He had a certain charm; well, at least I thought he had, which was very unusual for meeting for the first time."

"You mean you hadn't met Mr Donaldson before, even though he was a regular visitor to the club?"

"On Lieutenant, please, that's not correct. Mr Donaldson was certainly no regular. In fact, the night I slipped that card into his pocket was his first visit to the club. The club is for members only. One joins automatically on their first visit. I was on duty downstairs the night he arrived and even completed his membership card.

"So Donaldson joined the club for the first time that evening?"

"Yes. Our records downstairs will verify all this, and as far as I'm aware has never revisited."

"What if he used another name?"

Maria paused. "Yes, that's possible but he would have been remembered. I mean, most of our members frequent the club regularly. For whatever reason; fat businessmen, lovely guys, men whose wives are not giving sex to their husbands. All sorts. They all have their reasons. The only exception is the out-of-towners, as we call them, or a guy can come in here wanting company for the evening, pay the membership fee and we'll never see him again.

"So, Lieutenant, I can assure you, Mr Donaldson has only ever been here once. Have you met Steve Donaldson, Lieutenant?"

Chandler smiled. "Yes, I've had the pleasure.

"Then you'll know, he's a handsome man, one not likely to be forgotten if he uses another name. Which he hasn't. Ask Francoise if you like; she meets every customer as they come in after registration. She's been here the longest and knows everybody."

Chandler was perturbed. By all accounts he had proof from the letter that was found written by Nicky Martin, verifying that Donaldson had visited the club and Nicky on several occasions.

"Are you absolutely sure, Maria?"

Maria responded. "Absolutely, Lieutenant. In fact, I was hoping Mr Donaldson would have found my card and given me a call. I was sure he felt the same electricity as I did, but we can't all be winners."

"No, I suppose we can't," echoed Chandler. "Listen, I may need to talk to you again. Is there anywhere else I can contact you?"

"You have my number on the card, otherwise I'm here most evenings. How is Nicky, by the way?"

Chandler shuffled his feet, his head bowed. "Not good. In fact, she's in a pretty bad way. In a coma. It's touch and go at this stage."

"And you think Steve Donaldson had something to do with it?"

Chandler nodded. "The evidence against him is quite overwhelming. We have him in custody, so all you girls are quite safe for the moment."

"You will let me know if anything transpires with Nicky's condition?"

Chandler nodded. I've only a few more routine enquiries to make before finalising my case."

Maria was disappointed and her face and voice gave it away. "Are you sure you have the right man, Lieutenant?"

Chandler shrugged his shoulders. "All the evidence indicates it that way. Now, may I take a look at that membership book before I leave? I specifically want to see all entries for the night Steve Donaldson first arrived and became a member of the club."

Maria led Lieutenant Chandler back to the reception desk and located the necessary paperwork proving when Steve first visited and registered.

Chandler scrutinised the information and Donaldson's signature. He also noted that Frank Coulson's name appeared many times. He was obviously a regular.

"Here's my card, Maria. If you remember anything, no matter how insignificant or small you may think it is, don't hesitate to call me, day or night."

With that, Chandler departed and ventured back into the street. The weather had deteriorated and he felt cold.

Next day, Chandler was at his desk early. He had not had much sleep. His investigation at The Blue Parrot had not only hindered his case, but it had brought into doubt evidence that he had taken for granted. Maria's statement and the club's records proved that Donaldson was lying the first time he was interviewed in Nicky's flat after Frank Coulson's murder, but it also proved that he had never been in The Blue Parrot until a much later date, and probably the first time he really did meet Nicky Martin.

Chandler considered the fact that maybe Donaldson was dating Nicky out with the club which would explain the letter he had as evidence. However, the fact still remained; there were inconsistencies and Chandler being Chandler didn't like that. He remembered Steve's confession that he was being set up when first arrested, and it concerned Chandler that Donaldson had been constant on that score at least.

The rest of the evidence held against his suspect was still enough to put him in the frame for Frank Coulson and Nicky; the fact that he was the last person to have seen Louise Volosso alive and her panties were found in his apartment, spoke volumes. Old Mrs Winston, although not the best witness; Chandler felt she would still identify him. His case was not airtight and he swore under his breath at the very thought that he had a loose end.

"Hey, what happened to you, Lieutenant? Had a rough night? Were these girls at The Blue Parrot too much for you?" Johnston said, upbeat and cheerful.

"You could say that. They don't leave much to the imagination," Chandler replied, trying to offer a smile. "They know how to tease a guy; I didn't play of course, but that's not what's bothering me."

"Oh!" Johnston said, "What's up, Lieutenant?"

"I really thought we had this all sewn up. Some of our evidence and statements don't add up and I, Johnston, want to be completely sure before we take this to the DA."

"I thought you were being pressured by the Captain?"

"Yeah! I am. I wish we could link Louise Volosso with Nicky and Frank Coulson , to say nothing of that poor schmuck, Hunter."

"Well, I've got Gill Donaldson coming in this afternoon so maybe she'll still be able to help."

Chandler nodded. "Close my door on your way out, oh, and Johnston, I don't want to be disturbed, understand?!"

Johnston nodded then departed, aware that his superior was troubled and tired.

Chandler loosened his collar and tie, stretched his legs and feet on top of his desk, tilted his chair back, and closed his eyes.

Chapter 21

Johnston organised a complete sweep of George Hunter's apartment and was about to depart when he noticed the sepia photograph on top of the bureau. George Hunter was on the right hand side of a foursome. There was an attractive woman in the middle of three other men.

Johnston stared at the photograph in disbelief. It was Steve Donaldson and George Hunter, definitely. He had found a link. Old vets from the war. Who was the woman? Johnston wondered and who was the other man?

Johnston pocketed the photograph and returned to the precinct. He was pleasantly surprised when he met Gill Donaldson.

"I'll just inform the lieutenant that you're here."

"What's all this about?" Gill started.

"Please be seated," Johnston replied, then instructed a woman detective to serve Gill a coffee.

Johnston disappeared into Lieutenant Chandler's office. "Gill Donaldson's outside, Lieutenant."

"Good. Give her a coffee, I need to think before I see her."

"Lieutenant, I found this photograph at George Hunter's apartment."

Chandler scrutinised the photo. He recognised George Hunter instantly, then recognised his suspect. "That's Donaldson!" he exclaimed, pointing to the man on the left.

Johnston's eyes glinted a yes in agreement.

"Who's the broad?" Chandler asked, staring at his sergeant.

Johnston smiled, paused, and then answered. "That, Lieutenant, is Gill Donaldson and she's waiting patiently right outside."

A smile broke out across Chandler's face, his eyes showing the same appreciation.

"Show the lady in … please."

Chapter 22

The ambulance arrived at The Mount Sinai hospital in One Gustave L Levy place, and Clive stood to one side to allow the paramedics to trolley Ralph into Accident and Emergency.

The ambulance team had radioed ahead and, although the department appeared chaotic, medics were waiting to attend to their latest casualty. The paramedics were shouting their report findings and the condition of their patient as they handed Ralph Rosenberg over. Clive stood in silence and waited anxiously as his master disappeared along a busy corridor and through big, heavy swing doors.

It seemed like an eternity before Dr Hillberry approached and introduced himself.

"I understand you found Mr Rosenberg."

Clive nodded. "How is he, doctor?"

"What was Mr Rosenberg's state prior to his attack?"

"I've no idea. It was my evening off. I only discovered him unconscious behind his study door when I arrived for work early this morning. There was nobody else in the house, except for Emma the cook, and she was busy working downstairs in the kitchen. Karen, I mean Mrs Rosenberg, is normally there; in fact I served them both dinner before I departed last evening and they both seemed fine. Mrs Rosenberg wasn't to be found today so I don't know what happened or where she is."

Clive thought privately of Gillian's upset bedroom. Something serious had obviously happened.

Dr Hillberry stared back at Clive. "Mr Rosenberg's not good. He's suffered a major stroke and his heart gave out. He's very lucky you found him in time, otherwise ..." Dr Hillberry let his unspoken words register.

"Look, the next 48 hours are crucial. Have you any idea how we can contact Mrs Rosenberg? It's vitally important we speak to her."

Clive shrugged his shoulders. "As I've said, she would normally be at home, so I have no idea where she could be."

"Is Mr Rosenberg on any medication?"

"Yes. He takes aspirin to thin his blood and a heart tablet to keep the rhythm of his heart beating correctly, and some other beta-blockers for cholesterol. Can't remember all the names but I'm sure I could find out when I return to the house."

"Has there been any undue stress recently?"

"No more than normal, I suppose. Mr Rosenberg is like most people, he has good days and bad days, but he normally handles them well."

Dr Hillberry acknowledged Clive's reply then disappeared back into Cardiac Intensive Care Unit to check on his patient.

Clive waited at the nurse's station. There had obviously been an incident at the house given the state of Gillian's bedroom. Had Mrs Rosenberg and her daughter witnessed Ralph's attack and then just left him there, possibly to die? Clive closed his eyes, thinking the unthinkable.

Karen Rosenberg had checked into the Waldorf with the two girls who were once again sleeping peacefully. She had experienced her husband's anger before but never ever witnessed or received such violence.

Gillian's lesbian tendency was obviously too much for Ralph and Karen thought how it took time for even her to understand. After all, Gillian was a good-looking young woman, but she had allowed her to continue her relationship with Philippa. All said and done she'd never seen her daughter so happy. She would contact Ralph and arrange a meeting: sort things out.

It was the following morning. Karen had dressed early, allowing the girls to sleep in. She had telephoned home but there was no response. Clive would normally be in attendance by now, and yet the telephone remained unanswered. Maybe Ralph had returned to Amsterdam to be with his precious son Mark and work out his anger.

Her intuition told her otherwise as she replaced its handset. Casually she switched on the television in her bedroom suite.

NEWSFLASH!

"Billionaire Ralph Rosenberg, of the famous Rosenberg Diamond company was rushed to hospital after a major heart attack. Doctors say his situation is critical."

The news reporter then announced that when they had more information it would be disclosed as and when they received it.

"This is Danny McGowan, live from The Mount Sinai hospital, New York."

"Oh God! No!" Karen shouted at the television. She knew Ralph and knew how their differences and their marriage was strained but she did not want Ralph to die. Well, not yet, anyway.

Quickly she woke the two girls. "Gillian, we have to go to the hospital. Your father's had a major heart attack. Get ready now."

Gillian was still half asleep. "Hey, after his behaviour last night, I don't really care. Hope he friggin' dies!"

"Gillian, you don't mean that," Karen shouted. Now please, do as you're told. I'm ordering a taxi."

"So last night was all okay then," Gillian retorted, hunching her shoulders and holding her hands out, palms upward.

"Gillian, you're missing the point."

"Ugh! I don't think so. He's never liked me, far less loved me."

Karen glanced at Philippa, then at her daughter. "Gillian," Karen said, pausing so that her words would get maximum impact, "none of us can achieve anything positive if we do nothing. Let's go and visit him and get an up-to-date report on his condition. And you're included too Philippa," Karen said, smiling at her daughter's partner.

"Fuck! Fuck! Fuck! I hate him, mom! He's never liked me. If I'm to go it's only because of you and Philippa, but don't expect me to mourn if the goddamn son of a bitch dies."

Karen shook her head. She knew with Gillian's attitude there would be no reconciliation between her and her father.

She telephoned Ralph's New York office, which was in turmoil at the news. Mark Rosenberg had been informed of his father's condition and was on his way home from Amsterdam. Mark had attempted to contact his mother at the family home without success. He just assumed his mother was at the hospital and he would catch up with all the details once he returned to the United States.

Ralph Rosenberg was tough and resilient and the fact that Clive Richards had arrived early probably saved his life.

Ralph lay in his hospital bed and recalled as best he could the events and drama of the previous evening and immediately requested that his son, Mark, be contacted.

"He's on his way home already," Clive said, as he sat beside his master.

"Get Mark. I want Mark," Ralph muttered, his eyes fluttering between a conscious and unconscious state.

Karen, Gillian and Philippa arrived at the hospital. They went directly to intensive care.

"I'm Karen Rosenberg, my husband, Ralph Rosenberg; he was admitted this morning with a heart attack. May I see him please?"

The young nurse checked her records and instructed Mrs Rosenberg to wait. A doctor appeared moments later.

"Ah, Mrs Rosenberg, your husband is very weak. We're monitoring him and hopefully have stabilised his condition."

"Can we see him, doctor?"

The doctor observed the three women. "I don't think it would be a good idea for all of you, but you, Mrs Rosenberg, that should be alright. His butler, Mr Richards, is with him and may I say, if he hadn't found Mr Rosenberg when he did I don't think he'd have been alive just now."

Gillian mumbled something under her breath that resulted in Philippa digging her elbow into her.

Karen paused, digesting the doctor's statement.

"I see. Is Clive still with Ralph?"

The doctor nodded.

"I want to see my husband, doctor."

The doctor nodded again. "Very well. Follow me."

The doctor waved to Clive Richards to come away, which Clive immediately obeyed. "Mrs Rosenberg wants to see her husband. Has there been any change?"

"Not really, He just keeps asking for his son Mark."

The doctor acknowledged Clive Richard's comments then instructed him to allow Mrs Rosenberg to have some time alone with her husband. Clive stared into Karen's eyes, searching them for information.

"Mr Rosenberg," the doctor said quietly to his patient, "your wife is here."

Ralph opened his eyes and stared at Karen who was standing over him.

"Get out, get out bitch!" Then, without any warning his whole body started to shake, then jump. An alarm in the monitor started to buzz. Ralph's body was shaking all over, his eyes closed.

Karen panicked and shouted for assistance. Another doctor and nurse rushed in.

"He's arresting," the doctor shouted.

"Please, Mrs Rosenberg, wait outside."

Karen moved slightly. She watched the medics attend to her husband, wrestling to bring him back to normality. An injection was administered as the medics shouted the changes in his condition as the drug took effect.

"Mrs Rosenberg, please will you leave?" The doctor's eyes flashed at a nurse and shook his head in Karen's direction. The nurse led Karen out of the room and back to the nurses station.

"Please wait here and once we have Mr Rosenberg calmed down Dr Hillberry will speak to you."

"What actually happened in there?"

Karen stared back at the young nurse. "Look, I don't know. Clive, his butler, had left his bedside, his eyes were closed and when he opened them and saw me he just seemed to go into a state of shock. And then all that shouting and shaking and that jumping of his body started …"

The young nurse could see Karen was becoming upset and tried to console her.

"Okay, Mrs Rosenberg, that's fine. Stay here, we'll get you a coffee and then as I said, Dr Hillberry will bring you up to date." The nurse paused. "He'll be alright, you wait and see. Just be patient. Your husband is in good hands."

With that, the young nurse returned to assist the rest of the group who were attending to Ralph.

Clive Richards approached Karen.

"This doesn't concern you, Clive. Please go back to the house, make arrangements for me and the girls to return. Hold all calls and if the Press are around tell them that I will give them an up-to-date statement later, once we know Mr Rosenberg's actual condition."

"But I don't think…" Clive started to reply, but Karen interrupted.

"That's right Clive, you don't think. Anyway, you're not paid to think."

Clive stared at Karen in disbelief and supressed his inner feelings.

Karen then continued speaking. "I understand that you found him?"

"Yes, I did."

"Well, good for you, Clive. So without you he may just have died."

Karen's words and tone held a definite unpleasant note. Clive stood motionless, unable to respond.

"Now, go back to the house. You're not required here."

Clive understood Karen Rosenberg's words and was deeply hurt. He left the hospital and as instructed made his return journey by taxi to The Rosenberg residence. He would need to have everything ready for Master Mark's arrival. He hoped Mark would be there soon. He was like his father, and Clive liked the boy.

The thought crossed his mind that if Ralph Rosenberg died he knew instinctively that his position under Karen would be no longer attainable and he would be out before Ralph's body was cold.

What a sad situation they were all in. He made a silent prayer to wish that his master Ralph Rosenberg recovered and would once again be home and at the head of the family and household.

He knew only too well that Karen Rosenberg was a different predator, and one he couldn't cope with.

Chapter 23

Ralph's condition stabilised to the relief of his doctors who were still unaware that it was the sight of his wife that had sparked off his panic attack.

The doctor spoke quietly to Ralph, now assured his patient was perfectly calm.

"Your wife and daughter are outside, do you want to see them?" he asked, assuming an affirmative answer.

At the mention of Karen and Gillian, Ralph's condition changed. The doctor saw the shock expression return to his eyes and then once again Ralph's body started to shake uncontrollably.

Alarmed, Dr Hillberry immediately retracted his question.

"Okay, okay. It's alright. I'll send them away. You don't have to see them.

Ralph's expression changed. He was calmer now and his body stopped shaking.

Dr Hillberry now realised that whatever had triggered the heart attack was obviously to do with Mrs Rosenberg and their daughter.

"I'll just go and tell them that you're really distressed and can't be disturbed.

Dr Hillberry rose to go. Ralph raised his arm. It was heavy. He signalled the doctor to come closer towards him.

"Doc, I don't ever want to see that woman or her brood again, and I mean never. Promise me Doc. Do you understand?"

Dr Hillberry observed his patient. He was a strong, powerful, successful and wealthy man and yet at this time so unlovable.

He nodded at this patient but he didn't understand. Ralph's words were weak.

"Is Mark here? I want my son Mark. And is Clive, my butler, here? I will see him."

Dr Hillberry searched Ralph's face. "I don't think your son has arrived. As far as Mr Richards is concerned I'll go check."

Ralph opened and closed his eyes twice, signalling he understood.

"Get Clive and Mark, doctor," then he closed his eyes and fell asleep.

Dr Hillberry checked Ralph's pulse again before leaving his patient to rest.

Karen, Gillian and Philippa saw Dr Hillberry approach and Karen stepped forward.

"How is he, doctor? Can I see him now?"

Dr Hillberry appraised Karen. She was beautiful and he had read all about her in the social pages of the fashionable magazines that his wife bought, and couldn't understand how she, with all her money and family reputation, had such a bearing on his patient, Ralph Rosenberg.

"No, I'm afraid not. He's very tired and needs to rest. In fact, he's sleeping now."

"So, when can I see him, doctor?" Karen persisted.

Dr Hillberry once again appraised the woman in front of him.

"He has asked to see his son, Mark," he said hesitantly.

"And?" Questioned Karen.

"And that's all, apart from Clive Richards, his butler." Silence reigned between them.

"Did you tell him I was still here?" she said sternly.

"Of course."

"And?" Her question hung in the air again.

"It's not for me to judge, Mrs Rosenberg, but Mr Rosenberg has only permitted his son Mark and Mr Richards a presence, and right now he's too weak to have anything upset him. So with all due respect, as far as you and Gillian are concerned, there'll be no visits meantime."

Karen was aghast but Gillian was heard to mutter "good riddance!"

"Have you any idea, Mrs Rosenberg, when Mark will arrive?"

Karen smiled at Dr Hillberry but didn't answer. She just turned and walked away, but under her breath said "I couldn't bloody well care when precious Mark returns."

Mark's flight, Pan Am AM201B touched down on time but it was another hour before he cleared Customs and hailed a taxi.

"Mount Sinai hospital, please, and as fast as you can," he instructed the driver.

"Okay bud, you got it," then checked his rear view mirror and pulled out into the throng of the busy traffic.

Mark heard another newsflash on the driver's radio regarding his father's heart attack that brought comment from the taxi driver.

"It don't matter how much money you got, if it's your time to go, its time. I mean, take this guy Rosenberg. He's got all the money in the world, more than he'll ever need and yet he's no different to you and me in these circumstances. Okay, his money can buy the best of doctors, but hey, as I said, if it's your time..."

The taxi driver paused. "What do you think?" he said, eyeing his passenger through the mirror.

Mark didn't respond, he just sat quietly, listening to his ramblings.

"Yeah, all the money in the world means nothin' if you ain't got your health." The cab driver's voice seemed to be stuck in a groove. His voice had become monotone.

The driver's eyes flashed again in his mirror as he weaved his way through the traffic.

"Hey bud, you okay? You look a little agitated."

Mark responded this time.

"Look, I'm fine, just get me to that hospital, okay?"

Mark knew his panicked voice had given his calmness away. "Listen, you know that Mr Rosenberg they're talking about on the radio?"

The driver nodded, watching the road ahead and periodically checking his passenger in his mirror and pleased that his fare was about to engage in some conversation.

"Yeah," he responded. "The guy with the money."

Mark nodded. "Well, that's my father and I've just flown 4,000 miles to be here; now can you get me to that hospital without any more chat."

"Your father?" the taxi driver exclaimed, his eyes once again flicking between mirror and road.

"That's right, I just hope I'm not too late."

"Hey, hold on bud, you young Rosenberg?"

"Yes, yes," Mark replied.

"Well hold on son, its years since I've had such an emergency."

The driver swerved his cab, switching lanes, cutting other motorists up, the sound of horns indicating their annoyance.

"As I said, son, here we go."

The driver had switched on all headlights, his hand permanently on the horn, the pace of his vehicle quickening dramatically. Other road users sensing an emergency generally moved out of the way as the taxi accelerated, moving all over the road, Mark found himself being thrown about the large back seat of the yellow cab.

The cab screeched to a halt at the entrance to The Mount Sinai hospital with Mark leaping from its rear.

"You can either park and follow me in or just send the bill to Mr Mark Rosenberg. I'll make sure you're paid."

"I'll park and wait if you don't mind. I hope your Pop is okay."

Mark smiled for the first time that day. "Thank you, I'll see you inside. He then disappeared into reception.

The driver was about to re-enter his cab when two police motorcycles arrived, their lights and sirens blazing, blocking the yellow cab.

"Okay, mate, who the hell do you think you are, Dan Gurney?"

The cab driver laughed. "Had trouble keeping up with me, eh?"

"Licence please."

"Look officer, let me explain."

The motorcycle cops listened to his story. "Okay, once we've verified your statement we'll see."

One patrolman disappeared into the hospital while the other kept a watchful eye over his prisoner.

It seemed a long time before the officer returned to the cab.

"Okay bud, you can go, Mark Rosenberg has vouched for you, but don't go pulling any more stunts like that. You got an emergency phone it in next time, 'cos if you don't we won't be so polite."

The driver fired his engine and once the motorcycle cops had rode off, muttered out loud to himself "fascist pigs."

He checked the money the officer had given him; $100. "Nice one," he said out loud as he touched his hanging crucifix in his cab and prayed that Ralph Rosenberg would make it.

Mark was now at his father's bedside. They held hands. Tears were in Mark's eyes.

"What happened, dad, what caused all this?"

Ralph went quiet. He was happy to see his son, the only member of his family who turned out right.

"Don't ask. You're here, that's all that matters."

"I assume mom has been in?" Mark said.

Ralph withdrew his hand from Mark's.

"Son, that's all over now, I'll explain when I'm feeling better."

Mark didn't like the sound of what his father intimated, but he knew this was not the time for heavy questions.

"Okay, let's talk about you," he said. "What do the doctors think? Have they any idea what caused it? I mean, when will you be able to go home?"

"I don't know, son, but I'm fine now you're here."

"Hey dad, you should have been with me in Amsterdam and witnessing the cutting of that new diamond. It was fantastic."

Ralph smiled. He was pleased his son shared the same enthusiasm and passion as himself and wanted to know more, when Dr Hillberry arrived.

"I assume you are Mark? How was Amsterdam?"

"I've just been telling dad about the cutting of the new diamond, quite fantastic."

"May I see you a moment, Mark?"

"Sure," Mark replied and followed Dr Hillberry out of the room.

"I've been looking forward to meeting you," Dr Hillberry began. "Your father has been asking for you since he regained consciousness, so it's good that you're here. However, he's had a massive heart attack and stroke, God knows how he survived. He was lucky. Don't talk to him about business, even if he wants to, he's very delicate right now. And I don't think he realises just how ill he is."

"Is he going to be alright, doctor?"

Dr Hillberry paused. "We have to run some more tests. Once we're happy that he's fully stabilised."

Mark felt embarrassed and stupid. His burning eyes started to fill with tears, stinging them.

"Has mom been in to visit him?"

"Yes, she has, with your sister. But – how can I say this?"

"Say what, doctor? Tell me, I know something's not right between them. Tell me."

"Well, I'm not privy to all the facts, but let's say their meeting wasn't very amicable. In fact, your father had a major relapse when he saw your mother. We had to stabilise him again. He has requested that your mom and you sister do not visit. He doesn't want to see them. Now, I don't know your family affairs, except what I read in the Press. I guess whatever is going on between them caused you father's attack, and may I say he's lucky to be alive."

Mark was silent for a moment. He didn't understand. "Thanks doctor. I'll stay with dad. Keep him calm then when I get home I'll find out what's been going on. By the way, who found dad?"

"His butler, Clive Richards, I believe. Lucky he arrived early for his duties, otherwise..." Dr Hillberry let his words trail off.

"Good old Clive," Mark said. "He's been looking after all of us for many years. He's very close to dad."

"You go and take care of your father, Mark. He needs you to be strong at this time."

They shook hands and Mark returned to his father's bedside.

Mark sat with his father all night. His father was pleased he was there. They held hands and sometimes while Mark was talking their hands squeezed.

It was early in the morning; Mark was dozing. A twitch - a signal his father was awake - and attempting to communicate with him. Ralph had removed his oxygen mask and was trying to speak, his eyes rolling in their sockets, his mind still sharp but as yet unable to communicate his thoughts.

Mark immediately pressed the red emergency buzzer for help. A nurse appeared, repositioned Ralph's oxygen mask, then went in search of a doctor.

She no sooner left the room than Ralph removed his mask and was attempting to speak. The words were muffled but he found the strength to speak to his son.

"Find Gina and Lisa." His voice was faint but the names were crystal clear. "Promise me! You'll find them. Promise me! Please take care of them. They're your family."

Mark did not understand. He had never heard of these people, but realised whatever his father was trying to tell him was important.

"Gina and Lisa," Mark responded.

Ralph nodded his head, his strength being sapped away.

"What's their surname?" Mark asked, but his father had already lapsed into another deep sleep.

The doctor returned, replaced the oxygen mask and checked Ralph's pulse.

"Did he say anything?" the doctor asked.

"Not really. Someone called Gina and someone called Lisa. But it didn't make any sense." The doctor shrugged his shoulders. "That's all he said?"

Mark added, "Except that he wanted me to find them. Says they are family but I've no idea who they are."

"Did he give you a surname?"

Mark shook his head negatively. The doctor paused for a moment. It was obvious they were important.

"I think you should go home, get some rest, a change of clothes and come back tomorrow. If there are any changes I'll let you know."

"But what if he wakes up and I'm not here by his side?"

"I'll tell him you've gone to trace Gina and Lisa. You never know, he may even tell me who they are."

Mark shook his head. "Where do I start, doc?"

"Son, that's your job. Maybe Clive Richards, your father's butler will know some of these people, but I do know one thing, your father has given you a task and these people could make all the difference to his recovery."

"You'll definitely contact me doc if there's any change?"

Dr Hillberry nodded. "I promise."

Mark departed and took a cab home. The driver attempted conversation but soon gave up when there was no feedback from his passenger.

The large black and gold electric gates loomed into view between the white walls that boasted the Rosenberg estate and the family mansion in The Hamptons. Mark pressed the intercom button, identifying himself. Journalists approached, their cameras flashing, but luckily the taxi entered the long driveway before any interview could take place.

Another pair of eyes were watching from a short distance, undetected. The man stubbed out a strong black, Turkish cigarette before leaving the scene.

Clive Richards waited at the front door and welcomed Mark. They both went to his father's study and Mark sat down on the high-backed leather chair, behind the large double-pillared desk with its green leather inlay.

"How's your father?"

"He's stable meantime," Mark replied "but he's asked me to find a couple of people and hopefully, Clive, you'll be able to help me because I have never heard of them."

"Well, if I can be any assistance you know I'll do my best; I have always served your father well."

"I know that, Clive."

Clive smiled at his young master's comment. "So how can I help?"

"Dad has asked me to locate Gina and Lisa. I have no surname to go on; he muttered these names, saying they were as good as family, and then fell asleep. Have you heard of them Clive?"

Clive stood back, the silence between them obvious. Mark repeated his question, pressing for an answer.

"Sorry, Master Mark, the names sound familiar, but I can't place them."

"What are you not telling me, Clive?" Mark asked, sensing that Clive knew more than he was willing to divulge.

"Nothing, Master Mark. Please, sir, I beg of you. If I knew anything I'd be the first to help."

Mark appraised his father's butler. "You sure, Clive? You wouldn't keep anything from me?"

"Absolutely not sir," but the tone in his voice carried a lie. "May I go now?"

Mark glanced at the servant in front of him. "Of course, but should you remember anything, Clive, you will let me know, won't you?"

Mark's last remark stung the air.

"I'm going to go over some of father's old records. Maybe find some information."

Clive turned and vacated the study, leaving Mark to his task.

Mark was reading his father's personal diary, casually turning each page, as he searched for the names of Gina and Lisa, when Clive reappeared. Mark looked up acknowledging Clive's presence.

"Yes, Clive, what is it?"

Clive stammered, "Well, sir, your father …"

"Has someone telephoned from the hospital?" Mark asked.

"No, no, nothing like that."

"So what is it, then, Clive?"

"Well sir, I've known and served your father a very long time and I … I … well …"

"Do you have information about Gina and Lisa?" Mark pressed.

"Yes," Clive answered quietly, his head bowed.

"So you know, them? You know where they are?"

Clive remained silent for a few moments, then replied.

"Let me explain."

Chapter 24

Steve overheard George Hunter's name. He knew his friend was dead. Again, he asked himself why. George was an old army buddy who now worked in Social Security records department, and when necessary provided Steve with information. What was George's connection in all of this? This simple case of tracing Nicky Martin seemed to grow arms and legs.

Nicky must know something, but what? Gina, by all accounts, was Nicky's mother. Where was Gina? Only Nicky could answer that, and right now she was in hospital in a coma, unable to talk and lucky to be alive, and he was in a prison cell with no freedom to investigate the matter.

The peephole slid open.

"Stand back, you're wanted upstairs," the guard shouted, as he turned his keys in the heavy lock of the cell door.

Steve stood still as the police officer cuffed him and led him upstairs to Lieutenants Chandler's office.

"Un-cuff him," Chandler instructed, "he's not going anywhere; besides I've a little surprise for our man here."

Steve stared at Lieutenant Chandler.

"Johnston!" Chandler shouted. Johnston appeared instantly. "Bring Mrs Gill Donaldson in, would you?"

Steve turned to face his ex-wife as she entered Chandler's office. There was a moment's silence between them as they stared into each other's eyes.

"I don't know what they've told you Gill, but I'm innocent. Been set up, but don't know why." Gill stared back at Steve, emotional silence filling the air.

"Tell him I'm no rapist or murderer, Gill." Steve said, pointing at Chandler. Gill remained silent.

"For God's sake, Gill, tell him."

"I don't know what to say." Gill paused. "There's nothing I can say."

"Gill, tell the fuckin' lieutenant that's not the kind of man I am. Tell him!" Steve yelled.

"That's enough," intervened Chandler, stepping between them.

Gill now spoke, keeping her eyes on Steve's. "I don't believe Steve inflicted the beating or rape on that young woman. That's not his style." Gill's words hung in the air, both men waiting for her statement.

"But Steve can be cold, calculating and detached. You know that's true, Steve. Your training in the OAS taught you that."

"Gill, I'm not that person anymore. I'm a small town PI. I've got no superiors now, just my own time. I take jobs, got a reputation of achieving results, get paid, but that's it. I don't rape, murder or violate anybody and if I think a case is wrong I don't take it."

"So how are you involved with all this?" Gill asked.

Lieutenant Chandler stood quietly, patiently observing the two people before him. He was hoping some information would surface; something that would help his case.

Gill stared at her ex-husband. He was dishevelled and in need of a shave and a wash. "Did you sleep with this young woman, Steve?" The question hit like a bolt.

"What's that to with anything?"

"Did you? Answer me, Steve."

Steve shook his head and ran his fingers through his hair. "Yes I did. It was a one-off. But I swear; I didn't beat her. When I left she was sleeping like a baby.

Gill laughed in his face. "Steve, please, don't say any more."

"For God's sake, Gill, she's a lap dancer, picks men up every other night.

"Oh, so you fucked her Steve, couldn't keep your dick in your pants."

"It's not like that," Steve attempted to explain.

"Oh! What was it like, Steve? What was she like?"

Gill was crying now, her mascara running down her cheeks. Her meeting with Steve after all those years had not been a good one.

"Lieutenant, I want to go now. I will however confirm one thing. Steve and I met many years ago when he first joined the Marines. I was a nurse and he and his friend Andre were involved in a fight over a woman. He was badly beaten. I nursed him, we fell in love, married, had a lovely daughter and then he joined the OAS and it changed him."

"What are you telling me, Mrs Donaldson?"

"My name's Browne, not Donaldson, Lieutenant. I retook my maiden name when we divorced. As I was saying, that's his background. Maybe that will help you understand him. He's a good man, Lieutenant. Stupid sometimes, but he's not the type to commit these crimes. Now I want to leave." Gill paused, tearfully searching Steve's face.

"Thank you, Gill. Thank you."

"Hey, Donaldson, you're not outta here yet, not by a long chalk."

Steve got behind Gill. He held her between himself and Chandler, holding a letter opener he swiped from the desk. His quick action took both Gill and Chandler by surprise.

"You're not doing yourself any favors, Donaldson," Chandler said. "Put that down. Let Gill go. Let's talk about this."

Steve grinned. "Talk? Yes, Lieutenant, I'd like that. First, give me your gun, Lieutenant."

Chandler recoiled. "I don't think so."

"I'll kill her," Steve replied. "After all, you've got your case all wrapped up; one more won't make any difference."

Gill tried to move but Steve's grip was vice-like and she was rooted to the spot.

"Someone's setting me up, Lieutenant. I need to know why, and who."

Steve edged out of Chandler's room, now causing chaos in the outer office.

"I've missed you, Gill," he whispered in her ear. "I still love you." He managed to get to the street, still holding Gill hostage. The whole precinct had followed him out.

He kissed Gill gently, pushed her towards the police offices, dropped the knife, and ran.

Lieutenant Chandler put his arm around Gill to comfort her.

"Let me go! Lieutenant! Let me go!" she shouted. Steve was nowhere to be seen.

Steve ran several blocks; his first thoughts were to change his clothes, shave and find a safe place to hide. Chandler would have released his description to every unit so he would have to be careful. He thought of his ex-wife, Gill. She was beautiful; he'd been a fool to let their marriage fail. He was walking quicker than most and bumped into another pedestrian.

"Hey, watcha bud, look where you're goin'," the man shouted, as Steve continued on his way. In his possession was the passer-by's wallet, credit cards, money and identification.

His first move was a haircut and shave, and then he purchased some new clothes. The $400 he had found in the wallet was indeed lucky.

He vacated his last shop dressed in his new casual jacket and trousers, when he observed a police patrol vehicle creeping along the edge of the sidewalk. Quickly he changed direction. He needed help.

Steve knew George Hunter was dead but just maybe the information on Joe Marshall may still be available. He headed for the Social Security office, keeping a watchful eye out of any more patrols that would be searching for him.

"May I speak to George Hunter?" Steve asked the pretty, young assistant behind the counter. He was not prepared for her response as she burst into tears and left her post to contact her supervisor.

"It's Mr..."

"Alan Brunswick," Steve replied, remembering the identity of the man's wallet he had in his pocket.

"Please, why do you specifically require to speak to George?" the supervisor said.

"Oh, he's a personal friend; we go way back, but I haven't seen him for some time. Thought we'd catch up."

The supervisor considered his comments. "Please, come through to my office, Mr…"

"Brunswick," Steve repeated.

"There's no easy way to say this; George Hunter is dead. Murdered. A vicious attack."

Steve gave a saddened expression. Although he was privy to information he could not let his guard down, so appeared shocked and upset at the news.

After listening to the supervisor giving him as much detail as he knew, Steve gently asked his question.

"George was trying to locate another one of our buddies, a Joe Marshall. We were organising a reunion. Do you know if Joe has been contacted, or do you have his details where I could contact him?"

The supervisor now observed Steve more closely. "Excuse me, Mr Brunswick; let me see if I can help." He vacated his office and Steve watched as he spoke to a woman in the outer office, his arm and finger pointing in Steve's direction.

When he saw the woman with the telephone handset in her hand, he decided to leave. He quickly, but yet keeping an unhurried pace, vacated the building.

The supervisor and the woman returned to the office but Steve had gone. He knew he had to get off the streets.

Chapter 25

"The Downtown Hospital," he instructed the driver as he entered the yellow.

"City's busy this time of year," the taxi driver said, attempting to open a conversation between them."

"Just drive bud," Steve replied. "I'm in a hurry."

The cabbie glanced at his passenger through his rear view mirror, then remained silent for the remainder of the journey.

Steve paid his fare then took time to appraise the entrance and exits including the ambulance bays. He noted them all carefully.

He waited in a queue at reception. "I'm visiting a patient who's been admitted recently. A Miss Nicky Martin."

The receptionist checked her records. "She's on the seventh floor but no visitors are allowed. She's very critical." The receptionist went on to enquire about his relationship with Miss Martin, but Steve had already disappeared.

The seventh floor corridor was bustling and Steve observed the nurses' station. He needed to know Nicky's room number. Steve approached the nurse at the counter. "Miss Martin's room, please."

The nurse glanced at Steve. "And you are?

"Lieutenant Chandler, NYCP." Steve flashed the stolen wallet with its drivers licence, showing, but fast enough not to be read.

"Room 701, Lieutenant. Down the corridor on your right. I believe one of your officers is still on duty."

Steve thanked the nurse with a smile, and then proceeded towards room 701.

He stopped when he saw the patrolman sitting outside Nicky's room. Steve waited, then observed another officer exchanging places; one shift finishing and another beginning. Steve was considering how to gain access to Nicky when he was aware of a doctor in a white coat approaching the officer on guard, then after a brief exchange, entered Nicky's room. Steve backed off and stood against the corridor wall.

There was a loud buzzing alarm, and then hospital staff were running towards room 701. Nicky's door opened and the guard stood and faced the man in the white coat. He felt nothing as the swift, sharp stiletto blade cut his throat and he fell to the floor. The man in the white coat then disappeared towards the stairwell, the screams of other visitors witnessing the attack obscuring any view of the man or any chance of following him.

"Excuse me, excuse me," Steve shouted, his arms held high with one holding his wallet in the other. "Police! Let me through."

Steve relied on the fact that in the mayhem, nobody would verify his identity. He checked the patrolman's pulse. He was dead. Steve then entered Nicky's room. Nicky's monitor was going crazy. She was moaning.

"Nicky, it's Steve, did you recognise the man who was here a minute ago?"

Nicky started screaming. "Get him off me, it's him! Help me! Help!"

A doctor and nurse arrived.

"She's delirious," Steve said, playing for time. "It's the man in the white coat we're after," he said.

Nicky's outburst came. "It's him! It's him! She shouted, pointing at Steve.

"Where's that goddamn son of a bitch?" Steve exclaimed as he vacated the room. He worked his way back towards the exit. Another officer approached. Steve stopped him.

"We're a man down. Did you see a man in a white doctor's coat?"

"I'm with Lieutenant Chandler's team brought in for this case."

The young office looked bewildered. "The place is full of men in white coats," he replied.

"Get more back up. Disperse the crowd around our dead man."

The officer immediately responded, more in an automatic reaction than questioning Steve.

A moment later the office turned to interrogate Steve further, but he had disappeared.

Steve watched from a safe distance in the street as Lieutenant Chandler and Sergeant Johnston arrived at the scene. He did not see the other pair of eyes watching him.

Chapter 26

Clive sat down in an armchair across from Mark.

"It's at least, let me see, twenty; no, twenty two years ago when your father confided in me as his friend. I promised never to divulge his confidence to anyone … ever. However, given the gravity of the present situation, and the fact that your father has requested you to locate Gina and Lisa, I feel empowered to enlighten you regarding who they are."

"Clive, stop being longwinded; get to the point," Mark said, now anxious for the information he was about to receive.

Clive paused, wondering where to begin. "You were about five years old. The apple of your father's eye. Your sister, Gillian, would be three." Clive stopped speaking momentarily, as he recalled the years in his mind.

"Go on, Clive. Tell me, please continue."

"Well, your mother and father," again Clive paused. "Were not, shall we say…" Another pause. "Loving to one another. Don't misunderstand me, they needed each other in many ways, but the sparkle had gone. They were just two different people. Anyway, on one of your father's seminars he met a woman. They had an affair. Your mother was not aware of it, thank God, but I've never seen your father so happy. It was as if he had a new lease of life, especially when he was obviously seeing her.

"I found one of her lace handkerchiefs with the initial 'G'. It was in your father's coat pocket. I chose to say nothing. After all, it was not my business and in a professional capacity, being close to your father I said and did nothing. I had after all found out by accident.

That was when your father confided in me about Gina. He missed the handkerchief and confided his secret to me. Anyway, it doesn't really matter. The point is, I kept my promise to him. That is until now."

Mark stared at Clive. "Who's Lisa?" he asked, fearing the worst.

"Oh, Lisa, she's Gina's daughter by a previous marriage, some Italian fellow she married and it all went wrong. Anyway, time passed, then Gina just disappeared. Vanished. Your father discreetly attempted to find her but had no success. She just broke off their relationship. No reason given. Your father was in bits. He couldn't tell anyone. Well, he told me, but his remedy was to spend more time away from New York and concentrate on his business."

"Did you ever hear anything about this Gina and her daughter Lisa?"

Clive searched his master's young face. "No – nothing. It was never mentioned again, and that's all I know," Clive lied.

Chapter 27

Steve took a risk and returned to his apartment block. There was no patrol guarding it. He jimmied the lock of his apartment and entered. God, the place was a mess. The police had done a thorough job on it and his possessions. There was no point in staying here, besides, someone may see him. He needed somewhere to hide.

He righted his old leather chair, which was on its side, the bottom-lining all removed.

"Bastards," he said to himself. He had to think. Steve sat a while, then the thought crossed his mind. Maria, the hostess at the reception of The Blue Parrot. Maybe she could help? There had been chemistry between them; hopefully there still was.

Steve arrived at 603 45th Street, between Eleventh Avenue and Westside Highway. He wanted to go into the club but decided he had a better chance if he remained outside. He would catch Maria when she finished her shift.

It was cold, and Steve shivered as he shrank himself into the shadows.

Chapter 28

Gill Donaldson was back in Lieutenant Chandler's office, sipping a coffee. She had calmed down now, but seeing Steve after all those years had upset her.

"Mrs Donaldson, maybe you could expand on Steve's background? We have a lot of evidence against him; evidence that puts him at the scene of each of the murders, but we can't get access to his military file. It's coded, or some such thing, and no one can access it."

Gill listened to Chandler's words but her mind was blank as she sipped her coffee and stared into space.

"I don't really care what evidence you have, Lieutenant, but Steve's not a murderer; on a mission, maybe, but not young women for no reason. That's not his style."

"Ah, but there we have it. Our evidence proves he was the jealous type. He, we believe, was having an affair with this Nicky Martin. She was two-timing him. Call it part of her job, but Donaldson couldn't stand it when he found out he took his revenge. He didn't stop then either; he killed again, another young woman, but he was seen. Then there's this last one, a George Hunter. We can't quite connect the dots yet, but ..."

"George Hunter's dead?" Gill exclaimed, as her coffee fell to the floor.

Chandler rescued Gill, wiping her lap and hands.

Gill now stood. Chandler produced the photograph Johnston had found.

"This is you in this photograph. You, Steve Donaldson and George Hunter."

Gill took the photograph and smiled as fond memories came flooding back.

"We were in love, Steve and I. And George, well, George was always just there. Steve always befriended him. He was a loner kind of guy. I think that's why Steve liked him. The other guys used to make fun of him. He worked in administration; never shot a gun, never went on missions. Just paperwork, paperwork, paperwork.

"I'm sorry George is dead. He wouldn't harm a fly, Lieutenant, and one part of your puzzle is that Steve certainly didn't kill him. He would have given his life to save him; that you can be sure of. So, whatever evidence you have incriminating Steve, this particular death is not down to him."

"You sure, Gill?" Lieutenant Chandler asked.

"Lieutenant, apart from me Steve only had two friends; Andre Gomez and George Hunter. Andre was killed on a mission – that's Andre in the photo. It changed Steve but made him more protective of George. May I go now, Lieutenant?"

***

Mark sat motionless, his body numb, with the story that Clive Richards had just unfolded. It was obvious now that after all those years his father had not forgotten about this woman and her daughter.

His father was his hero. How could he do such a thing? Mark knew that relations between his mom and dad were strained. He'd grown up with that. He'd always taken his father's side but maybe he had misjudged the situation.

Mark then questioned, why did this Gina suddenly stop the affair? Why could she not be found? Did she have an accident? Did she die and his father not know? Then there was her daughter, Lisa. She surely would have surfaced. There must be something Clive is not telling. Maybe his father could, but his condition was fragile and Mark did not want to cause him any more anxiety.

He rang the push button bell in the study that would signal to Clive that his attendance was required.

Moments passed before a faint knock on the study door and Clive entered. Mark beckoned him to sit. He stared at his father's butler.

"Thank you, Clive, for sharing your information. I want to please dad, so I must find this Gina and Lisa. Do you have the surnames that will give us a start? I'm assuming, Clive, that I can rely on your assistance with this."

Clive sat there, and took a few moments. "Of course you can, Master Mark. Gina's marital name was Berio, if I remember correctly. Her former husband had dealings with, shall we say, unsavoury people of Italian origin. Whether that had an impact on her disappearance, I don't know."

"What about the daughter, Lisa?"

Clive shrugged his shoulders. "Don't know. Your father never discussed her, except to say how lovely and a fine young girl she was.

"Where do we start, Clive? Time, I suspect, is not on our side."

Clive nodded.

Chapter 29

Gina Gordino returned from church one Sunday and observed a car parked outside her mother's house. Two gentlemen in grey suits waited patiently, and as she approached, stepped onto the sidewalk in front of her.

The taller of the two men introduced himself. "Detective Cawarra. Mrs Gina Berio? May we have a word?"

Gina stopped, observing their identification shields in their leather pouches. "First, my name's not Berio, and second, I've nothing to say."

"No love lost between you, then?" Cawarra said.

Gina turned. Detective Cawarra observed her, then answered. "Okay! Okay! We thought you might?"

"Might what?" Gina interrupted. "Thank you, good day. I've lunch to prepare."

"We fished his half-eaten body out of the Hudson. Thought you'd be interested."

"Do I look as if I am?"

Detective Cawarra pursed his lips. "May we come in? It'll only take a few moments of your time; more a formality than anything else. Satisfying my boss and all that."

Gina did not want to admit the agents; after all, Peter Berio was in her past and she did not want or need to have that resurrected.

"I've nothing to say."

"Please," Cawarra insisted.

Gina considered his request. "Five minutes. That's all. Then you're gone. Okay?"

Cawarra again appraised the woman in front of him.

"Okay, agreed," he said, as he removed his hat and entered the Gordino household.

Detective Cawarra began. "I'll come straight to the point, Mrs Berio."

"I told you, it's Gordino now."

"Sorry, Mrs Gordino. Information has come into our possession, which linked your husband and his activities to, shall we say, certain families here in New York. The main link being to Michele Salvadori. We are seeking your help in our enquiries, even though Mr Berio and you were over a long time ago. Can we rely on you to verify certain things for us? We …"

"Stop right there, detective. As you said, Peter Berio and myself were over a long time ago. He doesn't concern me or my family, so really I've nothing to say. Besides, I never knew any of his associates, or indeed any of his business dealings. That was one of the reasons why we parted. I never knew where he was, or who with. Our trust broke down, so you see…"

Gina let her words trail off, although her mind was racing. She had made a promise to Joseph Cambrio, the councillary to the Salvadori family. She did not want them re-entering her life. Gina realised if the FBI or police were sniffing, it wouldn't be long before a connection would find its way back to Michele Salvadori, and even after all this time that could only ever end one way.

Detective Cawarra responded. "You sure, Gina? We can protect you and your family."

Gina just stared at him, but she conferred nothing.

Cawarra rose to go. "Here's my card, should you change your mind. Night or day, I'm available."

Gina took the card and glanced at it. "You won't be hearing from me, Detective," she said.

Gina watched from the window as their car sped off. She did not want any more upset in her life.

It was one week later when the black limousine slowed and pulled alongside Gina as she walked towards the park. Its tinted rear window slid down, revealing its passenger.

"Gina Berio? May I talk to you?"

Gina's heart skipped a beat. She recognised Joseph Cambrio's voice.

"This is not a good time, Mr Cambrio," she replied, as she kept walking. The limo kept its pace.

"Gina, we need to talk. Please get in."

"I'm not going anywhere with you, Mr Cambrio."

"Gina, please. Trust me."

Gina stopped, turned and smiled at Joseph."

"Sal, take a walk. Give Gina and myself some time."

Sal turned the engine off, vacated the driver's seat, and shrugging his shoulders walked slowly away.

"Come, sit with me, Gina."

Gina did not need this invitation, but she slid into the rear beside the Salvadori councillary.

"How's life been, Gina? It's been a long time since we last met."

"Not long enough, Mr Cambrio."

"Oh, Joseph, please. Call me Joseph."

"Okay, Joseph. I assume this is not a social call? What's troubling your family this time?"

Joseph Cambrio smiled.

"I like you, Gina. Always have. The first day we met."

"Mr Cambrio, get on with it. I've more to do with my time."

"Okay, well, we know Detective Cawarra visited you last week. What did he want?"

"Nothing."

Joseph laughed. "A social call, was it?"

Gina just stared at him. "You know I wouldn't tell him anything."

A brief silence reigned. "I know, Gina, but the clients I represent possibly think otherwise."

"What! After all this time, they think I'm going to squeal? We had an arrangement, Mr Cambrio. I've kept my side of the bargain."

"Then we have nothing to fear, Gina. It's just …"

"Just what?" Gina's eyes started into Joseph Cambrio's eyes.

"Peter's out of my life, he's dead I believe, so it's over."

"It's not Peter we're worried about, Gina."

"Then who, or what, is it?" Gina asked.

"It's Nicky."

"Nicky!" Gina shouted. "How? Where is she? What have you done to her?" Gina was hysterical now and started beating Joseph Cambrio's chest with her fists.

"Calm down Gina, calm down now, please. We don't have her. We've never hurt her, but she needs help. Needs protecting."

Gina was sobbing now. "How do you know? How? Tell me. I thought I'd lost her forever; never see her again. Where is she? Can I go to her? Take me. Take me, please Mr Cambrio."

Joseph sat back, fully realising now that Gina knew nothing of her daughter. Gina began to calm down.

"Tell me about her, Gina," Joseph enquired, comforting her with his arm.

"Tell you what? I fell pregnant with Nicky. She was beautiful but she was difficult. As she grew older we always fought. She never knew her father and I suppose she resented her life. Lisa, although not remembering Peter, still had photographs and as far as she's concerned, died in a road traffic accident."

Joseph Cambrio allowed himself a small smile. "He wishes," he said quietly.

"Well, Nicky had behavioural problems. The fights we had. Unthinkable. Then, without warning, one day she was gone. I tried to find her but she simply disappeared. I assumed she changed her name; anyway I never found her. I prayed and prayed, Mr Cambrio, but nothing, that is, until now."

"So what do you know?"

Chapter 30

Mark and Clive returned to the hospital. They spoke to Dr Hillberry.

"Your father is stable for the moment, but I'm glad you're here because he's been asking for Gina and you, Mark."

"Is Gina with you?" Dr Hillberry asked.

Mark glanced at Clive, then back at Dr Hillberry. "May we have a moment, doctor?"

The three of them stood to one side as Mark described Gina's relationship with his father, with Clive Richards backing up the story. None of them were aware of a young intern nearby, who listened intently.

"There can be no mention of this, doc. Do you understand?"

Dr Hillberry nodded, now fully aware of the complexity of his patient's situation. "We must keep Mr Rosenberg calm, at all costs. I suggest that if your father asks for Gina again, tell him you're dealing with it and you're waiting for a lead you're following. If we give him hope of her being traced we may just prolong his chance of recovery.

A telephone rang on the other side of the city. Jimmy Malone, a hotshot reporter with a nose and instinct after many years of experience, answered.

"You want a major scoop, Malone? I've got one for you, but it'll cost you."

Jimmy immediately started with pen and pad in front of him. "Who's this? $100,000. That's the fee … in cash."

"Here's the tip. Concerns Mr Ralph Rosenberg, you know, the billionaire diamond man who had a stroke and a heart attack?"

"So what have you got?" Jimmy replied, full in the knowledge that the Rosenberg incident was still fresh news.

"Meet me at the Maine Memorial, 59th Street, Columbus, in Central Park, tomorrow at 12 noon. Bring the money."

"Hey bud, give me something."

The line went dead. Jimmy knew enough between a crank call and the real thing. He recognised his caller's sincerity.

Jimmy read the note he made on his pad. He would meet the guy; get more information before any payment was made. Right now though he would pay a visit to the Mount Sinai hospital off 5th Avenue where Mr Ralph Rosenberg was admitted.

"I want Joseph Mendez, my lawyer," Ralph said, his oxygen mask muffling his words. "Get him now, Mark. He's to drop everything, I need him urgently."

"Fine dad, I'll see to it."

"Well go. Now. Phone him from here." Ralph had removed his mask; his eyes were large, forcefully confirming the urgency of his instruction. His eyelids closed momentarily as Clive helped him replace the oxygen mask.

Mark departed to find a phone booth. Ralph's room was silent as Clive Richards and his master were alone. Ralph extended his arm and Clive held his hand.

"We've been through a lot, you and I, Clive. It's important to me that you help Mark find Gina and Lisa. Promise me, Clive." Ralph's voice was weak but his mind was focused.

"I promise, Ralph. I promise," Clive said, squeezing his master's hand. Ralph retrieved his arm to be more comfortable, then fell asleep.

Gently, Clive Richardson rose and vacated the room. Mark was returning.

"Got Mendez, he's coming over in an hour, had to clear a few appointments."

Clive smiled. Good. Your father's sleeping, let's get a coffee."

Chapter 31

Steve was frozen by the time Maria appeared. The other girls shared a cab, but a private car collected Maria. It was an old Fiat and its exhaust fumes polluted the cold night air. Quickly Steve appeared and entered the other rear door.

"Hey, get out!" The driver shouted. "We've no money, so you're wasting your time."

Maria just stared at Steve and he returned her look. No words passed between them. The driver now turned around to face his daughter and the stranger in the rear of his car. Maria half smiled.

"It's okay, Pop. I know this man. Just take us home."

Maria's father glanced at the couple in the rear. "What am I, some kinda taxi service now?" then selected gear and moved off.

Steve mouthed a thank you. Maria only replied with a smile.

After kissing her Pop goodnight, Maria and Steve entered her apartment. It was awkward between them at first.

Maria's apartment was simply furnished, but tidy and homely. Steve broke the ice when he spied the goldfish.

"Oh, that's Freddie," Maria said, smiling.

"Hello Freddie," Steve said as he watched the fish rise to the top of the water searching for food. Maria watched Steve. It was obvious he'd been outside for a while.

"Can I get you a drink?" she said. "Coffee, or something stronger?"

Steve turned. "Both would be appreciated."

Maria started to speak, but Steve interrupted her.

"I didn't do any of the things they said."

"What things, Steve? I don't know what you mean."

"Oh, I just thought that Lieutenant Chandler would probably have visited the club, set you all against me."

Maria sat on the edge of her settee. "Did you do those crimes? Did you attack Nicky?" Maria's eyes searched Steve's face.

"Of course not. Someone is setting me up. My whole involvement was to find Nicky. She has a mother called Gina, but who or where she is. I have no idea. And as yet I haven't been able to find anything on Nicky's background, except she told me about Joe Marshall, but I've no info on him. My guy who was checking into that for her has been murdered, so that's a dead end. Nicky's involved somehow and I believe she doesn't even know about any of this. She's just a dancer at the club."

Maria listened to Steve. "You can stay here tonight. I'm afraid I've only one bed."

"Oh! … I'll be fine in the chair."

Maria smiled. "I'll get you organised and we'll discuss it all in the morning."

Steve nodded. At least he was off the streets.

He had settled into the chair as best he could and after his ordeal of his cell and the cold outside, quickly fell asleep. It was nearly dawn when he felt Maria's hand wakening him.

"Come to bed, " she whispered, as she gently led him to her bedroom.

Their intimacy and chemistry overtaking tiredness, they made love, each sensitive to the other's needs, feeling their way to ecstasy and satisfaction.

They now sat together and Steve was grateful to have her protection and the comfort she had provided during the night, but he was still a wanted man and it wouldn't take Chandler long to follow up the lead, linking Maria and himself.

"I've got to get out of here; you know that," Steve said, then added before Maria could reply, "I only want to help Nicky. She's involved in something, and someone wants her to suffer and I don't know why. I also have to clear my name if I'm to survive."

"What could Nicky be mixed up in?" Maria asked.

Steve shrugged his shoulders. "You do know that a further attempt was made on her life in the hospital? I was there. Only wanted to talk to her; witnessed a man dressed like a doctor leaving her room before all hell broke loose. They thought it was me and the trouble is, Nicky thought so, too. I need to talk to her, but I also need to get her out of that hospital."

"You can't be serious," Maria replied. "She's, she's all wired up, under heavy supervision. Anyway, it wouldn't be good for Nicky to be moved."

"Well, I, or we've, got to figure something out."

"I have an idea," Maria said, smiling.

Half an hour passed and Steve stood in front of a mirror with a black wig, dress, full makeup, stockings, and high-heeled sandals.

"I ain't wearing this," he said. "And as far as these things there," he said, pointing at the heels. "It's not friggin' possible."

Maria laughed. "Hey, from a distance you're not too bad. Besides, the cops aren't looking for a woman."

Steve sighed. That was at least true, but he felt he couldn't pull it off. "So, you expect me to walk about like this? I will get arrested, but for a different reason and ..."

"And nothing," Maria broke in. "Hey, honey, this is New York. Anything goes."

Steve afforded himself a smile. "I suppose I'm not too bad," then added, "if you're drunk and not particular."

Maria was on the telephone. "Yes, Pop, I want you to pick me up. I'll make dinner. Oh, and I'm bringing a friend with me!"

"That guy from last night, I suppose."

Maria hesitated. "No, it's a she, and her name is," Maria paused, "Jacqui."

"Oh, alright, see you in half an hour."

Maria and Steve practiced him walking in his new sandals.

"It's a question of balance and posture, you'll get used to it."

"My feet are aching. I can't do this. How the hell do you women do it?"

"Don't ask," Maria answered, smiling. "Now, let's try again before Pop arrives."

Steve was struggling when a horn peeped. Maria looked out.

"That's Pop, let's go. Now remember; straighten your back, now best foot forward."

"But my feet, oh! Ahh!" A heel collapsed on its side, and Steve lost all balance. "This is no good. Look, thanks Maria, but there's got to be another way."

"Steve, you can do it. It's mind over matter! Now, get that shoe on."

Another peep from Pop's horn signalled he was becoming impatient. With difficulty, Steve managed to enter Pop's car, incurring mysterious looks from Maria's father.

"Jacqui, I presume?"

Steve just nodded.

"Just drive, Pop, thanks for coming."

The car sped away as Steve glanced out its rear window.

Chandler and Johnston's car had arrived at Maria's apartment. Steve closed his eyes.

"That was close."

Maria turned to see the two detectives buzz her intercom.

Pop said nothing, but shook his head in Steve's direction as he whispered to his daughter. "This is the guy everybody's looking for, isn't it? The one that's raped and murdered those women. How, and what, are you doin' with him?"

"Pop! I can't explain that right now, just trust me, okay."

"No, not okay. Now, you listen to me." Maria had already moved over to Steve as they waited to enter her father's house. "Your mother would have had plenty to say, Maria, your mother would."

Maria gently put her forefinger across her father's lips. "Let him in Pop ..., please? It's cold."

Maria's father showed his displeasure as the three of them entered his apartment.

"You won't be able to hide, you know. Your picture is on all the newsreels and newspapers. You'll be found, no matter where you go."

"That's why Steve's going to stay here, with you, Pop."

"What! Are you outta your mind?! Holy Mary Mother of God, forgive me. He is not staying here, Maria. No, I forbid it. No! No! No!"

"Pop, please, just listen. Please, listen to him. If you then want him to go, then we both will."

"Maria …"

"No, Pop. I want you to listen to Steve. Don't prejudge, give him a chance."

Maria's father stared at his daughter. "Okay, okay."

Steve sat down.

"Can I get you something?"

Steve smiled. "Any slippers? My feet are killing me" The comment broke the ice between them and everybody chuckled.

Steve explained his whole case to Maria and her father, although he knew he was, for his first time being unprofessional, he did need help and all the help he could muster if he was to find the solution to the riddle of Nicky Martin and him being framed.

Finding her mother, Gina, would be a step in the right direction. Steve had found Nicky.

"Maybe Gina could unlock the puzzle. None of us at the club have ever heard of any Gina, but then none of us ever knew Nicky's past. She kept everything bottled up and, as you know, Steve, she has a volatile nature. One minute upbeat, the rest a time bomb."

Steve nodded. In the short time he had known Nicky, he realised how unstable she could be.

Pop made some coffee as they figured their next move.

Chapter 32

Joseph Mendez had cleared his appointments for the day. He sat at his client's bedside.

"A new will, Ralph? That'll take time. If it's only small amendments then we can refer to an addendum detailed sheet, which would obviously speed up the process. It also makes it easier if you decide to delete anything later."

"Joe, it's a new will I want; one that cannot be contested in a court of law. The changes I want to make are more than just amendments, so please settle back and take notes of my instructions.

"First, my wife, Karen, is to inherit nothing. That has to apply to all my assets: pensions, trusts, property ... in short, everything."

"I don't think that's possible, Ralph. As you wife she'd be entitled to ..."

"Entitled to fuck all," Ralph interrupted.

"But ... Let me explain. Even if you divorced her because there's no prenuptial agreement, she'd automatically be entitled to half."

"What? That bitch." Ralph was very upset and Joseph Mendez could see it.

"Have you and Karen had a disagreement? Are you going to divorce?"

"No – yes – well... We'd argued, more than that actually. I threw her out and that thing Gillian with her."

"Gillian?" Joseph echoed.

"Yeah, she's to get fuck all, write her out. See how she makes it with nothing, the way I did."

"Ralph – this is ridiculous, what you're asking. Look, whatever the reason, get yourself better, then we'll discuss this properly. I can see you're troubled, but stay calm and get better."

Ralph Rosenberg stared at his lawyer and replaced his oxygen mask.

"If you don't do as I ask," he muttered, "I'll find a lawyer who will. Now go, and if you want my business, come back when you're ready to comply with my wishes and have a method where my will can't be contested."

"Ralph," Joseph started, but his client and friend of so many years just turned his head away.

Joseph Mendez joined Mark and Clive. They were talking mainly about Ralph's wellbeing,

"Who's that?" Clive asked, making Mark and Joseph aware of the untidily dressed man sauntering about at the nurse's station.

Joseph turned back. "I'm sure he's that reporter, Malone. If he's sneaking about then there's a reason."

The three men walked passed Malone, ignoring him completely.

"I've a message for Mr Ralph Rosenberg," Malone told the nurse.

"He's not receiving any visitors," came the reply.

"Pity, it's pretty urgent. It's regarding his wife." Malone was fishing. He didn't know what to say.

"His wife?"

"Yeah! His wife."

"Well, as far as I'm aware, Mr Rosenberg doesn't want to see her. In fact, she and her daughter had to leave earlier.

"Oh! My mistake. I better check I have the right Rosenberg."

The nurse checked her sheet, then looked up, but Malone had gone.

So there was a story. A family secret or feud. Anyway, Malone thought. It's a start. Maybe his informant would enlighten him tomorrow.

Malone met John Park at the Maine Memorial.

"Listen, the price The Times will pay is $50,000. And we need to check out your facts before we print. We're not going to incur a lawsuit on your say so."

$50,000 – no, no, I said $100,000." Park replied. "When this story breaks it'll run and run and I probably won't have a job, so …"

"So nothin'" Malone interrupted. "You're trying to screw me over a conversation you overheard and who knows, you may just have got it all wrong."

Malone let his words penetrate. He didn't want to lose the scoop but he wasn't going to be a schmuck either.

John Park was silent. Malone and his newspaper had doubts, but he was sure what he heard was true.

"I'll give you a name; you check it out. If you're happy, meet me here two days from now – with $100,000 and you'll get your scoop."

Malone hesitated. He didn't agree or disagree. "So what's the name?"

"Gina – Gina Berio."

Malone searched his informant's face. "I'll be in touch he said, then departed.

Joseph Mendez returned to Ralph's bedside, hoping his client and friend had settled down and whatever altercation had erupted between Ralph and Karen would be over, and his instructions to alter the will put to bed.

"You got that new will?"

Joseph shook his head. "Ralph, you've had a stroke, heart attack; you're not well. You're not thinking straight; you're not …"

Ralph was angry now. For the first time his trusted lawyer was making judgements on him against his wishes.

"Stop right there, Joseph Mendez! I instructed you to create a new will and if you want to remain as my lawyer, I suggest you do so as instructed. Also,

I want divorce proceedings issued against my wife. She's no longer to be a part of the Rosenberg family."

"What! Ralph, what's going on here?"

"Let's just say she's been unfaithful."

"Ralph, we all know Karen loves the spotlight, that doesn't mean …"

"Joseph, Joseph," Ralph spoke. He was weak now. "I have proof. Photographs, everything. Times, dates. Hugh Sullivan and Karen …"

"Hugh Sullivan!" Joseph exclaimed. "He's running for the Senate."

Ralph sniggered. "Oh, he'll be running alright, but not for the Senate, by the time I've finished with him."

Joseph had never witnessed his client to be so vindictive and was still not at peace with Ralph's requests.

Joseph met up with Clive Richards and Mark. He did not want to impart the information he'd just received.

"Clive, you know about this Gina. She was married before, with her daughter, Lisa. Do you know her married name?"

Clive glanced at Mark. He had told him as much. Clive paused. "Berio – Gina Berio. Apparently her husband was involved or connected to a certain Italian family. Nothing to do with Gina, as I understand, but very unsavoury people. We don't want to go down that road."

Joseph Mendez searched his memory. "Berio. Berio. Thank you, Clive."

"Listen, I've some papers to prepare for Mark's father. I'll be back tomorrow. I may need you both here if signatures require witnessing."

Joseph departed. If his hunch was correct then a certain councillary he knew would verify the facts.

Chapter 33

Joseph Cambrio picked up the receiver. "Yeah?"

"It's Joe Mendez here, of Mendez and Mendez. Maybe you remember we tried a case some years back; you won, of course, got money for a Gina Berio?"

The name stung in Joseph Cambrio's ear. "What d'ya want? Who did ya say's calling? I don't want to talk on the telephone. Met me, one hour, Calvary Cemetery."

Joseph Cambrio replaced the telephone. A name from the past. A name he'd only spoken to recently regarding enquiries from the FBI. Gina had promised she would not divulge anything to the authorities, and yet here was a call from a lawyer. He didn't need any loose ends or trouble from Gina, especially after all those years. He believed her when she had told him only recently that her connection to Peter Berio and the Salvadori family would remain buried.

Fuck, fuck, fuck! He'd meet with this Joseph Mendez. Find out what he knew and, more importantly, what he wanted. He did not want to alert his godfather at this time; best to have all the information first.

Joseph Cambrio also remembered the condition of Gina's and her daughter Lisa's life being spared. He did not need his future jeopardised.

Chapter 34

Karen Rosenberg had initially extended her stay at the Waldorf. Gillian and Philippa, enjoying their opulence, service, and freedom being away from the Rosenberg mansion.

Karen spoke to her lawyer, Frederick Cohan.

"I advise you to move back into the Rosenberg residence. Your husband Ralph's in hospital, critically ill; you may have had a disagreement with each other, but …"

"Disagreement? That's an understatement," Karen broke in.

"Well, whatever," Cohan continued. "It is your rightful place to be in the matrimonial home, you and your family; besides, possession is nine tenths of the law and once you're esconded there it'll take a mountain and a long time to have you removed."

"He's having us cut off financially, and I know Ralph when he says he'll do something about it."

"Mrs Rosenberg, listen, you're wealthy in your own right. You're a Laithwaite, of Laithwaite's Bank, you're not going to be out on the street as long as you're in that house."

Karen considered the advice being offered, and although she had a determined nature she understood what she was being told, and anyway, it would be easier to negotiate with her husband from a position of strength.

"Thank you, Frederick. I'll organise to move back today. Speak to you soon. Gillian, Philippa, come on, we're going home."

Gillian didn't want to return. She never really understood anything. As long as there was enough money to pay her bills and keep her in her lifestyle, then she was perfectly happy.

"Do we have to?" she said.

"Yes, we do," her mother replied. "It's more important now, especially since your father's in hospital."

The girls made ready to return to the Rosenberg mansion in The Hamptons, while Karen made another phone call.

"Hugh? Karen here. I have to see you."

"I'm actually in a meeting just now, can I phone you back?"

Karen was not used to being fobbed off with excuses.

"Listen, unless you want pictures of us splashed all over the city, I suggest you meet me at the mansion. Two hours from now."

Karen didn't wait for a reply. She just hung up. "Ready girls? Good! Let's go home."

Hugh Sullivan's mind was racing. Karen's comments had rattled his concentration. He listened in motion as the other directors discussed the options of the meeting, but his mind was elsewhere. He checked his watch on more than one occasion, even lit a cigarette. He wanted the meeting to finish. He had to see Karen.

Hugh arrived at The Rosenbergs. "So, what's all this about?"

"He's got pictures," Karen replied, pouring a drink.

"What pictures?"

"What pictures do you think? Pictures of you and me."

"How? Where? Impossible."

"I can assure you, Hugh, darling – fact."

"But … we … you mean social events, that kind of stuff?" Hugh let his words linger.

"Pictures – pictures of us – at the motel. Pictures in your car. God, they're so cheap."

"How? I mean …"

"He's suspected us for some time; employed a rat-faced detective, even got tapes of our conversations. He's …"

Karen didn't finish her sentence. "The thing is, Hugh, right now, I can't afford to be seen with you, or you me. So let's cool it for a while."

"Cool it for a while? Karen, I'm running as Senator. Let's just call it all off. I can't risk anything ..."

Karen threw her glass at him. It missed and shattered off the library wall, its contents staining the bindings of the books on the shelves.

"I'll tell you when it's off. I'll also tell you otherwise, Mr bloody Senator, so don't start with me, or I'll expose you myself. Don't think I don't know about your other exploits: who you've paid, how you really do things.

"You're a real piece of work, Karen, aren't you? No wonder Ralph stays away. How stupid have I been?"

Silence fell across the room as Hugh prepared to leave.

"Next time, keep your dick in your pants, you son of a bitch," Karen shouted as she poured herself another Manhattan.

Clive Richards had heard the commotion and entered the library. He saw the broken glass.

"Everything alright, Mrs Rosenberg?"

"No, Clive, everything is not bloody well alright," she answered, taking a large gulp of her freshly poured drink.

"Karen, what's happened?"

"It's Mrs Rosenberg to you, Clive."

Clive felt the sharp rebuke.

"You're so close to him; it makes my skin crawl."

Clive closed his eyes, absorbing the words Karen Rosenberg inflicted.

"Where's Gillian?" Clive said, his eyes still shut.

"Oh, for fuck's sake, is that all you can say? Please leave, Clive; go speak to Mark. Visit Mr Rosenberg, do something, but just GET OUTTA MY SIGHT. GO! GO! GO!"

Clive was stunned by the outburst and shook his head. His heart was pounding now. He knew it was time, perhaps, to call it a day.

Chapter 35

Joe Mendez sat patiently in his Buick waiting for Joseph Cambrio to arrive. He could see the black Sedan approach and recognised its driver, even after all those years.

Joe stepped out of his car as the black Sedan came to a halt, its tyres crunching the chipped surface of the parking lot.

"I haven't got much time," Cambrio said, shaking hands. "What's all this about Gina Berio?"

"Do you know where she is, or what name she's using these days?" Mendez asked.

"Maybe. Look, you telephoned me wanting this meeting; what's it all about? Where does the Berio woman fit in?"

Joe realised Cambrio knew more than he was willing to divulge. "Okay, I'll come straight to the point. My client is possibly dying. He's making a new will and he wants to include her and her daughter Lisa in it, but doesn't know where they are. He hasn't been in touch for about twenty-odd years, but for some reason wants to make amends, or something like that. I've been instructed to locate her. I think he wants to see her one more time before he kicks the bucket. He mentioned the name Berio, and it struck a chord with me that you defended her all those years ago when an insurance policy was contested."

"You've got a good memory, Joe."

"You have to have in our game," Mendez replied.

"Look, Gina Berio continued her life as Gina Gordino. She brought up her daughter Lisa with the help of her mother. Gordino was the family name. Her own father had long since passed away, so it was just the three of them until, of course, the mother died. Gina relocated to Staten Island, and there was enough put by for Lisa to attend college. I've – we've never spoken to Gina in 20 years, so God knows what she's doing, or even if she's at the same address."

Joseph Cambrio lied. He'd only spoken to Gina a week before, after he found out the FBI were snooping about. He paused, expecting Mendez to contradict his statement, but the contradiction never came.

"So you don't have an actual address for her, then?"

"No, afraid not. Listen, the Berio affair was over a

long time ago and we intend to let sleeping dogs lie."

Joseph Mendez stared into the councillary's eyes searching for the truth, but only found a blank expression.

"So, who's your client, Joe? Who wants to include Gina in his will? Anybody we know?"

No, I doubt it, but you'll know of him."

"Oh!"

"Yes. Keep it quiet, will you? Rosenberg. Ralph Rosenberg."

"The diamond man?!"

Joseph Mendez nodded.

"Phew! Lucky Gina if she collects. Listen, if I can be of any further assistance to you, then you know where I am." With that, Joseph Cambrio departed, his car tyres raking up a dust cloud from the gravel car park as he sped away.

Joseph Mendez stood quietly. He had the feeling he had not been given all the information. He did, however, now have a surname – Gordino.

Joseph Cambrio was not pleased that Gina Gordino had resurfaced. If her presence became prominent then Michele Salvadori, his godfather, would need to be informed, and the fact that she was to be included in a will from one of the wealthiest men in America made the task of keeping her name out of the Press impossible, especially should Ralph Rosenberg die.

He decided, therefore, to check on Mr Rosenberg's condition. He remembered he'd been taken to the Mount Sinai hospital.

Changing direction, Joseph headed back to the city.

Chapter 36

Jimmy Malone stood at the Maine Memorial off 59th Columbus Circle. He waited for John Park to appear. He was about to leave when his informant ran towards him.

"Sorry, Malone. Bit of an emergency at the hospital."

"So, what have you got for us?"

"Are you willing to agree our proposal of $50,000?"

John Park inwardly wanted more, but also required to be realistic. Get what I can, he thought. After all, most of his information was overheard. He was also aware that if there was no merit in his statements Malone would certainly not be there.

"$50,000 is fine, but I want half upfront."

Malone shrugged his shoulders. "Okay, you got that." He now waved his arm above his head, which signalled another reporter to join them. He carried a sealed envelope with the $25,000 in it.

Malone handed it to Park. "It's all there. Now spill the beans, and it better be worth it."

"Okay! Ralph Rosenberg, the billionaire who was brought in with a stroke and heart attack has apparently requested that his son locate a certain Gina and Lisa, her daughter. Apparently the son didn't know of these people. Or what they're relationship to the old man was, but the words 'they're your family, find them' were said, and Ralph Rosenberg was very emphatic about it. He also dismissed his own wife and daughter Gillian. Barred them from visiting, so there's obviously a family feud."

"So what?! Every family has arguments and he's no different from anyone else; we've all got skeletons in the cupboard. You've wasted my time, Park. This isn't much of a scoop," Malone said.

"Oh! Sorry you feel that way, Malone. Does it change anything if I tell you that this Gina's married name was Berio? I've done some research on this. She was married to Peter Berio, who worked for a certain Italian family, the head of which just happens to be Michele Salvadori. Peter Berio disappeared after he viciously attacked and beat his wife, Gina. I think The Salvadori's took the appropriate action to cancel any trace to them. Berio's debts at the time were all repaid and this Gina was allowed to live with no questions asked. She had an affair with Rosenberg, so there's a good chance Mr Billionaire has a link to organised crime, and possibly the Salvadori family.

"I also have a friend in the coroner's department and a body, or what's left of it, was fished out of the Hudson recently, wearing concrete boots. I understand its identity is that of Peter Berio. It's all hush-hush meantime, but what the hell, thought I could make a few bucks being ahead of the game, and you, Malone, you and your paper would have the scoop of the century."

Malone reflected on the information he'd just heard. Ralph Rosenberg didn't like the Press. He barred them at every opportunity. Maybe, just maybe, there was a connection, and if there was a link to Michele Salvadori, it wouldn't be just the Press who'd have a field day.

Malone knew certain names in the FBI who'd be very interested. He smiled. "Okay John Park, take your $25,000 but we'll need more. Do you have or can you get access to Gina Berio's old records when she was admitted to hospital after her attack?"

John Park was not fazed. He was resourceful. The adrenaline of the money he was holding the ideal aphrodisiac.

Chapter 37

Steve, Maria and Pop sat in the small living room.

"Let's examine what we know," Steve said. ""We know Nicky's the daughter of this Gina, or we have to accept that information for now. We know The Rosenbergs are involved somehow. Nicky's been raped and beaten within inches of her life. Why?"

"Whoever did that, I believe, is acting on instructions."

"Why do you say that?"

Well, because the other murders committed to put me in the frame are too precise. Whoever did this to Nicky knew what they were doing. I was the fall guy, but someone further up the line is pulling the strings. I suspect the person who hired me."

"Who was that?" asked Maria.

Steve broke his confidentiality. "I think its Mrs Gina Rosenberg, but I don't know. It'd start to make sense to find her child but why then have her attached?"

"That's not correct, Steve. Mrs Rosenberg's name is Karen, not Gina. She's always in the social columns; always on the arm of some wealthy suitor like that Hugh Sullivan for instance, who's running for the Senate. And there's something else. If Nicky were left alive for a reason then why was a second attempt made on her life whilst in hospital? Nobody knew you'd be there."

Steve considered Maria's observations.

"I'm too old for this," Pop interjected. "And I'm not happy that you, Maria, have got mixed up in all this. Your momma would turn in her grave."

"Pop, please, let's find a solution. Stop complaining."

"Complaining, she says. Do this, do that. Pick me up, put me down, make coffee, don't make coffee. What am I to think?"

"Pop, don't think, go to the kitchen; make us all something to eat."

"Pop, Pop, Pop. You just boss me about all the time."

Steve now spoke. "Pop, listen, I'm very grateful to you and Maria. I'd have no chance without any of you."

"Steve, your face is all over the newsreels, in every bar. So where you going to go?"

"I don't know! But I want you out of here – understand?"

Maria now moved to comfort her father.

"Don't do that, that wouldn't work. He's wanted for murder and rape. I don't want you or me involved."

Steve felt bad. "Look, I'll go."

"No! Don't!" Maria said.

"But your Pop is right. Besides, I can't solve anything sitting here."

"Where will you go?"

Steve shrugged his shoulders.

Maria's father interrupted. "Listen, I'm sorry, please forgive me. You can stay. But only till you figure yourself a plan. I just don't want my little girl mixed up in anything like this. I love her," he said, smiling at his daughter.

Maria was quick to respond. "Oh, thanks Pop!" she yelled as she flung her arms around his neck and smothered him with kisses.

"Okay! Okay! Enough! Enough! I make some pasta. You!" Pop said, pointing at Steve. "You make a plan."

Steve nodded, his eyes saying thank you as Pop retired to the kitchen.

After dinner, Pop dropped Steve off at the Mount Sinai hospital. He was aware of the police presence, but moved casually with the crowds. It was visiting time. He made his way to reception.

"Looking for Ralph Rosenberg's room."

The receptionist glanced at him. He's not allowed visitors, except for his son and lawyer.

"I know," Steve said, "but I've been sent over to collect a document he was signing." He hoped it sounded plausible because he had just made it up in the spur of the moment.

"He's on the third floor."

"Hey, what firm did you say?" the receptionist asked but was too late, Steve had gone.

She was about to ring the third floor but her intake of customers put the incident out of her mind.

The third floor was busy. Steve remembered the attempt on Nicky's life, with a man posing in a doctor's white coat.

He quietly found a changing room. There were several white overcoats on hooks, and it wasn't long before he found one that fitted. Pen and clipboard in hand, Steve joined the throng in the corridor as he made his way to the nurses' station.

"Checking on Mr Rosenberg, nurse. Which room, remind me."

"First on the right," came the reply. Steve nodded and raised his clipboard as if acknowledging her reply, but used it as a shield to cover his face.

Two seconds later he came face-to-face with Ralph Rosenberg. Ralph's eyes opened. They were heavy, obviously sedated.

"Has Gina been in?" Steve asked, matter-of-factly, playing a hunch.

"Gina!" exclaimed the surprised muffled voice. "Is Gina here? You found her?"

Ralph's hand was struggling to remove his mask. "Is Lisa with her?"

Lisa echoed Steve. "Let me check."

With that, he vacated the room, full in the knowledge that there was a connection between The Rosenbergs and Gina. And who was Lisa? Maybe he meant Nicky, but he said Lisa. The thought crossed his mind of a change of name, but dismissed it. Gina was important to the old guy. He had to find out why.

Steve thought about his long-legged client, who he was now convinced was Karen Rosenberg. She had found out about Gina and her daughter, but the question still burned in his mind – why? And was Karen Rosenberg behind him being framed? Steve now suspected she was.

Next stop, the Rosenberg residence.

Chapter 38

The Godfather, Michele Salvadori, listened. "So what are you tellin' me, Joe? Gina Berio is involved with Ralph Rosenberg? He's going to include her in his will? How very nice of him. The Press will have a field day. And so will the FBI. They'll be all over us like flies on shit. This is all your doing, Joseph. All those years ago the problem could have been dealt with. Now it's come back to haunt us. What have you got to say, Mr Councillary? We listened to your reasoning. I … me … I backed you. I've treated you like a son. Is this how you repay me? Joseph, don't stand there like a schmuck. Answer me. Is this how you repay me for all my consideration?"

Joseph Cambrio couldn't explain. "An off-chance love affair, I don't think Rosenberg probably knew who she was. I mean …"

"Joseph!" Michele Salvadori shouted, "She, Gina Berio, is a direct link to us and our organisation."

"She doesn't know anything, Godfather," Joseph interrupted.

"Now you listen to me, Joseph, and don't ever interrupt me again – understand? She does; even if she is unaware of it. You do realise the consequences of this discussion? Michele Salvadori let his words sink in.

"Don't you, Joseph?" Don't you?"

"I think that would be a mistake, Godfather, I ..."

"Hey! Don't your think any further." Michele Salvadori stopped talking. "Talking is finished. Joseph, clear out your things; you are no longer councillary to our family."

"Godfather ... Please ..."

"Joseph, Joseph," Michele held him close, just as he would a son who'd let him down. "Be a man. Accept your responsibilities. But go, ... now," he whispered, in a stern voice."

Joseph Cambrio accepted his Godfather's decisions. He would clear his desk as instructed. Hopefully he would have enough time to warn Gina.

The Don summoned Marco. "Have Vinnie brought to me," he said dryly, his voice carrying an emotionless tone.

Vinnie appeared. "Godfather, how can I help you?" Whispered instructions were given and Vinnie left the Godfather's sanctuary.

Joseph Cambrio made a call to Joe Mendez. He wasn't in and so recorded the call with Joe's secretary.

He was in his car as he drove towards the large gates. His head was grasped from behind; his neck broken as he slumped over the steering wheel.

Vinnie took control and Marco joined him as they cleared the exit to complete their assignment and dispose of Joseph Cambrio's body.

***

The heads of all the other families were assembled.

"I have invited you all here to inform you that Joseph Cambrio no longer is our councillary; no longer a part of our family. He made a mistake in judgement many years ago. Some of you will remember Gina Berio, we ..."

Some hands immediately shot up in the air. Michele Salvadori acknowledged them but refrained to allow the individuals to speak.

"Apparently this Gina is linked with the famous Ralph Rosenberg and who I understand is ill in hospital. I also understand the Press and the authorities are keen to become acquainted with Mr Rosenberg and his interests, especially those of Gina Berio. Now, Joseph Cambrio accepted a condition all those years ago if we indulged in clemency. That condition, gentlemen, has been fulfilled. The purpose of this meeting therefore is to deal with the Berio woman and of course her offspring and Mr Ralph Rosenberg. I believe, and you will, no doubt, have read he is in hospital after a serious heart attack. Therefore, your job on that score should not be a difficult one. Find the Berio woman; find her daughter, Lisa. Put an end to this matter once and for all."

There was no need for further discussion. Don Michele Salvadori, the Godfather, had spoken.

Chapter 39

Steve observed the Press outside the Rosenberg Mansion. Maria had showed him a picture of Karen Rosenberg from a magazine and he now knew for certain that she was his client. The question still remained, however, why set him up? Nicky had been found. To what purpose, after all she had been brutally attacked, but not killed. Was that in the plan? And where was Nicky's mother Gina, where did she fit in all of this? Was she still alive? Steve now realised that Martin was not Nicky's real name. Old Rosenberg had got excited at the mention of Gina's name and he mentioned Lisa. Who the hell was Lisa?

Steve knew the answers to his questions lay somewhere within that house.

He now had a thought. When he had previously telephoned a posh English man had answered. He had not denied that there was no Gina when Steve asked for her by name. He just handed the phone to another; the woman of the house, Karen Rosenberg. So the butler was involved. He knew who Gina was.

Steve would start with him, find the connection.

Chapter 40

Lieutenant Chandler was at a loss. Steve Donaldson had just disappeared. Vanished like a locust in the wind.

"It's a big city, lieutenant," Johnston said, attempting to placate his boss.

"Yeah, but someone's hiding him, Johnston. We've allowed the media in on this. We exposed him, and ourselves. We haven't come up with anything or anybody who knows or has seen him. I'm getting pressure from upstairs. Someone's hiding him; got to be."

Chandler thought for a moment. "Let's pay another visit to that club, The Blue Parrot. I want a word with a certain Maria. You can come too Johnston, but keep your eyes in their sockets and your mind on the job." Chandler then added, "You are happily married, I presume?"

Johnston smiled, and answered, "Sure am, Lieutenant." He did not appreciate the significance of his superior's comment.

The two detectives entered The Blue Parrot nightclub. It had gone midnight. Chandler flashed his badge and asked for Maria.

"She's not in tonight, but Francoise may be able to help. Chandler eyed the blue-eyed blonde in front of him. "So where's Francoise," she said, glancing around reception. "She was here a moment ago, ah, yes, now I remember. She escorted a man into the club. He was quite unusual; a bad scar on his cheek, spoke with a foreign accent."

"Where is this man? Can I see your register?"

"Of course, Lieutenant."

Chandler's fingers ran down the last few entries. There was nothing unusual.

"Where is Francoise?" he asked again.

The young woman shrugged her shoulders. "Don't know; she should have been back by now. She normally works in the main part of the club, but tonight she stood in for Maria, who phoned in unwell."

Chandler and Johnston's eyes glanced at each other. Since that last visit to Maria's flat they had posted a surveillance car outside, and as yet no one had been seen arriving or leaving, which indicated that Maria was elsewhere.

"I'll go and find Francoise, lieutenant. Please excuse me."

Chandler and Johnston stood awkwardly, glimpsing other hostesses as they passed through reception to the inner sanctuary of the club.

The blonde girl returned. "Francoise is nowhere to be seen," she said now with a concerned expression on her face.

"But she was here?" Lieutenant Chandler asked.

"Yes, yes, and not long ago."

"I want to speak to the owner."

"Miss Sandy! She is never available!"

"She'll be available for me," Chandler replied, not in any mood to be dismissed.

A short time lapsed and a red haired woman appeared in a kaftan. Her makeup was too heavy and didn't really suit her. It also didn't hide the years her life had bestowed.

Chandler introduced himself and Johnston. "Is there somewhere we can talk?"

"Come with me, Lieutenant," Sandy said, as she led the detectives into private quarters.

"Now, how can I help you? What's Maria been up to?"

Chandler hesitated. "We think she could help us with our enquiries regarding Nicky Martin."

"Nicky? She's trouble. Always has been, but the punters love her. She's good for business but very volatile. Maria's smart and good-looking. How can she help you?"

"She's not in tonight," Chandler stated.

"No – phoned in sick."

"Miss Collins …"

"Oh, Sandy, please, everybody calls me Sandy."

"Okay, Sandy," Chandler said, smiling. "We believe Maria may be involved with Donaldson, our chief suspect who escaped custody three days ago. We believe Maria is either in great danger or she may be harbouring him." Chandler then produced the card she had put in Donaldson's pocket.

Sandy examined the card and Maria's phone number.

"We don't encourage relationships in the club. As you can imagine, it only leads to problems. I can't imagine Maria doing this. It's not in her nature. Nicky though; Nicky would go with anyone if it suited."

Sandy Collins was quiet, then offered "Francoise might know. She and Maria were close. Francoise has been here the longest. She doesn't sit with anybody, but she manages the club and the girls. She's on tonight."

"Miss Collins. Sandy. We've already enquired after her. She too is nowhere to be seen."

"That's odd. I saw her escorting a customer earlier tonight."

"Was it Donaldson?" Lieutenant Chandler asked.

"Well, I don't know, maybe. We weren't introduced." Sandy stood up. "Give me a moment." She instructed another hostess to locate Francoise and bring her back to the room. Time passed and there was a knock on the door.

A young hostess appeared. "We can't find her, Miss Sandy."

"Oh! That's not like Francoise. She's so reliable."

Another girl appeared. "Miss Sandy, come quickly. There's been an incident."

"What? Who? Where?"

"It's … it's Francoise. She's in the alley."

Sandy, Johnston and Lieutenant Chandler followed through the club, and outside to the alley. They found Francoise's body. Her basque was intact but her stockings were unclipped; her panties gone and her throat cut, her face ashen white with the loss of blood that stained in the snow.

"It's the same MO," Lieutenant Johnston said, examining her body.

"Damn, that son of a bitch. Where are you, Donaldson?" Chandler exclaimed out loud.

Sandy Collins had seen many a sight in her time, but she was not prepared for the one she witnessed now.

"Get the team down here, Johnston. Usual procedure, seal off the alley. No one is allowed to leave the club and I mean no one."

"That could be embarrassing, lieutenant," Sandy said quietly.

"I don't really care, Miss Collins. This is now a murder scene. Johnston, we must locate Maria. Hopefully she's still alive."

"Lieutenant, her father normally drops her off and collects her. She very rarely takes a cab or fraternises with customers."

"Her father? What's his name?"

"Pop," Sandy replied.

Lieutenant Chandler afforded himself a smile. "I mean his surname."

Sandy thought for a moment. "Bertollachi. It's Gabrielle Bertollachi. Lives in Little Italy, just off Mulberry Street."

"Johnston!" Chandler shouted.

"Got that, Lieutenant, right on it."

Chapter 41

Joseph Mendez was not happy. He couldn't contact Joe Cambrio. The trail to the Berio woman and her daughter Lisa had therefore gone cold.

Joseph meditated. "Clive Richards must know more than he's letting on, after all, he was very close to Ralph, being his butler and confidante."

***

It was not an easy atmosphere in the Rosenberg household, with Karen, Gillian and Philippa segregating themselves from Mark and Clive. Clive, of course, had to serve and obey Karen, but contact between them was strained.

"Are you visiting my husband today, Clive, with precious Mark?"

Clive remained silent for a moment, but knew he would be required to reply.

"Yes ... I understand Joe Mendez will be there too?"

"Oh, everybody will be there, Clive. Why is it you think he doesn't want me?"

"It's not my place to …"

"Not your place, Clive – huh, that's rich. It wasn't your place all those years ago to bed me either Clive, but that didn't stop you."

"Karen, I've no wish to continue this conversation."

"Oh, I see. So your little indiscretion is to go unmentioned."

Clive just stared at his master's wife. He had no intention of locking horns with her.

"So, Clive, how do you think Ralph will react when he finds out that Gillian is not his, but yours and mine? What do you think he'll do when he finds out that Nicky is his daughter and that's why Gina ended their affair? Do you think you'll be top of his favourites then, Clive? Well?!"

"Karen, the man at the moment is critically ill. You can't tell him. You can't."

"Listen Clive, you're the one who told me all those years ago about Gina and her phone call. I've bided my time long enough. Mr fuckin' Ralph Rosenberg and his precious family name will be exposed for the liar and cheat that he is. I'm going to take my revenge, and it will be so sweet."

Clive stood rooted to the spot. "You don't mean that, Karen. Think of Gillian."

"Gillian? Clive, I kept your secret, had your daughter, brought her up with Ralph thinking she was his. He's never liked her. So, how do you think he'll react when he finds out the truth?"

"He won't find out, Karen. Besides, he's too ill."

"Oh, you're wrong, Clive. He'll find out. Besides, I've already located his daughter, Nicky, and Gina won't be far behind me, and let me tell you, Clive ..."

Karen was enjoying her moment of destructive power. "He'll die realising that he never knew his true daughter. That, Clive, will be my revenge after all those years. You should be pleased too, Clive, you won't need to witness him bullying Gillian without a say. Without a father's protection."

"Karen, you're so vindictive. You're twisted inside; all this wealth and it still isn't enough. You used me, Karen. I grant you I was weak. I should have accepted my responsibilities for Gillian. We agreed that she would have a better chance in life if she was included as a Rosenberg."

"We were wrong, Clive. You were wrong. Anyway, it's all too late now. As I said, Nicky has been found. She's the girl in the newspapers; the one everybody's protecting from her attacker."

"Karen, what have you done?"

Karen blinked her long black eyelashes. "Not nearly enough, Clive. Not nearly enough."

***

Joseph Mendez had returned to the hospital.

"Joe, Joe. Good to see you, where's Gina?" Ralph said excitedly.

"Gina?! We're still working on that."

"But the doctor, the doctor mentioned Gina was here."

"The doctor?" Joe Mendez interrupted. "What doctor?" Mendez was not aware of any development. Had Mark discovered where this Gina was, and had not thought to confide in him?

"Excuse me, Ralph, just want to pop out, make a phone call, be right back."

Ralph once again replaced his mask. His breathing was heavy every time he removed it. "God, let me see Gina one more time", he whispered quietly to himself.

Joe Mendez put a dime in the pay phone and listened to the line ringing out.

"The Rosenberg residence."

"Clive, Clive it's me, Joe Mendez. I'm at the hospital. Is Mark with you?"

"Master Mark is in his father's study, going over some old papers, shall I put you through?"

"No, Clive, listen, meet me at the hospital as soon as you can. Bring Mark with you. Some doctor has told Mr Rosenberg that Gina was visiting.

"What? Mark has said nothing to me," Clive answered, and then thought about the recent conversation he had just had with Karen Rosenberg.

Chapter 42

The white Thunderbird exited through the large ornamental black and gold gates of the Rosenberg residence. Steve observed all the reporters clicking their cameras as it passed. A handsome young man ferrying a more elderly passenger was driving the car.

Steve hailed down a taxi. "Follow that T-Bird," he instructed.

"Nice car, bud. Hey, you a cop, or one of those reporters back there?"

"Neither," Steve answered. "Just drive, don't lose them. I'll make it worth your while."

The cab driver checked out his passenger through his rear view mirror. The thought never occurred to him it was Steve Donaldson whose photograph had been circulated throughout the city.

"That old man Rosenberg. All that money and at the end of the day if it's your time then we're all the same. What d'you say, bud?"

Steve didn't reply. He did not want to extend the conversation. "Just follow that car," he instructed.

"Okay, bud. Just tryin' to be friendly."

Silence reigned between driver and passenger for the remainder of the journey. Steve alighted at the Mount Sinai hospital as he watched the white T-Bird enter the parking lot. He watched the young man and his elder stride quickly into the hospital. He guessed it was Rosenberg's son and a relative, maybe a brother. He knew the drill now; obtain a doctor's coat and clipboard. He wouldn't require directions to Ralph Rosenberg's room after all, he'd already been there.

Steve watched as a greying, well-dressed man joined his two targets. All three shook hands, had a quick discussion, then disappeared inside.

Joseph Mendez, Clive Richards and Mark Rosenberg stood in Ralph's private room.

"Is Gina here?" the weak voice asked. "The doc said …"

Ralph's words trailed off as Steve, in his white coat, entered the room.

All eyes turned to face him.

"Good afternoon, gentleman. Let me tell you a story."

Steve had his hand in his coat pocket, his two fingers bulging like he had a gun. "Now, will you all introduce yourselves? Mr Rosenberg I know. Let's start with you."

Steve pointed his overcoat pocket towards Joe Mendez.

Joseph stuttered. "If you've come from the Salvadori family, you've wasted your time. Gina is not here, and none of us know her whereabouts. In fact, your councillary, Joseph Cambrio, will testify to that."

"And you are?" Steve said, ignoring Mendez's statement.

"I'm Joseph Mendez – Mr Rosenberg's lawyer. May we ask who are you?!?"

"You." Steve now pointed his coat pocket at Clive.

"Clive Richards, Mr Rosenberg's butler."

"And you?"

"I'm Mark, this is my father, Ralph Rosenberg."

"What's going on? Is Gina with you?" the bedridden voice spoke.

Steve, still keeping control by his illusion of a concealed weapon, spoke. "No, I've yet to find Gina. But I know Nicky. Someone did a pretty good job on her, but she's alive. She's young and strong and has a good chance of surviving."

Steve witnessed the bewildered faces before him, all except one: Clive Richards. He chuckled. "They don't know who she is, do they?" he started, staring at Clive Richards. "But you do. Don't you?"

"I … I …"

"It's written all over your face, Richards. Come on, spill the beans, or you'll leave me no choice."

Steve shuffled his fist and fingers in his pocket as if preparing to fire.

"Nicky? Who for God's sake is Nicky?" Mendez said.

"She's Gina's daughter, that's who," replied Steve.

Clive Richards' eyes fell closed for the second time that day. It was all going to come out. What the hell, he thought.

"Okay, gentleman, let me explain."

"Clive?" Mark said.

Ralph casually listened, his oxygen mask still in place.

Joseph Mendez said nothing. His training as a lawyer taught him to say very little.

Clive stared at his master lying in his hospital bed. "Ralph, how do I explain? Where do I begin?"

Ralph returned the stare of his confidante. "Tell me about Gina, Clive, and who's this Nicky?"

Clive shifted uneasily on his feet. "May I sit down?"

Ralph signalled with his eyes to the chair at his bedside.

"Remember, Ralph, all those years ago I found Gina's handkerchief in your overcoat, and you shared your secret of the affair you were having with her? Remember how she made you so happy?"

Ralph listened as his mind rolled back to the years long ago, picturing Gina and her beauty in his mind.

"I kept your secret, Ralph, as I promised, but maybe now's the time to tell you what happened.

Gina fell pregnant with your child. She was in a quandary. She didn't want to upset your family name and, realising the consequences of your relationship, she decided to end the affair. She never told you about the baby, and although you attempted to find her, she just vanished. She actually retook her old family name, Gordino. Gina Gordino, Lisa and Nicky.

"She telephoned the house. Spoke to me, told me she was alright and it was a baby girl. She named her Nicky. She made me promise never ever to tell you, and I swore I never would. Besides, there were other reasons for withholding the information."

Ralph was mesmerised, then slowly spoke. "Other reasons? What other reasons?"

Clive glanced at everybody in the room, and then back to his master. "Oh! They don't matter at this time. Just you get yourself better, then we'll talk."

Steve had momentarily forgotten about his hand imaging a gun in his pocket and now spoke.

"So, Nicky is Mr Rosenberg's daughter. Gina is the mother. That explains why your wife hired me to trace them. It doesn't, however, explain why I was set-up."

The others now all stared at Steve; they had forgotten about him as they held onto Clive's every word.

"I know you!" Mendez shouted. "You're the guy in all the newsreels, the one the police are searching for. The one who attacked Nicky."

"Nicky," Ralph had removed his mask now. "Nicky … I have a daughter, Nicky. A daughter with Gina."

Steve now pulled out his gun. Unfortunately it was his finger that he pointed at the men in front of him. "Hold it!" he shouted, unaware that his bluff could be seen.

Mark moved quickly but not quick enough for a pro like Steve.

"Calm down sonny, or I'll break your friggin' arm. Listen, all of you. I can help you find Gina. I'm a private eye. I've been set up for those rapes and murders, probably by the charming Mrs Rosenberg, but I've yet to prove that. I just want my name cleared. You want Gina? I can find her. Let me work with you."

Steve paused. "You can trust me."

"If we can trust you, then let me go," Mark said. Instantly Steve removed Mark from his vice like grip.

Ralph Rosenberg had already pressed the silent alert bell on his bed. Steve instinctively realised this was not the moment for a full discussion. Anyway, he had Gina Berio's other name; Gordino. He'd find her. He had to. Time was running out.

Steve opened the door as doctors and nurses ran in. "Mr Rosenberg's relapsed!" he shouted, then disappeared in the corridor.

By the time the occupants explained and followed, Steve was gone.

Chapter 43

Lieutenant Chandler and detective Sergeant Johnston arrived. They had back up in case Gabrielle Bertollachi, Maria's father, decided to cause trouble.

Further down the street two old men stood under an awning; discussing how it was difficult for them to still live in the area they'd known most of their lives. The rising costs saw most of their friends move away to Brooklyn, Staten Island, and some of them to East Harlem in the Italian Quarter.

"Hey, Gabrielle, isn't that your apartment block the police are visiting?"

Pop searched the street.

"I've got to go, Peter. My girl Maria needs me."

With that, Pop departed, but not towards his apartment; instead he walked in the opposite direction.

"Hey, Gabrielle, you don't live down there," Peter shouted.

Gabrielle just ignored his friend. He didn't turn around, just kept walking.

Maria telephoned her father's apartment. The tone just rang and rang.

"Hello, Lieutenant Chandler, NYCP. Who's calling?"

The line went dead.

"Who was that, lieutenant?"

"It wasn't Kris Kringle," Chandler replied.

"I suspect it was Maria Bertollachi. If she's not at The Blue Parrot and she's not here, where could she be, and who's with her father?"

Lieutenant Chandler paused for thought, then answered his sergeant. "With Steve Donaldson, Johnston, would be an educated guess."

A call came over the car radio.

"Lieutenant! Donaldson was at the Mount Sinai hospital. Apparently held Ralph Rosenberg, his son, lawyer and butler hostage, but when they attempted to apprehend him he escaped. Rosenberg, the diamond merchant; the one who took a major heart attack."

"The same," Johnston replied. "Where does he fit in all of this?"

The red flashing light was switched on and the car siren blew as Chandler and Johnston headed North West to Broadway and Fifth Avenue, and the Mount Sinai hospital.

Chapter 44

BILLIONAIRE DIAMOND MAN RALPH ROSENBERG LINKED TO ORGANISED CRIME

The headline appeared in bold capitals on the front page of The Times newspaper. Malone had given his editor enough of the scoop to warrant a run that day.

"Keep the pressure up, Malone, on your source, 'cos if this backfires your ass is on the line."

Malone smiled at Jim Clancy. "Is it ever anything else, boss?"

"Get outta here. Get the rest of that story."

"Sure thing."

Malone made some phone calls. He had work to do.

Michele Salvadori read The Times headline. "Who's this Jimmy Malone creature? Where's he getting his information? Marco, attend to this, and this Rosenberg, what's his beef, who's jerking his strings? Find out what he wants, it certainly can't be money. Oh, and Marco, any progress on the Berio woman?"

Marco knew his godfather did not like bad news. "Not yet, Godfather, but Porcelli and Vincent are working the streets. Something should break soon."

"Something better break, Marco. You understand?"

Marco nodded. He was well aware of Michele Salvadori's solution to a problem. The Berio woman had been an exception. His godfather would not be so kind next time.

Chapter 45

So now Steve knew who Gina and Nicky were, and the connection to The Rosenbergs. That still didn't explain Nicky's life. Where was her mother, Gina, now? Why was she not in touch with her daughter? There was obviously a chunk of her story missing.

Steve thought about Ralph Rosenberg lying in a hospital bed, and discovering that he had an unknown daughter from 22 years ago.

Steve passed a newsstand and saw the Rosenberg headlines. He purchased a copy of The Times and made his way to the nearest park.

If there was any merit to the article it would be bad press for The Rosenbergs. Steve also imagined a certain group of Italian families in the city wouldn't appreciate it either. Whether true or false, Steve reckoned it placed Ralph Rosenberg's life in danger. The fact that he was critically ill would only accelerate his demise. Steve thought about Nicky and all the punters she had entertained in her life, and if her mother Gina would also be threatened.

If Karen Rosenberg wanted revenge on her husband it would surely have been easy just to hire a hit man, and solve her problem, especially if the newspaper article was correct and The Rosenbergs were connected to organised crime. It also didn't explain of all the trouble that had been set in motion to put him in the frame for rapes and murders he didn't commit.

Steve furrowed his eyebrows. Hiring him to locate Nicky was one thing, but why involve him, or anybody else? It didn't make sense.

Steve now thought about Maria and her father. Indirectly, because of their connection to him, they were probably in danger, too. Anybody connected to the Rosenberg case would be taken out. Steve realised that included himself.

So, if Chandler and his team didn't get him, the mafia would.

Steve changed his mind about heading for The Blue Parrot. He would go to Pop's apartment in Hester Street, off Mulberry Street. He hoped he wouldn't be too late.

Maria had been alarmed when Lieutenant Chandler had answered her father's telephone and fearing the worst had made her way to Hester Street. A policeman stood outside the entrance to the apartment. Maria had to find out what was going on. She casually sauntered up to the officer.

"You look kinda bored," she said, appearing to be a nosy Italian from the neighborhood.

"Nothin' to be concerned about. Missing person, that's all. Hopefully he'll turn up soon, safe and sound."

Maria smiled, "good luck. Hope you find him."

"Hey, you from around here?" the officer asked.

"No, I live in Brooklyn."

The officer smiled. The Italian district around Mulberry and Canal Street had become very expensive and most of the original families had all but moved out. There were a handful of old friends who remained but even their days were numbered. Pop was one of them who didn't want to uproot himself. After all, his memories were here, even although most of his friends had gone.

Steve entered Kenmore Street off Lafayette, then after four blocks turned into Elizabeth Street, walked along, and turned right into Hester Street. He wanted to hurry, but paced himself, and then froze as he observed the police officer standing guard outside Pop's apartment. Steve continued into Mulberry Street and stole himself into an awning, shielding himself. He felt a hand touch him, and turned. He was so pleased when Maria fell into his arms. They hugged; then kissed.

"Hey, you two get a room," a voice shouted, from a passer-by.

"There's a café down the street," Maria said. "We need to talk. We won't be seen."

"What about your father?" Steve said, searching Maria's big, green eyes.

"Gone missing, by all accounts. He'll be out of his mind. We have to find him before the police do, because, Steve, he'll protect me but he'll offload you and just now I don't think that would benefit anybody.

"Where would he go?"

Maria shook her head. "Maybe my place? He has an old friend in East Harlem, but surely he wouldn't go there?"

"There's always The Blue Parrot," Steve offered.

"No, not really. He would only go there to collect me and he definitely would not be seen dead inside."

Steve allowed himself a smile.

"He doesn't approve of your lifestyle, then."

Maria shook her head. "Certainly not, but he loves me, and I'm all he's got."

Maria purchased some coffee and pastries. They sat quietly at a small table in the rear; Steve bringing Maria up-to-date with Nicky's identity and The Rosenbergs.

Chapter 46

Clive Richards, Mark and Joseph Mendez had returned to the Rosenberg residence in The Hamptons. All three sat in the large, opulent study, deliberating their situation and that of Ralph Rosenberg.

Karen was out of the house. She had a very private meeting with Hugh Sullivan. Philippa and Gillian had gone away for the day, so the three men could talk freely.

"What about this article?" Mark said, pointing to the headline in The Times.

Clive shrugged his shoulders. "I, for one, don't believe it. Your father never courted these kind of people, you should know, Mark, you've been close to him over the years.

"I don't think Mother would stoop to this kind of slander," Mark replied, then added "but as far as being close to dad, well, I've just found out I've a stepsister. I don't know what to think right now!"

"Well, I spoke to Joe Cambrio regarding Gina Berio. You see, she was married to a Peter Berio, as we discussed earlier, and he worked for that organisation. Apparently he attacked his wife, Gina and left her so badly beaten and raped that even his bosses couldn't condone his actions. They allowed a settlement for Gina and her daughter Lisa, which enabled them to start a new life. Her daughter Lisa was just a baby, so the families' overlords felt that nothing would be gained by killing them. I actually fought Joe Cambrio in court over an insurance claim, which was false, of course, but its proceeds gave Gina and her daughter Lisa a lump sum payment, which today would be no big deal, but 22 years ago would have been quite considerable. The fact that we now know she reused her maiden name Gordino, and resided with her mother, would allow her a fresh start and the money would go further. As far as your father's connection to organised crime, there is none; at least, not that I'm aware of."

"Clive, you've told us how they met, fell in love, and also how Gina fell pregnant with Ralphs' child, Nicky. I, for one, don't think Ralph was aware of Gina's first husband's escapades, which proves to me he had nothing to do with these kinds of people."

"How do we prove that?" Mark said.

"Well, I'm sure Joe Cambrio could verify a few points for us, but I've not been able to contact him."

"That, gentlemen, also concerns me." Clive Richardson remained silent for a moment, then spoke in his usual articulate English accented voice. "You think, Mr Mendez that this Joe Cambrio would have contacted you, especially after the article appearing in the newspaper."

Joseph nodded, then added, "that may mean, Mark, your father could be in great danger."

"How?" replied Mark, sitting forward, his body erect, the expression on his face worrying.

"Because these intolerable people don't leave any loose ends. The fact that someone has dropped a line to a newspaper journalist means there's at least smoke. In their minds, anyway. The authorities will investigate all your father's dealings. They'll want to look at all records and all transactions going back years, on the assumption that they'll find a link to Michele Salvadori or one of the families within his organisation."

"So what?" Mark replied, still not appreciating the severity of the situation.

"Well, it places your father's life in great danger. These people don't make threats, Mark, they just take action and worry about the consequences later."

The realisation hit Mark like a bomb. "What are we going to do?" he gasped.

Silence reigned again; then Clive spoke. "I suggest we enlist the help of the PI we met today. Oh, I know he's wanted by the police, but I think that will give him and ourselves an edge, and let's face it gentlemen, we need all the help we can get."

There was a long pause. Then Joseph Mendez agreed. Mark, with no other solution to the situation, reluctantly accepted the decision.

Clive Richards nodded his head. "How do we contact him?" he asked.

"Let me try Joe Cambrio one last time," Joseph Mendez replied. You never know what may turn up.

The meeting of the three ended; Mark needed time on his own. It had been quite a day, all things considered. He now understood what his father meant by Gina and Lisa being part of the family. There was also Nicky. He now had a stepsister whom he'd never met. God, what a day!

Clive kept his own company. He had personal business to reflect upon. Karen Rosenberg was behind all of this, but he couldn't allow her to destroy his life, or take Gillian and Ralph down with her.

He would need to confront her once again.

Chapter 47

Lieutenant Chandler was going berserk and, as usual, Johnston was taking the brunt of his superior's outbursts as Francoise's murder was bringing new attention from the media. It also put every club on the alert as their hostesses could be in danger.

The girls in The Blue Parrot all respected Francoise, and the fact that she never got involved with customers increased their danger. Why did the police allow a rapist and murderer to escape, and still be unable to apprehend him?

The focus on Donaldson's recapture was more acute now, especially with the festive season on its way. Nobody wanted to party and let their guard down while he was at large.

Lieutenant Chandler had come off the phone. His superiors were granting him an extended budget to increase manpower on the case, but they wanted results and they wanted them quickly.

"Where is that son of a bitch, Donaldson?" Chandler shouted at his sergeant. "He can't just disappear. Did you check out Maria at the club?

"Yes, Lieutenant, but she's still not appeared. Nobody's seen her, and we know she's not at her house, or her father's."

"Oh God, don't let her be next," Chandler interrupted.

Steve quietly brought Maria fully up-to-date with everything he knew; Nicky's relationship to The Rosenbergs via her mother, Gina. The murders of Frank Coulson, Louise Volosso; even George Hunter. He explained about the man who smoked the strong, Turkish cigarettes, and the Salvadori connection through Gina's first husband, Peter Berio. He sat back, realising how much trust and faith he had bestowed on Maria. A woman he hardly knew. He also realised that Maria's father; Pop, would not be so responsive.

Maria listened to Steve's statement without interruption.

"If what you say is true, then why has Nicky never made contact with her mother, or even The Rosenbergs?"

"Maria, Nicky actually doesn't know who she is. For whatever reason, she ran away from home; she didn't go to Ralph Rosenberg, her father, because she didn't know he existed. Anyway, there are many reasons why kids leave home. Not everybody has a loving situation. Sometimes we – I mean, kids – have no choice." Steve momentarily remembered his own experience, but dismissed the thought. He had no desire to rekindle his own story.

"Well, I know Nicky never spoke about her mother. All us girls have various reasons for doing what we do. Nobody really delves into each other's past unless the girl wants to discuss their business. Nicky was a loner; a hothead. Great for the punters, and the club. Sandy always made sure Nicky had the best, because she invariably brought in the most money. She seemed to be turned on by these men. Dancing was her thing, and no one could change that, not even Joe Marshall. He wanted to take her away from this life, give up her dancing. It wouldn't have worked, and I guess he was lucky to have escaped her clutches."

Steve had forgotten all about Joe Marshall. He never did receive that information from his friend, George Hunter. Steve reflected as he realised he never would.

"So, what's our next move, then?" Maria enquired.

"First of all, let's find your Pop. We need to make sure he's okay, and then get him on our side. Then I have to enlist the help of young Rosenberg and Clive, his butler."

"And how do you propose to do that, with the whole city searching for you?"

Steve smiled at Maria.

"Leave that to me," he said, as he kissed her forehead.

Maria contacted her boss, Sandy, at The Blue Parrot and was shocked to learn of Francoise's death. She and Maria had been close, and Maria could not hide the anxiety in her voice.

"Where are you, Maria?" Sandy asked, hoping she would be able to inform Lieutenant Chandler of her whereabouts, and save another of her girls.

"That's not important Sandy," Maria replied, as she hung up the handset in the phone booth.

She then burst into tears, as she imparted her bad news. Steve held her in his arms.

The next day Steve stood silently in Ralph Rosenberg's study. He was hidden by the heavy brocade drapes that hung like an iron curtain, keeping the room snug and warm.

There had been movement in the house, but as yet no occupant had ventured in his area. It seemed like eternity, then Steve heard the heavy wooden door open, and recognised the voices of Mark Rosenberg and Clive the butler. He waited patiently, hoping to catch their drift, and some more information of his case.

The two men were whispering, which Steve thought was strange. Had they sensed him and his hiding place, or was there another reason? He strained his ears but to no avail, then the large study door opened again. Were they leaving before he had his chance of speaking to them? Steve was proved wrong as he now heard a very authoritative, matter-of-fact female voice. He recognised that tone, and so peeped through the join where the two drapes met.

It was Karen Rosenberg. Full on as ever; still as striking looking.

"Clive, I'll be staying in for dinner tonight, you can let Emma know. I also need to talk to you …" she glanced at her son, Mark, then added "privately!"

Karen vacated the study, leaving a silence between Clive and Mark. Steve realised this was his opportunity and stepped into full view from behind the curtains.

"What the hell?" Clive shouted. "Call the police, Mark!"

"Stop! Listen to me, both of you," Steve said, raising his arms; the palms of his hands facing the two men. "I'm here to offer you my assistance. I believe, and I'm sure you both realised, that Mr Rosenberg's life is in danger."

"Oh, from you, Mr Donaldson?" Clive replied sharply.

"No, Clive, from a certain Italian family, and probably also his wife." Steve glanced at Mark. "Sorry, I hope I'm wrong on that one, but I have my reservations. It's just I don't have all the answers right now."

"Mark, call the police. Tell them we have an intruder in the house. Tell them we have their Mr Donaldson."

Clive let his instructions fill the air.

"I don't think so," Steve said, his hand bulging his pocket.

"Oh, you've pulled that one before, Mr Donaldson, it won't work a second time."

Steve produced his snub-nosed .38. "Oh, you think so, Clive?"

Mark and Clive stood aghast, both raising their hands.

"Oh, put your hands down, I'm offering my help, otherwise why do you think I'd risk myself breaking-in here?"

"Okay, Mr Donaldson, why? Explain yourself," Mark said.

Steve still pointed his gun. "As I said, the last time we met I told you I've been set-up; framed! Your mother hired me – that's one thing – but to frame me, and have all those murders planned, I can't understand. Your father has found a daughter he never knew he had, and you, Mark, a sister. There's also the newspaper article. I assume you've both read it? Someone is trying to not only discredit your father, but destroy the Rosenberg family. They want me to be a fall guy. Why? I need that answer. Clive, I believe you know more than you're revealing."

Clive Richards didn't reply. He kept his nerve.

"You and Mr Rosenberg obviously have something between you; why don't you explain that? Tell Mark, tell us both what it is you're hiding."

"Nothing, I'm hiding nothing. Karen; Mrs Rosenberg and I, I mean. This has nothing to do with me."

Steve knew he had hit a nerve.

"Clive, come clean. We can't resolve this issue, or save anyone else from being killed if you keep quiet."

"I don't know what you're talking about," Clive replied.

It was Mark who spoke. "It's okay, Clive, whatever is between you and my mother; you can tell us. You've always served my father so well, been there for him, what is it Clive? Tell us. Tell me, now."

Clive shuffled his feet. "It just happened, it wasn't planned. We ..."

Chapter 48

Maria had contacted her father. He was in East Harlem.

"Pop, you don't understand. Steve is …"

"No! No! No! Maria. It is you who does not understand. I wash my hands of all of this, and if you persist with this, and this man, then this time I wash my hands of you. This time, Maria, it's too much; too much."

"Pop, please. I need your help. We need your help. Steve is innocent, and another innocent man will die if you don't help."

"It is nothing to do with me," Pop paused, then said "and nothing to do with you, Maria. Get out now, while you still can."

"Pop! I beg you."

Maria's father fell silent. He shook his head. "I can't, Maria."

"You mean you won't, Pop."

Again, her father shook his head.

"You remember Francoise at the club, Pop?"

"Francoise, of course. She goes back a long time with you."

Maria hesitated. "She's dead, Pop. Murdered and raped." Maria let her words sink in. "And Pop, Steve Donaldson was with me."

Maria waited. Still her father did not respond.

"Pop, I need your protection. Something is very wrong and bad. It could be me next time … Pop … Pop, please."

Gabrielle Bertollachi studied his daughter. He loved her very much. She reminded him of her mother, and her memory flooded into his mind. She would not have denied Maria anything, and he knew that. Reluctantly, and against better judgement, Pop replied.

"So, where do we find your Steve Donaldson, and what do you want me to do?"

"Pop, Pop, thank you, I love you."

"I didn't say I agreed, but your mother would have wanted me to help you, God bless her. So Maria, I love you, you're my baby. Let's finish this thing. How do we meet with your Steve Donaldson? He may need that wig and outfit again if we're to move about this city with everybody searching for him."

Maria laughed as she thought of Steve in his disguise, and also with the huge relief that her father had agreed to help.

Chapter 49

"Clive, where are you?"

It was Karen's voice. She was returning to the study. Quickly, Steve re-hid behind the drapes; he prayed Mark and Clive would not give him away and co-operate with him.

Karen entered. "Ah, you're still here. I need to talk to you; I'll be in my room."

"Eh – excuse me Mrs Rosenberg." It was unusual for Clive to offer any excuse, but he mustered his courage on this occasion, as he glanced at Mark. Steve thought Clive was about to blow his cover. His gun was ready. "Young Mark has some papers to go over for his father. Is it okay if I come to you once I've finished here?" Clive paused. "It won't take long."

Karen, taken by surprise by Clive's excuse, stared at her son.

"Dad has requested some old information, and Clive was helping me sort it out. We shouldn't be long."

Karen appraised her son. "Don't be long, Clive," she said coldly, then added "I suppose I can wait a little longer."

"Thank you Mrs Rosenberg," Clive answered, well aware of Steve hiding behind the study drapes.

Karen returned to her room. She would shower and change for dinner. She opened her vast dressing areas walk-in closet, filled to the brim with all the top fashion house products.

"What shall I wear," she mused. "I've nothing to wear."

Steve reappeared. "Okay, gentlemen, do we have a deal?"

Both Mark and Clive nodded, and Steve returned his revolver to his pocket.

"Your father is in the Mount Sinai hospital. I think he should be moved."

"Moved?" both men echoed.

Steve nodded. "He's a sitting duck in there. The police can't fully protect him, anyway, they're concentrating most of their efforts locating me. The Salvadori family and associates will close down any link to them. It will look like an accident; disconnect his life support. By the time the medics will realise it'll be too late."

"What are you proposing?" Clive asked.

"I need you to help me relocate him to another hospital where he can receive treatment, but checked in under another name."

"You're mad. We can't just go taking Mr Rosenberg casually down a corridor without medical help. We wouldn't know where to start. His condition is critical," Clive said, "it can't be done."

"It better be done, Clive," Steve replied. "Because if we don't then I fear Ralph's condition won't be critical, 'cos he'll be dead. There's no time to lose. We must go now, tonight."

The Rosenbergs black, long wheel-based limousine glided down the driveway towards the large black and gold gates. Steve wore a peaked cap, as did Mark, who sat in the front with him. Clive was the passenger in the rear, and shielded most of his face with a newspaper.

Steve had planned it this way as the photographers at the entrance would automatically flash their cameras into the back of the limo, ignoring the front-seated occupants. He hoped that he and Mark would not be seen, and therefore nothing unusual would be reported.

Karen didn't hear the limo leave from the car pool. She was too busy pampering herself for her meeting with Clive Richards. Oh, she was going to have such sweet revenge before she confronted her husband with the truth.

They arrived at the limo entrance of the Mount Sinai hospital, and made their way towards Ralph Rosenberg's room; the three of them picking and adorning white coats, as Steve instructed.

"We need help. Mark, you speak to your father. Clive, I need your assistance." Steve grabbed a stethoscope from a table and hung it around Clive's neck. "We need a medic to help us with this next bit, and then we need an ambulance."

"You are mad. Mad," Clive said.

"Clive, it'll be alright. Generally, people just accept what they see. It's all perception. Act with a sense of urgency and everything will be fine."

Clive approached a young intern. "I'm Dr Windsor. Here to transfer my patient, Ralph Rosenberg, to the Memorial Hospital in Sleepy Hollow." Clive read the notes Steve had scribbled on his clipboard. "May I have your assistance, please? We have an ambulance waiting."

John Park searched Clive's face, and turned towards the nurses' station.

"Come on, come on, there's no time to lose," Clive, posing as Dr Windsor, said, with his cultured English accent.

John Park thought it strange, but who was he to offer an opinion? Besides, it was in his interest to be involved in any move of Ralph Rosenberg, which could only help when he next contacted Jimmy Malone of The Times.

John Park set up a trolley and portable oxygen and drip, which allowed Ralph to be moved.

"Does Dr Hillberry know about this," John Park asked.

"Of course," Clive replied. "It was he who authorised it."

John Park shook his head. "Strange, to go to a lesser hospital, but if that's the way of it, who am I to question anything?"

Steve held in his grin, and Clive helped wheel the trolley with his master on it along the corridor towards the lift, muttering to himself, "unbelievable."

An ambulance was secured, and Steve gave instructions to go to Sleepy Hollow via Downtown General hospital.

"Why are we making a detour?" Mark asked, concerned that his father would be travelling more than necessary.

"Because, Mark, that's where Nicky, your sister is, and your father's daughter that he's never met. I think it's time they were both united, don't you?"

Mark gulped. "Yes," he said, "but let's not be too long about it."

Steve smiled. "I don't want to be any longer than I have to be. I've other loose ends to tie up. Get the lights and sirens on, we're an emergency vehicle, for Christ's sake."

"That's cute," Mark stated. "No traffic problems."

Again, Steve smiled.

Picking Nicky up as a transfer from Downtown General went smoothly, and they then proceeded to Sleepy Hollow

It was a long journey, just under the hour, even with the sirens. Staff were on hand when the ambulance appeared. Mark and Steve, with the help of John Parks, informed the staff of their patients' conditions, Mark making it clear that a very large donation to the hospital would be forthcoming, if discretion and co-operation was given to his father and Nicky.

"Can you stay here, Clive? You too, Mark."

"No worries, I don't intend to be anywhere else."

"Good," replied Steve. "I'll be back as soon as I can."

With that, Steve borrowed a member of staff's car and headed back to New York and his office. He had not been back there for several weeks, and hoped it would be safe. He needed somewhere to think out his next move.

Chapter 50

"Godfather, we have soldiers all over the city, there's no trace of this Donaldson."

"What about Rosenberg and this girl, Nicky?"

"We acted on information, but both have been removed. Transferred, or something; Rosenberg from Mount Sinai, Nicky from Downtown General, but nobody's talking."

Michele Salvadori slammed his hand hard on top of his desk. "Marco, I ask you, do I look like a fool?"

"No, Godfather."

"Well, no one just checks out of a hospital without the relevant paperwork being completed; far less two people from two different hospitals."

"Yes, Godfather?"

"Don't 'yes, Godfather' me, Marco. Find out who's got them. Did we find the Berio woman?"

Marco lowered his head. "Not yet, Godfather. We traced her to her home, but she too has gone, but we know she calls herself Gordino now."

"And her daughter? Lisa, was it?"

"What of her?" Again, Marco gave a negative answer.

"Get out; get out of my sight, Marco. I am holding you personally responsible to find these people – you understand?" the godfather yelled.

Marco knew only too well what Michele Salvadori meant.

"I'll do my best, Godfather."

"Marco … just do it. Get it done. Tell me when you've located them. Call in as many favors as you require. We've got to shut this down, capisce?"

Marco nodded, and bowed to his godfather.

Michele Salvadori, in a softer voice, spoke once more. "Marco, dear Marco, many years you have served me and the family. I have faith in you, now go with my blessing, but find them."

Marco departed, leaving Michele Salvadori to reflect. He was getting too old for all this crap.

Across the city, Chandler's office was in chaos.

"So, somebody just waltzes into Mount Sinai hospital, removes Rosenberg without anybody noticing, or checking, and then in a stolen ambulance, abducts Nicky Martin from Downtown General and disappears? It's not friggin' possible. I bet that son of a bitch Donaldson has a hand in this. It smacks of his style. Oh! Excuse me, I'm just stealing a patient of yours," Chandler mimicked sarcastically.

"Lieutenant," Johnston interrupted.

"What is it? Somebody else gone missing? For Christ's sake, what are we running here?"

"Lieutenant, we just got a call, an enquiry from a woman. She wants to know why her limo was left abandoned at the Mount Sinai hospital."

"Oh, for fuck's sake! Oh, I just lost my limo, oh dear. Get outta here."

"Lieutenant, the woman was Mrs Rosenberg."

"What! So her car has been stolen and used as part of deception and abduction of her husband. It gets worse, Johnston. Fuck!"

"Lieutenant, she categorically states that the only person with access to its lock-up was her son Mark and her butler Clive Richards."

"Your point is?"

"I think if we locate them, we'll find Mr Rosenberg, Nicky, and our friend, Donaldson."

"Okay." Chandler began to compose himself. "Check every hospital and clinic in and around New York. They can't have gone far, especially given the condition of the two patients. Get back to me if anything turns up."

"Oh, there's one other strange thing."

"Yeah, what's that?"

"Michele Salvadori's limo was seen on Manhattan toll bridge, heading towards the city. Now, you know that man never comes out of that fortress without good reason."

Chandler pondered. "Maybe the article in The Times has got legs to it. Maybe there is a connection between Salvadori and Rosenberg. Are we tailing him?"

"Yes sir, two cars, normal procedure."

"Okay, keep me posted. I'll bring the captain up to date, then I'll be right with you."

Chapter 51

Steve stealthily moved towards his office. There was no police in sight. He was grateful for that. He had arranged to meet Maria, hopefully with her father, in order to plan their next move, reuniting Nicky and Ralph Rosenberg. He now had good news to tell Maria.

His office was in darkness, the closed sign still on the door from the last time he had been there. He entered, allowing his eyes to adjust to the dim room.

"Don't move a muscle mister, if you want to see another day," the woman's voice said from a darkened corner. "I'm armed, and don't think I won't use it if I have to."

Steve shrugged his shoulders. Whoever it was, it wasn't the police, and it certainly didn't sound like a member of the mob.

"What do you want?" Steve asked.

The woman's voice was hesitant. "Just answer this question. Did you attack Nicky Martin and beat her after raping her?"

Steve paused before responding.

"Well, did you, Mr Donaldson?"

"So you know who I am," Steve said. "May I ask who you are?"

"Never mind. Just answer the goddamn questions."

Steve sighed. "No, I did not."

"The police think you did," the woman said. "Looking for you all over, so what's the story?"

Steve reckoned he'd nothing to lose. If he took evasive actions in the dark, someone was sure to be hurt. The shots would be heard and the whole district would be overrun with cops in minutes. He therefore decided to tell the truth. He had nothing to lose.

"I was hired to find Nicky. I was set up – why? I don't know. Someone has taken a lot of trouble to make sure I'd be put away for a long, long time. I don't know the reason; all I know is that I had to locate Nicky, and possibly her mother, Gina."

The woman's voice sounded from the dark corner of the office. "Gina? What do you know about Gina?"

Steve was curious so he continued, keeping his mind sharp. "Gina Gordino. She's Nicky's real mother. Nicky Martin is just a front name. Apparently, old man Ralph Rosenberg had an affair with her; Nicky was the result but he never knew, and neither did Nicky. She's had a hard life; became a dancer in one of the clubs on the street. Not the best lifestyle to have as a young woman. I bet her mum misses her."

"Is she going to be alright?"

"I hope so," Steve replied. "Got a good chance. I've relocated her beside her father, Ralph Rosenberg. I don't know how long he's got, but at least they'll be together for a while. She …"

"Stop! Don't say anymore," Gina said, as she lowered her gun and stepped towards Steve out of the shadows.

"I'm Gina Gordino," she said, extending her hand.

Steve sighed with relief. "Well, pleased to meet you, Gina."

Both smiled at each other when a horn beeped urgently from outside.

Steve strode to the window and peeped out the corner of his blind. It was Pop's old car. Maria had found him.

Steve turned to Gina. "Would you like to see Nicky and Ralph one more time?"

"Oh, Mr Donaldson. Do I, do I."

"Okay, let's go. We haven't much time."

Steve and Gina Gordino entered Pop's car, Steve making the introduction.

"Hey. How many people involved in this thing," Pop said. "It's like a zoo. And I don't like it, and I don't like you, Mr Donaldson."

Steve just smiled as he glanced at Maria, and then Gina.

"Pop, just drive to the destination." Memorial Hospital, Sleepy Hollow."

A pair of eyes observed silently as the watcher hailed a cab and another strong, Turkish cigarette butt fell to the ground.

The taxi followed but kept a discreet distance behind Pop's car. The taxi driver as usual attempted conversation but was ignored, and therefore silence dominated the journey.

The taxi, without warning, pulled over.

"Hey, what you doin? I told you to follow that cab."

"Hey, bud, this is way off my beat. Not even my jurisdiction. Where we going anyhow?"

"I've got the money," his passenger said, realising time was of the essence to catch up to Steve Donaldson and his party.

"Look, you some kinda weirdo? Follow that car. You think this is the movies, eh?"

The taxi driver never felt a thing as the sharp stiletto blade slit his throat.

Pop spoke. "Sleepy Hollow's too far. It'll take us an hour at least."

"I know, Pop, I've already done that journey twice today, there and back, but it's far enough out of the city to be completely safe. No Lieutenant Chandler, and even the Salvadori family won't think of it."

"This is madness. I tell you again, madness. I don't even know these people. Maria, help me out here," Pop said to his daughter.

"Pop, let it go. We're going to reunite these lovely people with their family, get Steve's name cleared, hopefully bring the real murderer to justice, and be able to continue our lives safely."

"Aahh! I don't like it."

"Mamma would have said ..."

"Your mamma's not here, Maria. I am. I'm doing this thing, but I don't like it."

They all fell silent as Pop travelled his car ever onward towards Sleepy Hollow.

Steve glanced out of the rear window. There was no one behind them. Then, as he began to turn back, he glimpsed the faint glow of headlights, and with their reflection the car behind was travelling at speed.

"Pop, you make this thing go any faster?"

Pop didn't answer, but Steve felt the sudden increase as Pop floored the accelerator. The lights behind were gaining on them.

Pop's car took the turn-off for the hospital.

"Pop, could you stop a moment, please?"

Pop brought his car to a halt, but kept its engine running.

"Look, I've something to do."

Maria was now alarmed. "Steve, what is it?"

"Oh, nothing really, but we may have been followed. I just want to make sure. The hospital reception will be expecting us. Give them my name. Gina, you tell them you're Nicky's mother. Now, I left Ralph Rosenberg and Nicky in the same room. It's actually a ward of four, but they're the only two in it. So there'll be plenty of space to sit and catch up. I'll be along as soon as I can."

Steve kissed Maria as Pop shook his head.

Pop's car sped off towards the main hospital entrance while Steve hid in the trees at the side of the road. Five minutes lapsed, then he heard the engine; its gears were changing down as it slowed.

The yellow taxi passed him, its illuminating sign unlit, and Steve could see the outline of its driver. Steve stiffened as he recognised the face and black feroda hat.

The taxi slowly entered the car park, and came to a halt in a solitary parking bay furthest from the hospital entrance.

Steve watched as the man walked into reception, but instead of going to the desk went immediately to a payphone booth. He dialled.

Steve watched as the man replaced the handset, then with a frustrated expression on his face, redialled. Steve wondered who he was calling. His hunch was to Karen Rosenberg, but she was in The Hamptons; a long way away.

That bought Ralph Rosenberg, Nicky, and Gina time. Time that they had all lost and time right now that Steve needed.

Chapter 52

Michele Salvadori arrived at the Mount Sinai hospital on One Gustave L, adjacent to Fifth Avenue, with his entourage.

"What you people running here?" he said out loud. "Where is Ralph Rosenberg? You say gone, you don't know. Someone took him. Stole an ambulance. What's goin' on here? This is a hospital, for Christ's sake."

"Now, Mr …" Dr Hillberry started, attempting to calm his visitor's outbursts.

"It's Mr Salvadori, Dr … Hillberry," Michele said, reading the nametag.

"Well, Mr Salvadori, I'm afraid I have to …" Dr Hillberry's voice trailed off as he realised Michele Salvadori's name.

"Mr Salvadori, let me explain. I … I …"

Michele raised his hand. "You have to do better than that, doctor. Where did they go? You, or someone in here, must have cleared them. Someone must have known what equipment, medicines, he required. Someone, doctor. Someone like you."

"Mr Salvadori, please, I can assure you. I don't …"

Again, Michele Salvadori spoke. "I don't do – don't. Marco, Vincent, take this man outta here. And find out where Rosenberg is."

"Luciano, any news?"

"No boss, but Maggio has found out that the girl in the newspapers, you know, the dancer that was beaten, has also disappeared. Apparently a doctor and an ambulance collected her. Said she was being transferred."

"Transferred? To where, Luciano?"

Luciano shrugged his shoulders. I don't know."

"Does Maggio know?"

Again, Luciano shrugged his shoulders. Michele Salvadori mirrored him.

"Stop doin' that, you stupid son of a bitch. Why are you still here? Speak to Maggio, find out – FIND OUT!" Michele yelled. "God, I'm surrounded by idiots!"

Sirens were heard and instinctively the Godfather realised it was the police.

"Okay, let's go." Michele signalled to the rest of his soldiers with his forefinger. "You all better start to find this motherfucker."

Lieutenant Chandler arrived, just as Michele Salvadori vacated the scene, amidst all the commotion he left behind.

"You heard him say Downtown General on William Street," Chandler repeated after interviewing a witness.

"Johnston, let's go, we have a lead."

Chapter 53

The telephone rang and rang at the Rosenberg mansion. Karen heard it ring but assumed Clive Richards would answer it; after all it was one of his duties.

The ringing was persistent, its tone continuous.

"Oh, for Christ's sake! Clive, Clive, answer that telephone."

No reply came. Karen did not appreciate that Clive Richards and her son, Mark, were long gone while she had been busy pampering herself.

Karen, now infuriated, answered the call.

"I told you never to call me, especially not here."

"I know," the voice said. "But I thought you should know that Mr Rosenberg has in fact been reunited with Nicky, and if I'm not mistaken, her mother Gina as well."

"How? Impossible. Where are you?"

"This is going to cost. I've been put to a lot of trouble."

"No, you listen. I paid you. You went over the score. You were supposed to frame Donaldson, but you've obviously over reacted."

"Don't you want to know where they are?" the voice carried on calmly, ignoring his employer's patronising. Karen stopped talking.

"Of course, tell me."

"Another $20,000."

"What! Don't be comical."

"Okay, bye," the voice said, then paused for effect.

"You still there, Luther?"

A soft chuckle broke out down the telephone line.

"We have an agreement?"

"We have," Karen replied. "Now, where are they? And are you with them?"

"I'm with them here in the Memorial Hospital in Sleepy Hollow."

"Sleepy Hollow? Where's that?"

"777 N Broadway, Winchester County."

"But that's over an hour and a half."

"Yes it is. I wouldn't waste any more time," Luther said, then chuckling again, "I'll look out for you," as he hung up.

The white Mercedes sports car departed The Hamptons, speeding past reporters at the gates of the Rosenberg mansion. Karen was driving. Her silver white pearl handle gun lay on the passenger seat.

"You're gonna pay, Mr fuckin' Ralph Rosenberg," she muttered, as she headed north.

Luther returned to the taxi. He'd wait for Karen to arrive, then they'd all have some fun. He lit up another Turkish cigarette, inhaled deeply, and then blew the smoke out of the window into the cold night air.

He was unprepared for Steve's attack.

"Got you this time, motherfucker."

Steve held him by the throat. "So, you like raping and murdering women? You like stealing their panties, beating them senseless? You're sick, pal, you know that? Sick. Now, who are you working for?" Steve yelled, inwardly aware of the answer. He just required confirmation.

"Who?" he yelled again, when no response came. "Why was I set up? Is it Karen Rosenberg?" Steve shouted, as he slapped Luther's face.

Luther was tough enough and wriggled. He dropped his cigarette on the carpet floor, which allowed him one hand to be free, and retaliated with all his might.

Steve and Luther beat each other in the confined space of the taxi, the dropped, lit cigarette taking hold on the passenger floor. The pointed silver stiletto pierced Steve's abdomen, but luckily didn't penetrate, as Steve administered a karate chop on Luther's throat. As Luther fell back, stunned, and dropping the knife, Steve twisted Luther's head, and broke his neck.

"That's for George Hunter, you bastard."

Steve felt the pain where the stiletto had penetrated, and rolled out of the car, the snow stinging his wound.

An explosion erupted as the car burst into flames. Steve witnessed Luther's body on fire, but knew the assassin would feel nothing; he was already dead.

Steve was unaware of the other charred body of the taxi driver in the trunk, as the car's petrol tank exploded, incinerating everything within.

Alarms rang in the hospital when staff witnessed the explosion of the car in the parking lot. Steve limped back inside and was given immediate assistance.

"I have to speak to Maria," he said, struggling for breath. "She's with Ralph Rosenberg and his daughter we brought in earlier."

"You need attention, Mr…"

"Donaldson," Steve replied. "Patch me up. I must talk to them"

Steve entered the private ward where Ralph Rosenberg and Nicky lay side by side in separate beds; Gina talking quietly to both of them. Clive Richards and Mark sat at the end of Ralph's bed, listening as history was being unfolded.

Maria and her father sat together in the middle of the floor, witnessing everything.

Steve entered, and Maria rushed towards him, alarmed that he was obviously hurt. She embraced him.

"I'm okay," he said, removing her arms from around his neck. "How's everybody here?"

Gina turned and smiled. "I think we're all going to be alright now, thanks to you, Mr Donaldson."

Steve smiled, relieved that it was all going so well. But he knew there was another piece of the jigsaw missing that needed to be exposed.

Chapter 54

Michele Salvadori and his troop descended on the Downtown Hospital like ants in a heap. The Godfather was in no mood for excuses, and after much painful persuasion, received the information of Nicky's transfer and Ralph Rosenberg.

"Where did they go? You better tell me, or you'll wish you were dead by the time I'm finished with you."

The frightened medic shook his head. "I don't know." Then within a few moments of increased pain administered to his vital organs, replied "The Memorial Hospital, Sleepy Hollow."

"Sleepy Hollow, where's that?"

Vincent stepped forward, and whispered in his godfathers' ear.

"How far is it, and how long till we get there?"

"'Bout an hour, boss, if the traffic is light."

Michele Salvadori wasted no time. "Let's go, before the cops arrive."

Lieutenant Chandler and Detective Sergeant Johnston arrived at the Downtown Hospital five minutes after the Salvadori party had departed for Sleepy Hollow.

Chandler was given all the information he required.

"Shall we radio whoever's in charge down there in the County Sheriff's department?" Johnston asked.

"Yeah, no, wait. Hold fire," Chandler replied, his brows down, his mind working quickly. "How far did you say Sleepy Hollow is?"

Another officer shrugged his shoulders. "About 33 to 40 miles, maybe, say, 45 minutes to one hour, depending on traffic and weather."

"We'd cut that time with our emergency sirens," Chandler said, still obviously deep in thought.

"Johnston, that newspaper article referred Rosenberg being linked to the mob and especially the Salvadori family. There's obviously a connection between this Berio woman and Rosenberg, which may just give us the link to Salvadori and the rest of his family."

"What are you suggesting, Lieutenant?"

"I'm suggesting we don't involve those clowns at the Sheriff department in Sleepy Hollow, they'll make things too obvious, and before we know where we are, we'll lose Salvadori, the girl, and any connection to the Rosenbergs. I think we should handle this on our own; bring them in at the last moment just to keep protocol correct. We certainly don't want them bungling this one. I've waited a long time to get Michele Salvadori. I don't need some fat-arsed sheriff playing the lone ranger and balsing it up."

"What are you suggesting, Lieutenant?"

Chandler looked at his watch; he was calculating the journey. He realised that if the Salvadori family had only left five minutes before he arrived at Downtown Hospital, there was very little point in charging down the roads and expressway, all lights blazing. They would invariably overtake Salvadori, and that Chandler did not want.

Getting to Rosenberg and the girl, Nicky, was one thing. Catching Michele Salvadori red handed was quite another. Besides, there may not even be any link, but he and his department would have a better chance of a conviction on any score if he apprehended the Godfather in question committing a felony.

"Johnston, as I said, we'll handle this one ourselves. We'll bring in the County Sheriff at the appropriate time, but for the moment let's give them the time to really dig themselves a hole."

Johnston appreciated how his boss was thinking. He didn't agree with it all, but had no choice but to go along with his superior.

A telephone call was made from a public telephone booth within the Memorial Hospital at Sleepy Hollow.

Malone's desk phone rang out. "Hello, Jimmy Malone here, who's calling?"

"John Park," the voice said.

"Ah! The intern."

"I'm at the Memorial Hospital, Sleepy Hollow. I have Ralph Rosenberg reunited with his daughter that he wasn't aware of, from an affair twenty-odd years ago. I have Gina Berio, now Gordino here, who was the woman involved; the one formally married to Peter Berio you know, with the link with the Salvadori family. Do you want your scoop?"

Malone was at a wall map next to his desk. He'd traced Sleepy Hollow's location with his forefinger. It was a fair distance, but the scoop would be worth it.

"Okay John, I'll be with you as soon as I can."

"Malone, bring the money; the other $25,000." John Park let his words hang in the air.

Jimmy Malone, however, had his location. He didn't care whether Park was paid or not, he would have his scoop. So who cares?

"Sure thing," Malone replied; then hung up.

Chapter 55

Michele Salvadori and his soldiers proceeded in convoy. They headed northwest on Beekman Street towards FDR Drive, and then Willis Avenue Bridge, taking them towards the Interstate Deegan Expressway and the Willis Avenue Bridge. They merged onto I-87 N, a partial toll road, their journey so far consuming 22 minutes. The I-87 N was the main road to Sleepy Hollow; they would be travelling on it for probably half an hour, so Michele Salvadori sat back, his mind tortured with his next move.

Chandler and his NYCP green squad cars were not far behind, and it was unusual to see so many following one another without any emergency lights flashing, or sirens wailing. This was a pursuit all right, but more of a trap set to catch a wise old fox.

Lieutenant Chandler knew he would need all his guile to land his quest. He would also require the cooperation of the local sheriff for Sleepy Hollow, but there was time enough for that.

Another vehicle travelled more recklessly than the other convoys of Salvadori and Chandler, the driver fuelled with hatred and revenge; one thing on her mind.

Karen Rosenberg's Mercedes hit the interstate 10 minutes after Salvadori, but five minutes before Chandler's convoy.

Karen was now on the toll road; she could now release the power of her well-engineered motor that lay beneath the hood. It wouldn't be long before she could face down her husband, and with Luther's help give him the full realisation of what he never had; then with complete relish take it all away from him.

Karen smiled, her green eyes aflame with the passion and the thought of the pain she was about to inflict. The snow was becoming heavier, but Karen kept pressing her accelerator. She felt good. This had been a long time in coming.

Steve was pleased that Ralph, Gina and Nicky were together, even if Nicky didn't completely understand all that was happening.

Gina spoke to her daughter. "I'm so glad I've found you, Nicky. Lisa and I have missed you. Thank God you're still alive. It's going to be all right now. We're together again."

Nicky was listening, but didn't respond.

"This is your real father, Nicky; Ralph. Ralph Rosenberg. You'll be loved and cared for at last,"

Gina said, as she felt Ralph squeeze her hand lightly, signifying his agreement.

"We've a lot to catch up on," Gina continued.

"And what if I still don't want to catch up?" Nicky said, obviously still in a lot of pain.

Gina was taken aback. "I'm sure you don't mean that, Nicky. After all, we …"

"After all what?! Who's this fairy godmother? He doesn't know me, and I don't know him. Don't know if I want to …"

Ralph was becoming agitated at Nicky's outbursts. He removed his mask, and although his voice was weak, spoke with conviction.

"Young lady, listen, please. I am your father, I just didn't know. Don't speak to your mother that way; she was trying to protect me. She thought her love for you would be enough to shield you from a messy scandal, which would have been the case, had my wife, Karen, known all about this. I'm only sorry that I've never known you till now, as I would have loved you, taken care of you, spoiled you, given you every opportunity the wonderful world has to offer."

"Yawn, yawn, heard it, mister. You'll love me, take me away from my dancing, and take me away from my friends. I'm doin' alright. Understand. Got it?"

Gina withdrew her hand from Nicky. "Nicky, please. Let's make amends, please."

"Nicky, let's make amends, love luvvie do," Nicky mimicked. "It's been 22 friggin' years, mom. Since Mr Righteous here left."

"Nicky, I've already explained. Ralph didn't know," Gina answered. "I broke off the relationship when I found myself pregnant with you. I didn't want hand-outs, or a compromised start to a relationship. A situation that would have ended in disaster for all concerned."

"Oh, yeah! Yeah yeah," Nicky said.

"Hey, young lady. Nicky, don't you talk to your mother that way. She sacrificed everything for you, including me. So don't start with her ..."

Ralph was about to carry on when Nicky started to cry.

"I'm sorry mom, I'm so sorry, I shouldn't have run away." Tears were welling up in her eyes, stinging the bruises where Luther had beaten her.

"It's alright, baby," Gina said. "It's alright."

Nicky was always volatile; up one moment, down the next.

Chapter 56

Karen's Mercedes flew passed Michele Salvadori's car.

"Someone's in a hurry," he observed, as the white German sports car took exit 9 to Tarrytown and Sleepy Hollow.

"If that broad keeps that up she'll end up where we're going, the Memorial Hospital, but it'll be in the back of an ambulance."

Little did Michele Salvadori know who the driver of the sports car was, or that he'd confront her in the next 20 minutes at the Memorial Hospital in Sleepy Hollow.

Lieutenant Chandler was on the I-87 N. He too was travelling fast, but being careful not to jump ahead of his target.

"Lieutenant, do you think it's time now to alert the local sheriff? Our ETA at the hospital is about 30 minutes away. They'll need time to organise themselves," Johnston added, before his boss replied.

Chandler deliberated for a moment. "Give it another 10 minutes. Let's get closer. The less they're involved, the better."

Johnston nodded. "I just thought it could make the arresting procedure complicated if we attempt to do all this on our own. There's no point in putting their nose out of joint Lieutenant, wouldn't you agree?"

Chandler glanced at his sergeant, and then smiled. "Thank you, Johnston. You're probably right. Radio back to Headquarters, have them contact the sheriff out at Sleepy Hollow, then tell him to contact me and await further instructions."

"Thank you, Lieutenant. You know it make sense." Chandler sat there, quietly staring ahead at the road and at the heavy snow that was now falling.

"I'm going to get you this time, Michele Salvadori, you son of a bitch," he said to himself under his breath.

A small Ford Compact overtook them; then realising it was a police convoy, held back and joined them from behind.

Malone realised he had enough time to achieve his whole scoop; no point in getting a ticket and missing all the fun. So he sat confidently tapping his fingers on the steering wheel, as he too took exit 9 to Tarrytown and Sleepy Hollow, along with Chandler and his squad cars.

Chapter 57

The private ward was full of emotion when Steve spoke.

"I'm glad you're all being reunited and becoming reacquainted with each other, but we have another player in the pack that I feel should be exposed."

"What are you talking about?" Clive Richards said, as he shuffled his feet.

"Oh, you may well ask Clive, 'cos you know exactly what I'm talking about, don't you?"

"I haven't the faintest idea what you mean, Mr Donaldson," Clive replied, with a surprised expression on his face.

"Oh! Well, let me help you out, Clive. When the woman who hired me left me a contact number, I rang. You answered. I'd recognise your very polite English accent anywhere. I had occasion to do it again in the middle of the case, when I was employed to locate Nicky. You, again, quite rightly, answered, except this time I asked for Gina. You didn't inform me I had the wrong number, you never even questioned 'Gina who'? You just handed the telephone over to another woman. Clive, you knew who Gina was," Steve said, pointing at her sitting between Ralph and Nicky. "You knew who Nicky was, Clive. You knew she was Ralph's daughter, but she'd run away from home many years before and couldn't be found. But you knew her, Clive. She had to be found if your plan was to be successful."

"Plan? What plan? This man's talking rubbish. Must be the drugs they've given you for your pain of your wound."

"Clive, sit down. My head is as clear as yours. You're involved in all of this."

"What! Don't be ridiculous. I've served Mr Rosenberg here for years; why should I do anything that would jeopardise or compromise his safety? You're barking up the wrong tree there, Mr Donaldson."

"Oh! You think so, Clive? You know as well as I that Karen Rosenberg employed me to find Nicky, gave me Gina's name, too. How do you think she found out about Gina and her daughter, Nicky? How, Clive?"

"I don't know. Mrs Rosenberg has many acquaintances; anyone of them could have …"

Karen appeared. "Oh shut up Clive, you'll get yourself into, what; what is it you English say? A fandangle?" Karen said, laughing, holding her automatic pistol with the pearl handle at arm's length, ready to fire at anyone who moved.

"Mother, what is going on in here," Mark said, standing up.

"Sit down, Mark," Karen shouted. She continued to smile, then changed her expression to one of distaste as she observed her husband lying wired up to machines.

"Holding hands, are we? Oh, how lovely. You and your whore Gina, together, and this slut of a daughter. Quite a reunion, wouldn't you say?" Karen started laughing again. "Don't move, Mr Donaldson. You've accomplished much more than I gave you credit for," Karen said.

"You didn't make it easy," Steve replied. "In fact, I'm not supposed to be here at all. Your monkey tried his best, but he won't be joining us."

Karen's arms started to shake as she held her gun, now aware that Luther would not be backing her up.

"It's no use, Karen," Steve said. "You can't win this one; it's over. Put down the gun; we'll settle this amicably."

"Yes, Karen." It was now Clive Richards who now spoke. "Give it up. You can't win; none of us can. Well, maybe Nicky. She's found her father at long last. That's got to be a good thing."

"For fucks sake, Clive, tell them. Tell Ralph; tell everybody. I want Ralph to know before he dies."

Clive started shaking. "We've lost, Karen. Ralph and Gina have Nicky, let it go."

"Let it go? What! You spineless son of a bitch."

"What's this about, Karen?" Ralph said. "I don't understand. I'm missing something."

Karen laughed. "Oh, you're missing it all, Ralph."

"Listen Karen," Ralph continued. "I did have an affair with Gina here," Ralph said, smiling at her, "but it ended a long, long time ago. There's never been anyone else, only you. You know that. I've never strayed since. That's the truth, Karen."

"And would you have stayed with me had you been aware Gina was carrying your child?"

"Karen, it was a long time ago. You can't ask me that today."

"Oh yes, Ralph, I can. Would you have brought up another woman's child? Would you, Ralph?"

"Karen, Karen, you've had many affairs, put yourself in that position."

"Oh, I have, Ralph, believe me, I have."

"What do you mean?" Ralph asked.

"Are you going to tell him, or am I?" Karen shouted, now waving her automatic in Clive Richards' direction.

Ralph looked at his butler. "What is it, Clive? Not you and Karen? I don't believe that. You're no more her style than chalk and cheese. Ho! Ho!"

"Karen, Karen," Ralph said, shaking his head.

Again, Karen waved her gun. "Clive, tell him."

"No, I can't."

"No change there then, you spineless oaf."

"For Christ's sake, tell me what?"

"Gillian's not yours, Ralph."

"What? What are you saying?"

"You were away. I was bored. Clive and I, well, we had a thing; pardon my expression. Gillian was the result. Rather than expose myself, Clive and I came to an arrangement. I'd have his baby. It would be our secret; you'd never know. Gillian would want for nothing; kept in a lavish lifestyle. Kept with your money, Ralph. Clive's part of the arrangement was to be able to see his daughter grow up in a wealthy environment with a better chance of being successful, rather than a single, out-of-work butler who could not have provided anything for his daughter. At least me having the baby I retained her, my lifestyle and Clive retained his job. He watched her grow, loved her as a father, although he could never show her his true affection. But I did, Ralph. She had me in her; unlike you, Mark. Oh, you're good looking, intelligent, but you've always been a daddy's boy."

Ralph started to tremble, his mind too ill to absorb the information and confession of his butler and Karen.

"Good, good, shake some more, you bastard, because I haven't finished."

"Karen," Clive said, "Stop. Enough."

Karen was wired, taking pleasure in witnessing her husband squirming.

"By the way, Clive kept your dirty little secret Ralph, but the day came when you bullied Gillian just too much; the final straw. He couldn't have his daughter treated like that, and he came to me.

Again, Ralph's body jerked, his breathing heavy, irregular, signals on the monitors going haywire.

"Yes, Ralph. Listen, listen. I want you to suffer. I wanted your daughter Nicky to suffer. Luther went overboard but I wanted you to know the same hell you took out on Gillian; your mental torture, your constant loathing of her.

"She's a lesbian," Ralph struggled to say. "No daughter of mine would."

"Oh, listen to the great Ralph Rosenberg. Protect the family name, Ralph. Did you know what your real daughter has been doing for a living? Well, I'll tell you. She's a fuckin' pole and lap dancer on the street. Different fuckin' men, every fuckin' night, Ralph. That's your daughter. Yours, Ralph, not mine."

There was a shuffle in the corridor as Michele Salvadori entered the ward. Instinctively Karen was distracted, turned and fired quickly. Michele fell to the floor.

Steve saw his chance, and attempted to disarm Karen, but she swung uncontrollably, firing her gun wildly. Maria had run to protect Steve; she didn't make it. She took the bullet in the heart.

Her father knelt beside her; then ran at Karen, who was still out of control. He also received the same array of fire. He fell, crawled to his daughter and held her hand. Maria was dead. He knew it. Gabrielle Bertollachi died instantly.

Michele Salvadori's men burst in, and seeing their godfather, filled Karen with an array of bullets, her body wriggling in nervous spasms as she fell to the floor, dead.

Chapter 58

Lieutenant Chandler and Johnston arrived into the mayhem, their team of backup really appreciated. The local sheriff had played his part but was smart enough to give Lieutenant Chandler the lead; after all, he didn't really want all the paperwork that would be necessary, especially when it involved a big hood who was out of his jurisdiction. The fact that he was involved as local sheriff in a supporting role would stand him in good stead, without blemishing his career.

The exchange of fire that executed Karen Rosenberg resulted in the police crews taking down many of the Salvadori family soldiers, giving Chandler's New York City Police control as Michele Salvadori lay dead on the floor.

"Well, Lieutenant, it's a bit of a mess, don't you think?" said Johnston.

"Oh! I don't think it's all bad Johnston; after all, we did get a result."

"A result?" Johnston echoed. "How?"

"Well, Michele Salvadori's dead. What could be better? Less paperwork; the DA can't complain. No public waste of money or court case that he can slip out of. And he's dead, Johnston."

"You know, what goes around comes around."

"Funny old world, isn't it?" Chandler said, as he checked on the other casualties in the ward and corridors of the hospital.

"Johnston, make sure everybody's particulars are taken; then book them. Oh, it's been a long day, but a good one."

Chandler approached Steve. "So, Donaldson, tell me your story. How do you fit in with all of this?"

"As I said, Lieutenant, I was set up. Employed by the deceased here," he said, as he pointed to Karen. "I was to find young Nicky and her mother, Gina. I wasn't aware of the connection to the Rosenbergs, or indeed Gina's history, until I got well into my investigation."

"I've only your word for that, Donaldson. I'll still need to take you in. You're a wanted man. You can't be seen to be just walking around. Johnston, take Donaldson to my car. Cuffs won't be necessary under the circumstances."

"Please, Lieutenant, can you give me a few minutes?"

"You're not going to give me the slip again, are you?"

"No, Lieutenant, I'll come quietly."

Nicky saw Steve. "Hello," she said calmly. I never did thank you for protecting me from the man who killed Frank, did I?"

Steve turned towards Chandler, then back to Nicky. "That's okay. Just you get better; get back together with your mom here. You've a father to get to know and a brother," Steve said, pointing to Mark.

Gina smiled. "You also have a sister, Lisa, who loves you, Nicky."

Nicky smiled. She closed her eyes a moment. "I think I'll be alright now. I want to be part of a family. I do, mom, I do."

Ralph was also calming down, but his anxiety rose again when Clive Richards passed, being led away by a police officer.

"How could you, Clive? How? Why! I always trusted you; never forgot you Clive. Why?"

"Ralph, it wasn't planned. You were away; it happened. What can I say? I love Gillian, but couldn't tell her the truth. It ate me up. Karen flaunted the situation every chance she got; I wanted to get back at her."

"And so you told her about Gina, and obviously about Nicky."

Clive bowed his head, and nodded. "I'm ashamed, Ralph. It was never supposed to go this far. We just wanted to make you aware of how it feels to suffer a huge loss. I lost Gillian. Lost my dignity. Couldn't give her the normal things, like love; be there on birthdays, special days. Oh, I was around, but I had to observe from a distance; watch my little girl grow up without being able to hold her, guide her, or …" Clive paused. "It was hard, Ralph. You actually have no idea, well, that is, until now. Find Nicky, and you too, Gina, make the great Mr Rosenberg suffer, but as God is my witness, I – we – never planned to take it this far. We – I just wanted you to experience the loss I had for years."

Clive continued with his confession. "Karen wasn't easy; you know that, of course. Oh, she had many suitors and you hit the mark with Hugh Sullivan, but you see; she had to go one better. She employed this vagabond murderer; Luther. I tried to dissuade her, but her hate brought a hellish revenge that she wanted to inflict on you. Luther was out of control. He was a monster, and worst of all, he enjoyed his work. I look at you, Nicky. This was not supposed to happen. Please believe me, Ralph. When I found you unconscious behind your study door that morning, I wanted everything to stop. I knew something had happened, but I didn't think of Karen. I just wanted to save you. I don't expect your forgiveness just now, but maybe over time you may come to understand."

Clive glanced at Karen's dead body, now covered with a blanket.

"She was beautiful. She loved life. She loved herself. Maybe too much."

Steve knelt beside Maria and Pop, who were also covered with blankets. Steve had not cried since the day his mother had died, while his father drank in a bar. It was the first time since his wife Gill that he'd began to fall in love again, and now Maria was gone; all because of some stupid revenge from high-powered people who didn't really appreciate how lucky they were in this life.

Steve jumped at Clive. "You bastard. Bastard! Do you know how many people have died through your sheer selfishness? Do you realise the pain you have caused to innocent people who were not involved in your sordid affair with your master's wife? Do you? Do you, Mr Richards?"

Again Clive felt belittled and ashamed.

Detective Sergeant Johnston led Steve away, uncuffed as instructed by Lieutenant Chandler.

"I'll need statements from everybody," Chandler said. "So settle down, nobody will be going anywhere for some time."

"Sheriff Wayne."

"Yes, Lieutenant?"

"Organise an interview room. Liaise with the hospital here."

"You got it, Lieutenant, no problem."

"Ah, there he is; the little ray of sunshine. Always there, no matter where, no matter when," Chandler said, as Malone entered.

"Well, thank you, Lieutenant!" Malone replied. "I do deserve this scoop."

Chandler smiled. He didn't like the Press, or Malone, but over the years he had his uses.

"Did you get the dudes in the burned out taxi, Malone?"

"No, followed you in, Lieutenant. Thought that's where the action would be."

"Well, I suggest you check it out. By all accounts, there's two bodies; one of Luther, the real murderer, and the charred remains of who we assume was the cab driver; poor son of a bitch. Just unlucky with his fare."

Malone never allowed emotion to interfere. His job was reporting from live events, and he was good at it.

Chapter 59

Ralph Rosenberg lay quiet. It had been quite a day. Gina and Nicky were by his side, Mark making light conversation, struggling with what had transpired.

"Where is Lisa?" Ralph asked. "What does she do? How old is she now?"

Gina smiled. "She works in the financial industry. She has a rented apartment in Cherry Street, and commutes every day. Lisa's 29 now, and gorgeous."

"She always was, when I knew her. Is she married?"

Gina hesitated with her reply. "No – she was close once, but he ran off with a dancer, and …" Gina could have bitten her tongue. "Sorry Nicky, I didn't mean to …"

"Hey Mark, its okay. I understand the type. Lisa is better off without him, that's a fact."

Gina smiled awkwardly.

"What about you, Mark? Are you seeing anyone?"

Mark appreciated being included in the conversation. "Actually, no. Like Lisa, I've had my moments, but I spend so much time abroad with dad and the business that it's difficult to cultivate a proper relationship."

Gina fished in her handbag. "Here's a picture of Lisa, taken a year ago."

"She's very pretty," he said. "Can't imagine why some guy's not snapped her up, and intelligent too, working in finance."

Nicky began to feel second class again, as Mark stared at the picture in his hand. He wanted to meet this girl.

"What is it, Nicky? Why are you crying?"

"I was hoping for a new start, a family to be part of, but when I listen to how well Lisa is doin', how well your doin' Mark, while I've made a mess of my life, there's no chance; I can't compete. I'm useless. Worthless. It would have been better had that Luther guy killed me. I'd be outta my misery."

Ralph removed his mask. He recognised a cry for help.

"Nicky… Nicky, please listen to me. You are my daughter. Your life is about to change big time. You'll be given all the opportunities you want, but more importantly, Nicky, whether you embrace them or not, you'll always be loved. I will always love you, just as I love my son Mark here. He's your stepbrother, so don't think that way. Believe in yourself. Whatever it is you want to do, I'll help you."

"I only know about dancin'. Dancin' is my life, and it's not exactly the kind you'd want your daughter to be doin'." Nicky turned away.

Ralph was silent for a few moments. "I'm sure you're very good at the type of dancing you do, and I'm sure plenty of young women would love to learn to dance. I bet there's more to it than just hanging round a pole or dancing on the floor. I mean, a dancer has to be super fit, nimble, have natural rhythm, all kinda things; you'll know better than me about that. All I know is, to achieve and be a good dancer ain't easy."

"So?"

Ralph thought again. "So why don't you set-up a school; teach them. Prepare them for the entertainment industry. Yes, that's it; Nicky's Dance School. What d'ya say?"

Nicky was stunned. Nobody ever took her interests seriously enough. The men she frequented were only ever after one thing. She'd seen her friends be abused too, and when too old or not fit enough for the punters, they were discarded, like waste fodder back to the streets.

"Mr Rosenberg," Nicky began.

"Hey kid, call me dad."

Nicky smiled nervously. It seemed awkward to have a father. "I like it. I like that idea. It's good.

Thank you, thank you dad," she whispered, as she fell into a deep sleep.

Chapter 60

The next few months brought many changes. Ralph, after some time back at the Mount Sinai hospital, was allowed to return home. His condition prevented him from flying, and so Mark took his rightful place, attending to business, albeit with his father's guidance. Gina Gordino visited regularly, and although Ralph wanted her to move into the mansion, she was happy enough to remain in her own home on Staten Island. Nicky had moved in with her and had given up her job at The Blue Parrot on the famous street.

Lisa kept her apartment and still worked in the financial district, but her fondness for Mark was growing, and any time he was home the pair were always together.

Ralph had made his peace with Gillian and Philippa too. He allowed them to live with him until they found a suitable place of their own. He had also deposited $1 million into Gillian's account, plus a monthly allowance. It didn't make up for all the wasted years of arguments, but the recent train of events had made him realise just how important family were, and he had known Gillian since she was born. In fact, he felt more like her father now than ever, and accepted her as her own person.

Lieutenant Chandler's case made the headlines; Jimmy Malone's scoop taking priority for The Times newspaper. The district attorney couldn't complain about lack of evidence as an avalanche of suits were brought to justice, and the very fact that Michele Salvadori was dead was a huge result in itself. His stranglehold on the city and other territories were unravelling. For once the authorities had the upper hand.

Joseph Cambrio's body was fished out of the Hudson, and a proper funeral and burial given.

Joe Mendez attended, as did Gina. After all, she did owe Cambrio her life all those years ago, and Mendez as mourning a friend and professional colleague.

Clive Richards for his part was sentenced to 10 years without parole. He would never be able to retain a position of trust ever again, and although Clive knew he wasn't totally to blame for all that had happened, he was remorseful enough to take his punishment.

Gillian visited him regularly, and although they

couldn't be together, each made up for the lost years and looked forward to the day of Clive's release, when they would be reunited properly as father and daughter.

Chapter 61

Steve Donaldson was released after helping Lieutenant Chandler with the case. They parted with a mutual respect for each other.

"You could always come back, Donaldson. I could use a good man like you."

Steve smiled. "Thank you, but no thanks. Anyway, I like my own space. Got too long in the tooth for other people's rules. Most of my life, Lieutenant, I've had to run to someone else's tune. I've paid my price; I just suit myself now."

Steve shook hands with Chandler, then with Johnston.

"Hey, if you hotshot guys are ever passing and want to visit small guys, don't be shy, pay a visit. It'd be nice. Oh! On second thoughts," Steve said, "maybe you should call first."

Chapter 62

Donaldson sat in his old swivel chair. Ralph Rosenberg had paid him a handsome bonus, which enabled him to redecorate his office. His water cooler had even been refilled, and although they didn't fit in with the new décor, his old desk and chair still remained.

Steve was reminiscing of the Rosenberg case, how different it all could have been. There was a knock on his door.

"Come in," Steve shouted.

"Good morning, Mr Donaldson," the young woman started. "You were recommended to me."

She was attractive. Steve turned his chair away, averting his eyes.

"I need to know who's paying me. Some background of why you want to employ me. It would be most of the cash upfront, my fee is..."

Steve swivelled back, his new client was seated.

"I'm well aware of your conditions and results, Mr Donaldson. Shall we proceed on a need to know basis?"

THE END

About The Author

Born and raised in Lanarkshire, Scotland, I ran a successful business in the construction industry for thirty years before moving to Harrogate in North Yorkshire to become an hotelier with my wife Marion. A passion for reading crime thrillers led me to write the first book of the 'Jigsaw' series featuring private investigator Steve Donaldson set in New York in the late 1950s.

As I suffer from epilepsy due to an accident suffered when I was one year old, using modern technology is a huge challenge, but with the help and support of Indie Authors Scotland I have been able to publish the first of the 'Jigsaw' series.

As I am now retired, I have more time to pursue my passion for writing as well as visiting all my family in Scotland.

Innocent Death

A preview of Book 2 in

The Jigsaw Series

Coming soon

Chapter 1

A blue-eyed blonde with an attractive figure sat across from Steve. "As I said Mr Donaldson, on a need to know basis."

Steve sighed. He didn't need this. The death and loss of Maria was still fresh in his mind and right now he did not want a repeat of the Rosenberg case. Claire Monroe uncrossed her legs, stood, extended her hand to seal their contract but Steve just sat there, making no movement and making no commitment. Claire hesitated for a moment and then withdrew the gesture. She turned to leave in full anticipation that the private detective would make an effort to stop her. It was not to be.

She opened his office door, the lining of her skirt rustling against her body and departed, the clicking of her heels echoing down the dimly lit corridor. Steve watched from his window as she crossed the street.

The quick movement from the dark-coloured car at the kerb was unexpected, its speed and direction finding its target as it ploughed into her then continued on its way.

A crowd gathered around the dead body of Claire Monroe as Steve closed his window blind, his mind in turmoil.

He knew instinctively Claire's death was no accident.

Chapter 2

Back in his apartment Steve poured himself his second Jack Daniels. He left the bottle uncorked as he felt his need for the liquor would not be done with for this evening.

Claire Monroe's death was recorded as a hit and run, but Steve suspected otherwise.

"On a need to know basis," he said, repeating Claire's last words to him before leaving his office and walking to her death.

Whatever she had died with her, but whoever killed her wouldn't know that. She had obviously been followed and someone knew that she had visited him. Claire had wanted to employ him and yet had been reluctant to impart all the information she had, drip feeding him as and when necessary. She didn't appear frightened or even nervous but for whatever reason she had obviously been holding something back.

Steve pondered a variety of questions that ran through his mind.

What did she know?"

Who was involved?"

Why had she not gone to the police?

What was her background?

Why had she felt the need to employ him?

He never found out, all because of her condition of employment, proceed on a need to know basis. So what was it the she couldn't divulge completely and what could be so important that she had been eliminated?

Steve mulled the questions over and over. He didn't know the answers and, at this stage, he could walk away, but the fact remained whoever had killed Claire Monroe would believe that she had imparted what she knew to him. She was dead. Was he next? He certainly was implicated.

His telephone burst into life, Steve stared at the instrument but didn't answer. Instead he switched off his lights and moved quickly to the window. The ringing stopped abruptly. He scanned the street below, his observant eyes recording any movement. He saw no one. He switched the lights back on and within seconds the phone began to ring again. Hesitantly he picked up the receiver, the line was live but nobody spoke.

"Hello! Who's calling?" Steve asked. "Come on I know you're there."

Silence reigned, and then the line went dead.

www.ingramcontent.com/pod-product-compliance
Ingram Content Group UK Ltd.
Pitfield, Milton Keynes, MK11 3LW, UK
UKHW020415250726
13967UKWH00007B/2649

9 780993 033605